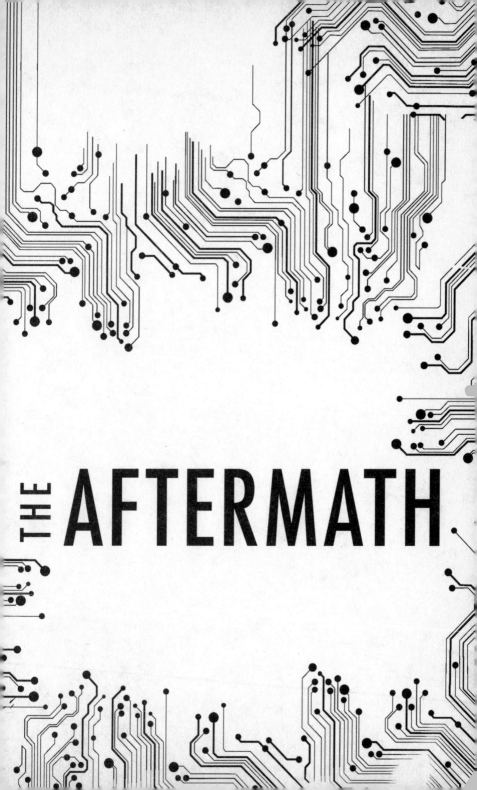

THE AFTERMATH

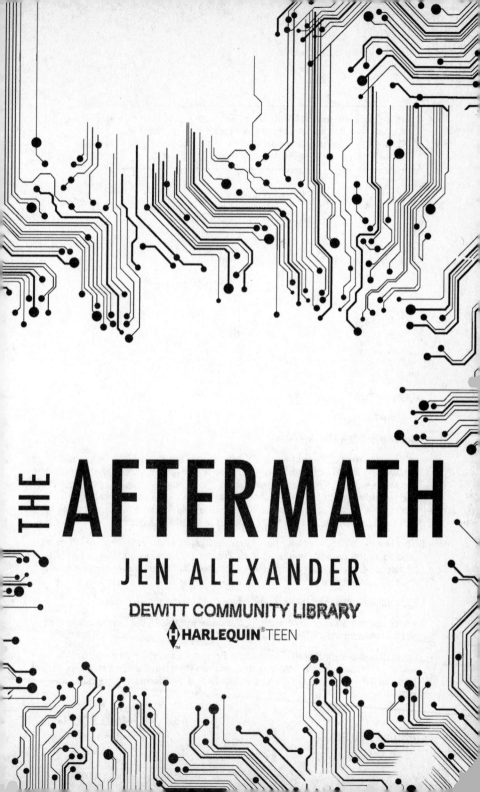

THE AFTERMATH

JEN ALEXANDER

HARLEQUIN®TEEN

Recycling programs for this product may not exist in your area.

ISBN-13: 978-0-373-21132-6

THE AFTERMATH

Copyright © 2014 by Jen Alexander

Printed in U.S.A.

To Taryn, whose support and advice is incredible. And to you—
yes, you—for picking up this book and giving it a chance. Thank you.

PROLOGUE

Late May

Frigid air gasping against my skin yanks me awake.

"Wonderful." I climb off the sleeping bag I slept on top of the night before. When I went to bed, the heat was blistering, unbearable—the complete opposite of what I'm facing right now. "They screw with the weather right after we hit the jackpot."

A few feet behind me, someone snorts. I shoot a look over my shoulder at April. Blue-lipped and shivering, with wet strands of her flaming-red hair plastered to her forehead and around her shoulders, she looks as if she won't be able to manage a coherent word.

Instead, her calm, even voice surprises me. "We'll be fine," she says as she walks over to the pile of items we procured the day before on a raid and begins gathering them together. "I've checked the area, and the weather's not that bad. The important thing is we get back to our shelter so we can make all of this count. I wonder if Mia's been fi—" The rest of her sentence catches in the back of her throat as her eyes land on the row of sleeping bags across from where she's squatting.

"Where's Mia?" April asks.

Slowly, my gaze turns to where Jeremy, Mia and Ethan, the other members of our clan, lay down the night before. Jeremy and Ethan are sitting up on their sleeping bags, but Mia is nowhere to be found.

Where is Mia?

"We're better off without her," I say to April, feeling my heart sink at the bitter words I can't seem to hold back. "And you're right—we should go. Our shelter is waiting."

"Will she be replaced?" April demands, and my stomach hardens at the harshness of the question. Our friend has gone missing and April's already wanting to know how soon we'll find someone to take Mia's place, make our group stronger.

When did April—any of us, for that matter—become so cold?

"No." When I shake my head, she storms outside and into the cold. I somehow stay cool and collected as I finish packing up the bulk of our new supplies with the boys. When April returns a few minutes later, shivering twice as hard as before, she doesn't speak to me nor does she mention Mia again.

In fact, there's no more mention of her at all as our group prepares to leave the abandoned garage that was our shelter last night. Fear slivers down my spine as I think of the raid we'd gone on just before finding this place, where we'd ripped apart a flesh-eater den, freeing their living captives before making off with all the weapons and supplies we could carry.

Where is Mia?

Just before we venture out into the snowstorm, I face the rest of my group. "We'll be fine."

We walk through the blizzard for what feels like days, rarely stopping, until, finally, we return to our windowless safe room and sleep like the dead. In the months that follow, it seems we never have enough food, despite the constant raids for energy bars and water bottles that barely sustain us. Missions to free captured Survivors from flesh-eater dens, and the fraying bonds between the members of our clan, are the only remnants of the humanity we'd once known—a time in my life I can't even remember because I had awakened in this world with no recollection of my past. Who was I before all this? Was I carefree and loved, a girl with a family and a real home? Or was I manipulative, like the person I've become, this person who has killed other people time and time again? Even though everything I've done is out of necessity—the need to survive—the longer we live this way, the less human I feel.

Sooner or later, there won't be any humanity left to salvage.

Some days, I can barely even bring myself to string together a coherent sentence, letting silence and barked commands take the place of the complicated emotions I feel. And other days, I awake unsure of myself. When was the last time I ate something? How long did I black out for this time? Who was I before this world became such a wasteland?

Our world went to sleep in the spring of 2036, when the sky opened up, releasing asteroids. Releasing blizzards and hailstorms and then a heat wave that blistered the land. Releasing death. When Nashville and her inhabitants awoke hours—maybe even days—later, we were all as good as dead. Our only source of food came from the few factories untouched by the storms—mostly there were protein bars, but sometimes we were fortunate enough to find other food. We prayed for water, for rain.

We hoped for a miracle.

We'd christened our new world The Aftermath. There are the cannibals—flesh-eaters. And then there are people like myself. Survivors. We possess honor and loyalty. We scavenge for food, not flesh. We're willing to die or kill for the safety of our friends. And we choose our clans with care because they must be prepared to do the same for us—because one must be so careful these days.

My group's changing, though. Mia, who'd been with me since I awoke in this world of tainted water and dry soil and chaos three years ago, has been missing now for months. I told the others that we'll be fine without her, but I was lying.

Mia's disappearance has left me disoriented and hopeless. Every time I think of her, I want to embrace the bittersweet darkness that swallows me when I close my eyes.

But sometimes I dream that I'm someone else. A girl with dark hair who doesn't worry about hunger or thirst or running from flesh-eaters.

In her world, those sorts of things don't exist.

CHAPTER ONE

August

I can smell a storm coming in. It's an earthy scent that I can't ignore, especially when we're running low on water and I can almost feel the raw ache of thirst in the back of my throat. We need the rain.

I draw in a deep breath to make sure I'm not imagining the scent, but now it's even stronger, intermingling with the decayed odor of a music shop that caught fire last week.

A few days ago, after we'd raided the little souvenir store across the street from it, something had driven me to go inside. I'd found what was left of two Survivors within the remains of the building, lying side by side on a bed of smashed records and charred instruments with their fingers interlocking.

Focus on the rain, Virtue. Not on death.

Today, the air is damp, and I swear I can feel my skin drinking the moisture in, but until the first drops fall, I won't get my hopes up. Not when the sun is so bright that it seems as if it's mocking me.

The last time I expected rain, positioning empty water bottles on the roof, it hadn't come for nearly two weeks.

Remembering those thirteen miserable days of thirst and uncertainty is just enough to take my mind off the dead couple in the music store, but it's not a welcome change of thought. So, I refocus again—this time on the reason why I came up here in the first place.

I haven't eaten in days.

I squat down on the roof of the jail we've lived in for the past two months. Midafternoon sunlight hisses at my bare shoulders. Perspiration drips from my forehead, blinding me and making my binoculars oily to the touch.

Across the street is a courthouse. It is imposing, gothic, with gargoyles lurching off the roof and bronze sculptures protecting the ground. It's beautiful, even in this world that has fallen on its face and refuses to stand back up, but I'm more interested in the elderly couple that has taken up across the street than the building's beauty.

They're not the first to move into the courthouse since my group sought out shelter here. And I've got a feeling they won't be the last. They have no clue we exist. When there's a real threat, and there always is, they won't know that, either. Not until it's much too late.

"Spying on the neighbors again, Claudia?" Ethan's voice startles me, and I drop the binoculars to my chest, jumping up hastily. Although the ledge I'm standing on is several inches higher than the roof deck, my green eyes are level to his—he's that much taller than me. With the sun as a backdrop that makes his dark blond hair seem like a halo, he's ethereal. If it weren't for the knife sheathed to his side and the dried blood smeared across the front of his jeans, he'd be out of place in this run-down landscape.

"Didn't think you would be around," I say. I peek over my shoulder at the courthouse. "They have food. Bet they have water, too."

"So you are spying."

I nod and hop down from the ledge, skidding a little on the gravel. Ethan steadies me, holding either side of my waist as he draws me to his body. His grip is too tight and it momentarily takes my breath away. But instead of pulling away from him, I move in closer, tucking the top of my head underneath his chin. Being near Ethan has always made me feel safe, and even now it gives me the confidence to follow through on my plans.

"I'm going in, and I'm taking as much as I can carry with me," I say.

Ethan groans. "It's risky. I mean, they're so close and—"

"Don't worry, I can handle it," I promise, sliding my hands into his back pockets. I gaze up at him, and he tucks stray strands of my short blond hair behind my damaged ear. "They just left. Now's as good a time as any for me to go in." At last I shrug away from him and take a couple of steps backward. Tilt my head to one side and await his response.

"I'll go with you, Claudia."

"No offense," I say, placing my hands on my hips and shaking my head, "but I'm pretty sure I can handle this one by myself. You should work on inventory while I'm gone. April swore she did it last week, but she screws everything up."

He stares behind me at the winged lion gargoyle on the corner of the courthouse. After a long moment where I doubt he'll continue to argue with me, the sides of his mouth quirk up. "Come on. You and me. Mini-quest."

Ethan comes up with the most ridiculous names for raids. Quests. Mini-adventures. Field trips. Jeremy and April never call him on it, but I often want to. Still, if I have to pick anyone to hunt for food with, he's the one. Ethan is strong and quick.

When he stands watch, I never fret about guarding my throat because when he swears he'll protect me with his life, I never doubt him. On the other hand, clearing out the courthouse *is* a simple task that I can easily manage without any help.

"You really don't have to come, you know? I wasn't kidding when I said I can do it alone," I say, and he laughs.

"Oh, I know you can, but I wouldn't be able to get anything done knowing you're in that building by yourself."

I feel my lips move into a slow smile. "Suck-up."

Hunger twists my stomach into tight coils, and I almost suggest we take the elevators to the basement. Although it's available, we shouldn't use electricity here. As far as shelter is concerned, working lights are a rarity, and nothing attracts flesh-eaters like a brightly lit building. That and a functional commercial-size oven.

"How long have they been gone?" Ethan climbs into the roof hatch. He jumps down effortlessly, then glances up at me. I use the ladder, gripping the slippery metal rungs as best I can. When I reach the bottom, he slides his hands under my arms and lowers me to the floor.

"Fifteen minutes."

"And you're sure they have food?"

I shoot him a look as I grab my bag from the stool by the staircase and shrug it onto my shoulders. "Am I ever wrong? Like I said, you don't have to come—I can handle it by myself."

He blinks a few times before shaking his head, then starts down the steps. I follow close behind, trying to disregard the noise that erupts from the pit of my belly and echoes off the metal and concrete.

There's no natural light on the jail's ground floor, so we use flashlights. I think this part of the building was once used to in-process prisoners. Rows of tiny cells extend along both sides of the hallways. Each room has a steel door, just like the ones upstairs, but these cells have bulletproof windows, too. Expletives and drawings of body parts are etched into the glass. Ethan once said that the prisoners must not have liked seeing each other locked away.

At the end of the hallway is a door, which leads to another corridor.

I loathe going into this hallway because it reeks of waste and mold and what I swear is a decaying corpse. It also runs directly into the courthouse basement. I want to pull the collar of my T-shirt over my mouth and nose, to breathe in the scent of harsh soap and sweat so I don't suffocate from the stench. But since doing so would prevent me from detecting any odors that are out of place, I carry on and hope I don't get sick to my stomach.

"I'm, uh, sorry for the other night," Ethan says. He isn't covering his nose, either. His face is so expressionless, I wonder if he notices the scent or if he's simply grown accustomed to it. "About what I said, you know."

"It's fine."

He'd admonished me for not taking better care of my health after I'd returned from a raid sunburned and so breathless I couldn't move or speak. The only thing I wanted to do was curl up on the flat green mat in our safe room and rest. Instead, I'd gone back and forth with him for nearly half an hour. His concern was both endearing and frustrating. How can he expect me to have excellent health when we are constantly facing death to get what little we do have?

"No, it's not. It just makes me so angry. That we have to go on like this."

Ethan rarely talks about being bitter with the hand we've been dealt. Out of everyone in our clan, he seems to accept what happened three years ago the best, focusing on the present so that we can do whatever it takes to survive. That's what draws me to him. I reach out in the darkness and thread my fingers through his. "Thank you...for everything you've done for me," I say as I squeeze his hand.

He exhales, blowing wisps of hair out of his eyes. "Just know, I'll do whatever it takes to stay here... I've never been with anyone like you—not even before all this."

My heart lurches, and I swear it's about to explode from my chest. What does he mean when he says not even before all this? I want to ask him about it, but my body seems to have a mind of its own, and instead I silently wrap my arms around his neck, gazing up into his hazel eyes. He lowers his head until our lips touch.

"Me, neither," I say before releasing my hold on him.

We stop in front of the metal door to the courthouse, and he bends his head to fish an oversize key from his pocket. I sneak a glance at his face under the flashlight. He's smiling. Maybe my words helped ease his mind.

After returning the key to his pocket, he pulls his knife from its holster. "You coming?" he asks, taking a few steps into the pitch-black basement. I squint when he beams the flashlight on my face. And to think I was the one asking him if he wanted to back out of the raid.

This is the last place I want to be.

My head bobs up and down, and I hold out my hand. Allow him to pull me into the dark after him.

Once we reach the first floor of the courthouse, there's no use for our flashlights. The people living here are almost asking for flesh-eaters to attack because every corner of the building is lighted and cool. If it wouldn't almost certainly mean death before sunset—my skinny body becoming someone's meal—I'd stay here in the air-conditioning.

"They live on the third floor," I say as we walk briskly through the lobby. It's surprisingly clean. The last squatters were disgusting.

We take the stairs. Again. There's a buzzing hum of electricity all around, and a working elevator, but we still climb three flights of steps to avoid notice. I'm out of breath by the time we find the courtroom the couple has made their home base. My belly is on fire, and all I want is to rest, to lean against one of the benches to steady myself.

I join Ethan on the other side of the room instead.

Kneeling down behind the jury box, he bites his bottom lip. "Where did they get all this?" I see the top of his head moving—he's taking count of the supplies. "There's so much food and water... Hey, give me your bag, will you?"

Usually he's the lookout while I load the bags because I'm faster. Today, I don't object. I toss him my empty backpack, and it lands quietly on the front row.

"Be quick," I order before stepping into the lobby.

My tennis shoes tap softly on the beige tile floor as I pace in front of the door. I feel that at any moment, I will drop from hunger and yet I can't keep still. I am not particularly patient, but when it comes to a raid, I try to have some restraint. Stealing someone else's resources is a quick way to wind up dead. And it's the thieves who are hasty or greedy that you see bloated on the side of the street or beaten bloody and left slumped against a building.

I am still thinking about food and water and pacing frantically when I realize I'm no longer alone. The sound of a gun cocking and the bittersweet scent of menthol make me freeze.

"Turn around," orders a soft female voice. "Hands on top of your head."

I do as I'm told. I twist around so slowly that the rubber soles of my shoes make a drawn-out squeaking noise. My heart nearly tumbles out of my chest. For a moment, for whatever reason, I'm sure it's Mia. My friend who decided she was better off somewhere else shortly after we celebrated freeing several people from a flesh-eater den. But then I blink a couple of times. Other than the dark hair and eyes, this person looks nothing like Mia.

This woman is middle-aged, not seventeen, and has a gaunt, dented face. She is nearly shirtless and so skinny I can count the bones beneath her translucent skin. Tattered cargo pants hang low on her hips.

Her feet are bare, worn and bruised. If not for the Glock aimed at my forehead, I wouldn't be afraid of her at all.

But there is a gun pointing at me, and the person holding it is not on my side. If I'm lucky, she'll shoot me now instead of trying to breed me with a male captive in hopes of making more food. I've heard about flesh-eaters doing this because babies are so fat.

"Need some help holding that thing?" I ask. My bold words surprise both of us, and she sneers. Lowers the gun until it's aimed directly between my eyes. My chest contracts, but I don't stop talking. "Go on. I dare you."

"You dare me?"

There's a gun in her hand and my fingers are clasped above my head and I'm goading her to kill me. I am a sadist. I am terrified out of my skull.

I nod and smile.

Instead of firing, she laughs at me. Her bony body shakes hard—like a skeleton dangling about. I only hope she's loud enough for Ethan to hear. "You're not getting out, girl. You're worth too much for me to let that happen. Question is—" she twitches her head toward the closed courtroom door and grins "—how many more we taking with us?"

We.

The word makes me want to scream. Of course she's not alone—flesh-eaters raid with their entire clan. I take a tentative step toward her, and her nostrils flare. "Do. Not. Move," she warns.

I take one more step. Two. Then three. I feel as if my muscle and bone have turned to jelly, but somehow I walk with confidence. If I pretend I'm not terrified, then maybe—just maybe—I'll survive this day. It's worked before, more times than I can remember. Still, I can almost smell my fear intermingling with her pungent minty scent; can practically feel the cold barrel of the gun. I am that close to her now.

My lips move into a mocking grin. "Go on," I challenge.

The next few moments are a complete blur. Ethan shouts something, and the woman turns in his direction. I rush forward. The gun goes off, and I'm trembling with my arms around this skinny creature that wants me dead, unsure which of us is wounded. The echo is so thunderous, and I'm so numb, it takes me a moment to realize Ethan is saying my name, telling me to let go.

The woman collapses to the floor. She's motionless, and I watch as a crimson stain spreads across the chest of her skimpy tank top. Then, her chest expands, a gasp bubbles from her throat and her eyes bulge open.

"I— Where—" Wild brown eyes shift up to me. I want to disappear, to melt into the floor, but I stand still as a statue, staring down at her.

"Help me," she whispers. Her voice sounds different—there's an accent now that wasn't present before. "I feel it. Get it out of me!" She thrashes around, grabbing at her scalp, and I draw in a deep breath. The wound is right under her heart, not in her head. She must not realize this because she yanks her hands through her matted hair. Begs me, over and over, to get it out of her.

"What?" I want to ask. "Get what out of you?" But I say nothing to the woman as I watch her. I don't even look at Ethan when I say, "She's been around a long time. Worth a lot of points."

Suddenly, it feels as if the space around the three of us is rotating, like a revolving door. I have no explanation for what I just said, but it sounds so familiar. Like something I heard or said once before, but I can't quite grasp where or when. Or why.

What the hell is wrong with me today?

The woman stops moving, and this time I know she's dead. Burning pain consumes my chest. For a moment, I wonder if we were both hit.

"We should get her things," Ethan whispers. He throws my bag at me. A few protein bars fall to the floor as it hits me in the chest. "Hurry!"

I keep my eyes away from her face, which is partially covered by her limp arm. Swallow back the bile threatening to come up. Focus on stuffing my bulging bag with the brown-eyed woman's belongings— one coat, a copper-stained pocketknife, a box of matches, a half-empty bottle of codeine syrup.

"Hurry," Ethan says in such a calm voice my shoulders tense up. He's looking right at me, at what's left of the woman, and he's completely expressionless.

I grab the gun, swing my bag onto my back and rise to my feet. "There are probably others like her in the building." My voice is collected, detached.

Ethan processes this for a moment, flicking his hazel gaze from the elevator to the staircase. Finally, he tightens his grip on his knife and starts toward the elevator. I sprint after him, but my brain is screaming at me, *Coward. She needed your help and you just stood there, staring.*

I don't know the person I'm leaving behind—the decisions we made when our world came to an end took us on two different paths—but I still feel like a traitor.

It almost seems fitting that when the doors of the elevator squeak open, we come face-to-face with another stranger—a boy with dark shaggy hair and eyes so gray they seem black. I stand unmoving, ice crawling through my veins, as I take this intruder in. He's dressed entirely in black and he's weirdly clean—more polished than anyone I've seen in the past few years.

"Don't tell me you're—" Ethan begins, but I don't catch the rest of his words because the other boy swings something at him. Ethan ducks, and the object collides with the top of my head and sends me reeling back. Darkness closes in.

CHAPTER TWO

I seldom have dreams. And when I do, when I'm fortunate enough to close my eyes to something other than the nothingness that seems like death, it's always the same; I dream I'm someone else. A girl in a world without pain and hunger. The dreams are nice, and I always dread waking. Not once have I had a dream I wanted desperately to leave the moment it began.

Until now.

I'm standing beneath short rows of fluorescent lights, gazing down at a white metallic machine. It's as long and as wide as the empty casket Mia and I found on a street corner last year after a torrential storm, but one end is rounded and there's a thin glass panel running along the length of the top. Transparent tubes extend like tentacles from the bottom of the machine into even more machines with dozens of buttons and multicolored lights.

And on the other side of the glass, inside the metal coffin, there's a body.

I watch quietly as a mechanical arm slides back and forth on the girl's bloody face, like a pencil scratching lines across a blank sheet of paper. The girl in the machine is so still and quiet, I'd think she was dead if it weren't for the slight shudder of her chest.

There's a loud beep behind me, and the metal picks up its speed on her skin. The coffinlike machine begins to make a humming noise, and when I lean in close to the glass, the girl's injuries gradually start to change. Her skin is being made whole again.

Small forehead, V-shaped scar at the hairline.

Straight freckled nose.

Lips that have spoken my every inadequate word for the past several years.

I am looking at myself.

I want to run away. I want to end this dream now and go back to my world, a world that's filled with the type of fear that I understand. But instead of backing away, I tap my fingers on the glass and suck in an impatient breath. "This is taking entirely too long." The voice I speak in is soft—almost childlike.

The voice is not my own, but I've dreamed of it before. I'm that other girl again.

"You would be better off going home to wait as she's horribly damaged," someone else says.

"She fell on her face after she was hit. It's nothing you can't fix."

"It's not her exterior that I'm so concerned about—the Regenerator can easily repair that damage."

My gaze is finally dragged away from my broken body and settles on the woman speaking. She's bent over a desk, squinting down at a computer screen. She taps the screen a few times, and the machine behind me makes a grating noise. A see-through image of someone's head drifts up over the desk. Even though it's neon green, with grid lines running through, I can tell that it belongs to me from the round face and nose shape. The woman touches the screen again, and the projection changes to a floating model of a brain.

"Making sure she hasn't received any brain damage will take additional time," the woman explains.

I walk in a circle around the machine. This…thing that is slowly repairing my body's injuries. My shoes clacking loudly on the tile floor are the only sound other than a steady beep from the machines. Heels. Even if I could find a pair, I'd never wear them outside of a dream because there's no place for impractical shoes in my world.

"Spare me the technical doctor talk, okay? How long will it be before I can have her back?" I demand.

The woman lifts her eyes to the side of the white machine where I'm standing over myself. She swallows hard and fumbles with the last button on her white coat. "With all due respect, Miss Olivia, there are other characters far more advanced and with the newest technology that—"

Even though this is a dream and I'm somebody else, that name makes me go cold. I want to wake up. I want this dream to be over now.

"I don't want another," the soft-voiced me snaps. "I want her."

"But her vitals are incr—"

"Perhaps you didn't understand me, Dr. Coleman. Or maybe you lack the skills to perform what you were hired to do. This is who I want, so fix her!"

Dr. Coleman touches her screen again. The brain changes back to the image of my head, and then the entire projection sinks down, disappearing. "She came close to dying this time."

"If she dies, then you will, too. Make her right again."

Again.

Again?

Wake up. Wake up right now. This is all wrong…

Dr. Coleman sighs heavily and grabs something off her desk. As

I step aside so she can walk past, I catch a glimpse of it. Long and silver—it looks like a square flashlight. She positions her hand over a blinking light on the side of the Regenerator. The machine beeps five times before the glass panel flips open. My body shivers visibly as Coleman brushes back strands of my blond hair.

"Are you sure you just don't want to wait until—"

"What I want is her functional within forty-eight hours," I say in the strange voice. "And don't shave her head this time. She looked hideous the last time you did that. And no new scars, either—she already has plenty."

Wake up. Please.

I want to turn away as Dr. Coleman presses the square black tip of the tool to my scalp. But my thoughts and actions in my dreams are just the same as reality. Severed. The body inside the machine comes fully to life when the doctor holds down a button on the device. Screaming, thrashing against dozens of metal arms sketching over the rest of its injuries. Somehow, I'd failed to notice them before.

Wake up!

At last, I untangle myself from the nightmare.

And the pain of the girl who is struggling inside the machine coffin with the broken body—now it's all mine.

CHAPTER THREE

"I hate when that happens."

My first words when life rushes back into my body are so nonchalant, they nearly knock the breath out of me all over again. A throbbing ache claws the left side of my face, pulsating from my jawbone to my temple and, finally, to the top of my head. I try to open my eyes. They are so sticky, and I'm so weak, I only manage to part them enough to see slivers of bright light and dark faceless figures moving about. My breath quickens as panic surfaces in the pit of my belly and digs its way into my chest.

Where am I?

"Welcome back," Ethan says. I can detect a hint of a smile behind his voice. Just like three years ago when we'd first met, right after a flesh-eater had attacked me, taking a chunk of my right ear with him.

"Welcome to The Aftermath," Ethan had said before helping me up. Then he'd touched my bleeding ear and added, "We better get that fixed. Wouldn't want you to bleed out the first day in."

Now I should feel more relief he's alive. That I am with him and not fenced in by rotting flesh and half-dead emaciated captives in a flesh-eater's den. But I can't. My head is aching, and the sensation slinks through the rest of my body, leaving a bitter sting wherever it touches. Like poison.

"Here," Ethan says. A wet cloth covers my eyelids. "Better now?"

No. Not even a little. How could it be better when my head feels as if it's about to explode and I've no recollection of what happened to me? The only thing I remember after being hit by the boy with the dark gray eyes is a string of horrible nightmares.

A vision of me stretched out and bruised in a machine, with tiny mechanical hands repairing my body, flashes through my mind. I swallow back a sour taste in my mouth.

No, nothing is better. And I have a sick feeling in the pit of my stomach that things will become much worse.

"It's perfect," I say, my voice scratchy. Raw. Suddenly, I don't want to open my eyes. I want to stay like this, curled into the fetal position with my head ablaze until I gather my bearings. Piece together my broken memories.

My eyes open anyway.

Ethan's face hovers over mine. He is smiling widely, despite the open cut on his lip. But for the first time, his eyes startle me. They aren't injured or anything like that, but they're glassy, like hazel marbles. My hands suddenly feel clammy. In the three years I've known Ethan, I've never felt wary around him.

Until today.

"I'm glad," he says. His fingers intertwine with mine, and I feel weightless as he helps me to my feet.

We aren't in the jail, I realize as he pulls me to him and into a suffocating embrace. There are no cell doors, no chipping blue paint or exposed piping or opaque windows. This place is open and well-lit, thanks to its many windows, and I know it well. It's the museum in the Park. Once, I'd found a tourism brochure with a picture of this place tucked inside a tin box in a crawl space. The paper was so old that I could barely make out most of the tiny typed print, except for the words "Tour the Parthenon." I can't imagine anyone wanting to tour this museum now, though. These days, it overlooks a lake that's slowly drying up to reveal a makeshift burial ground.

Dozens of pillars enclose us. Two stories above, light gleams through windows in the beamed ceiling, illuminating splashes of graffiti and blood on the columns. And positioned behind the concrete—with missing heads and appendages—are sculptures that seem to turn accusingly toward me.

Coward, they seem to say.

Inside, I wince.

"I know you said you didn't want to come here, but it was so close to the other place," Ethan explains, leaning against one of the pillars. He glances away, and my heart jumps at the sight of the long gash that runs from the nape of his neck to just by his throat. I want to reach out and touch it. Ask him if this is what happened to him on our raid, if he knows what happened to me when I went under. If he knows what happened to the boy who came out of the elevator.

"I hope you're not upset," he whispers.

I stare at Ethan for a long moment, studying his injuries. I feel as if I'm about to pass out from my own. Did I speak to him deliriously, words I've now forgotten? I have no memory of talking to him about living here. And even though I would've argued against it because this museum practically screams to be raided, I don't understand why he'd think I'd be upset.

I'm not angry. At the moment, I'm just thankful to be alive. I don't want him to stress over me when he's so badly injured himself.

Maybe that's what's wrong with him. He's just worried. That's why his eyes look so strange—it has to be.

"You have the survival instincts of a toddler. And you listen like one, too," I say.

No, my words are all wrong. The opposite of what I need to say to him.

He nods quickly and pushes himself from the concrete. "If it makes you happy, we'll move immediately." His blank, serene expression is back. Like everything is normal. Like he doesn't feel the inflamed cut beneath his chin or the bruises that mutilate his face.

I feel them for him, and I'm creeped out.

He nods toward the back of the building. His movements are so quick and wobbly, I want to reach out and steady his head. "This is The Save for now. Open areas are a pain in the ass, but the rest of the building is too small to work with. Come on. I'll show you where we've stored the food."

I shuffle slowly beside him. Sharp pangs make my stomach tighten. My head feels like a jar and someone is clenching the lid, twisting and wrenching. I twitch. Blink. And once again, I see my body motionless, the long silver device pushing against my scalp.

This is the first time one of my nightmares has stayed with me outside of sleep, and it terrifies me.

"Which one?" Ethan's soft voice brings me back into the museum. He dangles two protein bars in front of my face. "Double chocolate or vanilla milk shake?"

Chocolate, I think, but a toxic cocktail of frustration and pain, coupled with disgust at the sickening images in my head, suddenly replaces my hunger.

"Vanilla milk shake," I find myself saying as I snatch the bar from his hand.

"Nice, she's up."

Ethan and I both turn to face Jeremy. He perches against the rusted doorway, twirling a butterfly knife like it's a toy and grinning. "You were gone far too long, Claudia Virtue, but I'm glad you're finally back. It's not the same without you. You're way more interesting than April."

What isn't the same? Raids? I draw a dizzying breath in through my nose. I am dying to demand an explanation. To force them to give me a play-by-play of the events following the woman's death in the courthouse and the brief appearance of the gray-eyed boy dressed in black. But all I manage to do is take another bite of the stale protein bar and stare idiotically between the two of them.

"Thank you both for completely going against my wishes and lying about it. It really makes me want to throw you both out of my clan." There are a million thoughts racing through my head and none of them are being verbalized— Instead, everything that I've managed to say has been a confusing mess.

Jeremy winks at me, but it looks so unnatural a shiver creeps through my body. "Don't be so dramatic, Claudia." He kicks his heel against the door frame and starts to walk off. "I'll catch you in a bit. April and I need to go finish clearing out the jail," he calls out.

"I really should get rid of all of you," I say.

"Don't be like that, Oliv—"

"Don't call me that!" I snap, focusing on Jeremy's back as he walks away. Even though Ethan didn't get a chance to finish his sentence, my heartbeat speeds up. He was about to call me Olivia, I think. The name from my nightmare. The name of that other girl. How does Ethan know about that?

"Don't bend your own rules." I grind the tip of my index finger against Ethan's bony chest. "Never call me that."

I don't understand the painful disconnect between what I'm thinking and what I'm actually saying today. Why am I bringing up the rules? Within our clan, there are only two rules: never leave one another behind. And never break. Up until now I was certain the rule about breaking referred to us bringing up who we were before The Aftermath—what good did dwelling on things we couldn't remember do us?

Now I'm not sure what it means.

"Rules are meant to be broken every once in a while. Besides, we almost lost you, and who knows what would've happened then."

I never cry, but I want to right now. From frustration. And from the numbing ache in the center of my head. I am going insane. That's the only thing that makes any sense. I turn to Ethan and open my mouth to speak, expecting a dam to burst and all my questions about what happened after I was knocked out to come rushing out in a deluge. But all I say is, "April's the one who wanted to move to this place, huh?"

No. That's not what's important to me. Not what I need to say.

The left corner of his mouth tugs up. He stares out of the store-room to where April is touching the giant statue that's the centerpiece of the museum. "How'd you guess?"

I look at April, too. Her head is lowered so that her red hair tumbles around the faded golden feet. That statue makes the end of society bearable for her— She's never said so, but I figured that must be the reason she's drawn to it. After every successful rescue mission or raid, she comes here. The thief and her shrine.

April's lips move for a few seconds longer; then she presses her lips to the golden shield the statue carries. She looks up at us, smiles at Ethan, waves and finally disappears out a side door.

Maybe April is ecstatic now that this is our home, but her obsession is the last thing that matters to me. I hate myself for my inability to say what's needed. I close my eyes to ground myself. And for that moment, I am no longer in the black mold-infested storage room of a dilapidated museum. I don't even think I am in my world at all.

I am outside it, looking in from a white room.

There are flashing red lights embedded in the ceiling at each corner of the room—ten of them in all. Every light is turned in my direction, like spotlights. The only furnishing in here is a plush leather chair that's empty. And all around the chair are large video screens that completely cover all ten sides of the wall.

In front of me, the side of Ethan's face and body fill one of the displays. Two years ago, we took up residence in a movie theater on the far side of town. One of the screens was faulty, playing the same old movie on a monotonous loop. Every time I walked past it, I saw bits and pieces of the film, a movie about car racing. This bright room reminds me of that theater except the picture quality is vivid, not crackled and grainy. Ethan is so lifelike I wouldn't know he was an image if I couldn't see the white border snaking across the top and bottom of the ten-sided room.

Ethan stares at the statue, and someone says, "I'm glad we didn't have to change things—bring in another character." It takes me a moment to realize the person talking is the one in the blindingly white room and even longer to grasp that I am not that girl. Our voices are completely different—hers is soft and whispery.

The same voice from my dreams.

Am I asleep now?

Is everything that's happened to me today nothing but a strange dream that I'll awaken from, ready to look for more food?

Ethan's smile illuminates the entire display. I observe, transfixed, as he reaches out. On the screen, his fingertips seem to brush back and forth over an imaginary object. "Me, too. We'll get out of here soon, okay? I promise. Maybe…it's time to leave the others—just you and me. So the game can be fun again."

"Hmm, I don't know about that. There's that pesky little rule about team size, remember?" the girl in the white room asks. This time I hear my voice, too, speaking in unison with her. "We should stay put right where we are. At least for the time being."

I startle, and when my eyes fly open, the screens are gone, replaced by the museum itself. Ethan is in front of me—real, touchable. I tremble softly, praying he does not notice how my breath bursts in and out. He strokes my cheek with his thumb and forefinger. Exactly like the motion I saw on the display in the decagon room.

His hand stops moving, pausing right under my lower lashes on the left side of my face. He stares down at me. My heart drums violently inside my chest. I try to swallow, but my mouth is so dry, my tongue is glued to the roof of my mouth. What just happened? What's happening to me?

At last, he gives me a smile. "We have more chance of staying alive with them. You know this already, Olivia," he says grimly.

Olivia. Here I am, my heart in my throat and my body numb, and Ethan is saying her name again. I rise on my toes and run my lips along his cheek. All this is happening, but I am not the one doing it. I'm too stunned to move. "Stop calling me that, Landon," I hear myself say in a low whisper.

A chill races through my bones.

Who is Landon?

Ethan laughs and pushes me back. "Got to go for a little. My mother…"

He does not have a mother. Ethan is just like me and doesn't remember anything before the apocalypse and doesn't know anyone named Olivia. Isn't he?

"Claudia?" he asks.

Things seem to move in slow motion for the next few moments.

"Go tend to your mommy," I say. "It's time to give Claudia a rest anyway—her health level is crap. Log back on in three hours?"

"See you then."

Log back on to what? I should know exactly what I mean—after all, it's me saying these words, my voice!—but I don't, and inside, I am screaming.

"Yes, see you then," I say, just before an electric tingle begins in the center of my skull, oozing down my face and body until it mutes each of my senses.

When the prickling sensation stops, I find myself under the statue, staring up at a large crack in its head. In the background, I hear crackling food wrappers. Hushed whispers. Above the statue, the night sky creates a dark canvas over the windows.

When did it get dark? My head throbs as I try to remember what I did after my strange conversation with Ethan. Nothing clear comes to me, just fuzzy images. I am sick of distorted pictures and forgetfulness.

A light flickers across the statue's concrete face, and I think I am the one holding it. There's no way I can be sure, though.

I am not in my body.

For the second time in one day, I'm on the outside, in the white room with the red flashing lights.

The girl in this room—the girl whose eyes I stare out of—shakes out her pale hands. On the screen a sleeping bag cracks up and down. Dust floats from the fabric before the bag drifts to the floor.

"Hungry?"

We turn to the right, to a screen where Jeremy's brown eyes greet us. They look empty—exactly like Ethan's eyes. I feel this person's head nod, hear this girl's voice and mine simultaneously say, "Didn't think you'd save anything for me."

I watch the screen in a mixture of horror and curiosity as it changes. The museum fades into the background. At the very top, THE AFTERMATH is written in a gritty block font with every few letters distorted and the color of blood. Just under that, on the right of the screen, is my photo followed by several rows of information.

Name: Claudia Virtue
Date of Birth: 04/22/2023
Blood Type: B Negative
Height: 5'3"
Weight: 101 Lbs.

This is the same data written on the bent, peeling ID card I found in my back pocket when I woke up three years ago—the only difference is the photo and my height and weight are all current. At least, I assume my measurements are recent. I've never come across a scale, though I have taken up counting visible bones when I wash up in the privy.

Beneath my personal information are a bunch of words and numbers. Long colored bars.

Life. Eighty-six. Green.

Health. Seventy-one. Yellow bar.

Sustenance. The number beside this is low—thirty-three—but I watch as it raises and the red gauge slowly changes color. Forty-two, red. Fifty-one. Sixty, orange. Seventy-two…yellow. The Health numbers have changed, too. Low eighties and neon green.

The girl moves her finger across the empty space in front of us. The red X at the top of the screen glows. My picture and the information collapse, showing the museum again. The others are lying on their bellies in a circle around one of the pillars, on top of sleeping bags with their flashlights creating a ring of light. The girl takes one step forward. Transparent letters flash in the middle of the screen. *Walk Mode*. She taps her palm out once and the picture gradually zooms in on my friends. The girl flicks her hand two more times, the screen stills and she stands right above Ethan.

Through the girl's eyes, I can see a stray eyelash on his cheek; I can count the strands of hair falling onto his bruised forehead.

He tilts his face up and smiles. The cut on his neck looks so much worse on the screen, and I want to shout at him. Shake him until he shows some emotion other than contentment, does something to address his awful wound. "It took you forever," he says.

"I was at thirty percent," I listen to myself say. "It always takes more time when that happens."

"Stop doing that so much, will you?" April's voice says from my left side. When I turn to her, I am back in the museum, back inside my own head and body. "We'll never finish this game with your character getting sick or beat up at every turn."

The corners of my mouth feel as if they're ripping open as my lips are coerced into a smile. I catch a glimpse of my reflection in one of the dark windows. My face isn't damaged like Ethan's. There's not a new blemish in sight; even my sunburn is gone.

And as I sit, listening to the others talk and responding with someone else's words, I come to terms with something terrifying.

My reality isn't at all what I believed it to be. It's not even real.

I'm some sort of puppet, and this girl, Olivia, is the one pulling my strings.

CHAPTER FOUR

An hour later, I tell the others that I'm ready to leave. This is something I always say before I go to sleep, sometimes losing consciousness for hours and days at a time, and for the first time I understand why—it's not me that's leaving. It's the girl, Olivia. Ethan draws me in for a kiss as usual, stroking my blond hair from my forehead as he promises me we'll be together again soon. Then April and Jeremy mumble goodbyes.

But for some reason, this time it's different. I don't black out like I normally do. At least not entirely. I feel the numbing static from earlier start in the middle of my head, but when it reaches my eyes and ears, it pauses. For the next hour the pricking sensation slides up and down my entire body, dragging me in and out of darkness like a chaotic light show.

And then, consciousness. I'm awake in the museum, in our safe room. Every shelter we've ever lived in has The Save—a space we hide out in to rest. It's where I am when I lose consciousness, and when I come to after a lapse. I've got a suspicion The Save has a function other than what I believed it to be.

My eyes fix straight across from me at Ethan's hazel ones. They're open and emotionless. His lips are drawn into a thin line. What are we? *Where* are we?

How did I get here?

I feel my right eyelid twitch, feel the muscles in my fingers tense as I try to move them. Am I human? If The Aftermath isn't even real, how do I know I am?

What am I?

When I'm sucked back into unconsciousness, I'm hit with a terrifying string of nightmares. At first, I dream of the boy in the elevator, with his clean face and dark eyes. My time with him is fleeting—just long enough for him to give me a crooked smile and cover his lips with his index finger. "Good night, Virtue," he murmurs. Then he swings out at me, rendering me unconscious, sending me to another dream world that's even more terrifying.

Men and women in crisp dark suits stalk in slow, deliberate circles around me like vultures. They're so close I can smell them—the scents of vanilla perfume and cigar smoke and foul-smelling armpits mingling together—and I feel sick to my stomach. There's no food left in me to vomit, though. I must have gotten rid of it all earlier, after...

There is something I can't remember—something important—but it refuses to come to me.

"She's the first," a man says from the back of the crowd.

The first what?

A woman touches a few strands of my hair—it's long in this nightmare—and studies me carefully. She reminds me of an owl with her large light-colored eyes and bobbed salt-and-pepper hair. "I was told she performed exceedingly well in the War trial. When do you plan to put her in?"

"Tonight," the man in the back says. The woman smiles at me. She has small teeth, like a piranha.

I want her to stop touching me. I don't want to be in this dream any more than my last nightmare, the one with the metallic white machine and the mechanical arms. But I can't leave. I'm standing perfectly still, letting these people appraise me. And this time I'm certain I'm in my own body.

"I'm a human," I plead, but this only seems to amuse the group of people. They smile at me as if I'm a small child speaking her very first words. A man wearing a black-and-gray-dotted tie touches the top of my head. I shriek as pain blisters my scalp.

"I've heard The Aftermath's designers did an excellent job constructing the game's world. My business partner toured the game and says it's the most realistic one yet, with the asteroids and ruins," the man says, ignoring how much agony his touch is causing me. He shoots a look over his shoulder.

The smug voice behind everyone replies, "Physical reality is always realistic, but I agree. The Aftermath is a winner. Claudia is perfect— a symbol of dedication and progress." When the crowd separates and the man walks forward, I can't make out his face—it's blurry—but I know I want to hurt him.

I've never wanted anything so much in my life.

"And let it be known, I am dedicated to this cause," the man adds, and applause erupts around him.

My nightmare disintegrates the moment I fling myself at him, my fist tight around the sharp needle I find hidden in the waistband of my starched pants.

My eyes open, and I'm back in my body, staring around The Save. I am human.

And I know with conviction that my dream—at least the second one about the crowd—was a memory, something that happened to me before The Aftermath. As I lie on my side, my arm falling asleep from the weight of my body, I'm ecstatic—or as ecstatic as a person who just found out her life is a fake can be. My first memory. My first genuine, frightening memory that doesn't involve The Aftermath.

I am not just some virtual person stuck in a reality that was created by computers. I am something else. Something called a character. A human trapped inside an intentional hell that's been created by designers—other humans. These are my last thoughts just before the electric current that makes my teeth chatter descends upon me.

And this time, it powers me down completely so that there are no more memories.

"We need to plan a massive raid," I'm saying to my clan when the other girl inside my head flips the lights back on. I'm positioned on top of my sleeping bag in a sitting position with my legs crossed at the ankles. "It's been too long, and I feel like I'm losing my touch."

"Losing your touch?" April turns her gaze toward me, and my shoulders lift in a shrug. "*Okay*, what are you thinking, Claudia?"

"We could go to The Badlands," Jeremy suggests, rolling a bottle of water to April. That's where we'd found her a couple of months ago. The Badlands are a part of the city where a bunch of flesh-eaters live inside and around a football stadium—a death trap that's only intensified by the massive sinkholes in the football field and where some of the buildings once stood. When the flesh-eaters are finished with their victims, those holes become a resting place for the dead.

The Badlands are about five miles south of here, and the last time we made the trip there, we killed several flesh-eaters. Raided everyone we came in contact with, cannibals and Survivors. Everything we did was dangerous and reckless, and I remember it all.

When I realize that I am inside the white room again, I don't think I'm the only one those memories belong to.

"If we go to The Badlands, we'll have to use points to upgrade weapons. It's not like we can just go in with knives and a few guns," April complains. On the screen, she's twirling the ends of her red hair around her skinny wrist. Three twirls. Unravel. Four twists. Unknot. I remember all the times I've told her she should upgrade to a haircut.

"That's how you'll get caught," I'd told her once. "Some flesh-eater is going to snag you by all that stupid hair and I'm not going to do a damn thing to save you. I don't care how many points you offer me."

At the time, I'd inwardly cringed over how callous and heartless I sounded. How confusing my words were, when truly I'd do just about anything to keep my group safe. Now I don't think it was myself at all saying that to April.

"You have to spend points to make points," the girl in the white room says in sync with me inside the game. "Unless you're too afraid of failing, April. If that's the case, maybe you'd be better suited for another group. One that moves at your pace. I'm sure you'll finish up by the time you're twenty-one."

"Olivia—" Ethan begins, but he quickly corrects himself. "Claudia…maybe we should save The Badlands for later. Give ourselves another month or two to load up on some better weapons, get some new supplies."

Olivia, the girl in the ten-sided room, doesn't say anything for several seconds. She taps her foot against the white laminate floor. She's wearing heels. Just like in the nightmare that I had after I was hit in the courthouse.

But I don't think that was a dream, either. It must have been what was happening to me at that very moment. Could it be that the Regenerator and Dr. Coleman are both real? At last, I hear Olivia sigh. "You, too, Ethan?" He nods. The way he moves his head so quickly can't be good for the gash under his chin. "Fine. Let's do things your way this time. See how well we manage."

I can tell she's livid, though, by her sharp, jerky motions. She slams her hands out in front of her, which pulls up a screen that lists supplies. There are weapons—every knife and gun and hacksaw that's come into my possession over the past three years, as well as my clothing and the little bit of food I currently have. The Glock is on this list, and so is the cold-weather jacket I took from the woman at the courthouse.

More than thirty-six months of my life, summarized on ten over-size screens.

"But just so you know, I've plenty of good weapons to go to The Badlands." The center screen focuses in on April as Olivia and I say this. She starts to say something else, but then there's a knock on the door behind her. "What?" she snarls, turning around.

"Your car is waiting upstairs to take you to your academy," a woman says.

"I'm not going today."

"Don't be ridiculous. Get off now or I'll come in and disconnect you."

When Olivia twists back to her screens and the game, she is seething. Her hands are flushed as she works her way through the various menus, and I imagine her face is just as red. I wonder what she looks like. "Ugh…I've got to go to class. Hopefully, I'll be back tonight."

A minute later she opens a screen with a square in the middle that reads, "Gamer Name" (GmrGrl06) and "Password," which is so small I'm unable to read what it is. Below that information is a purple horizontal block with the word *Logout* inside of it. When she slaps her hand over the bar, the images on the screens disappear, leaving nothing but transparent glass.

This is when I completely lose her, and I find myself in the exact

spot I was the night before. Flickering in and out of consciousness.
One moment there's blackness—so dark it's as if I don't exist at all—
and the next I'm in her head for a few seconds, observing flashes of
what she sees. A world made of buildings that are whole and vehicles
that aren't rusted and broken and people who aren't emaciated and
hopeless. A world that is vastly different from The Aftermath. This
change in cognizance happens so often and so quickly that when I find
myself partially awake inside the museum, surrounded by a bunch of
blank faces, my head is reeling from dizziness.

My hands ball into fists.

Because I will them to.

"Wake up," I try to say between my clenched teeth. It comes out
sluggish and barely audible—the static current is slinking down my
face. "Get up and fight this."

Before I go to sleep again, I think of Olivia, the girl in the decagon room. The girl I've dreamed about.

The girl who operates a character named Claudia Virtue in The
Aftermath.

It's all a game to her, and she's controlling me. Olivia.

My gamer.

CHAPTER FIVE

A day and a half of wavering in and out of Olivia's mind and consciousness passes. I can't figure out why it's happening, but being inside her head is better than being lifeless in my own. When she next comes back to the game, and I'm completely aware of myself, it is daylight, raining. Thunder rattles the skylights and reverberates off the sculptures. I'm immediately greeted by April. Ethan has told her we must find a new place to live because the museum is no longer a viable option. Apparently, he wasn't kidding when he said he'd change shelters for me.

No, not for me. For my gamer.

For Olivia.

I shrug into a thin gray hoodie, and I'm powerless to stop myself from stupidly venturing out into the humid storm. Everything feels different now that I'm aware a stranger is in my head, responsible for my forgetfulness and the inconsistency between my thoughts and movements and words. I want time to absorb this revelation, to try and figure out why I can think for myself but not even lift my own hand if I wish to. What I don't want is a new useless mission that may get me killed.

I'm more afraid than I've ever been.

"Jeremy's coming, too," April announces. She pulls her empty bag over her shoulder. I study her carefully. The way she buckles her holster of weapons around her waist—it shimmies down to hang low on her hips, just above the waistband of her shorts. I study the robotic way she flips her red hair over one shoulder. The way her blue eyes stare me down. Unfocused and glassy, just like the rest of my clan.

"Five minutes—that's all I'm waiting. I don't have much time today," I say. I imagine Olivia in her brightly lit room, checking the time every few seconds as she glares at April's image on the screen.

Jeremy takes another two minutes. He's dressed in ragged jeans and a T-shirt with a faint stain on the sleeve. I remember this shirt—it's the one he wore when he and Ethan ransacked a flesh-eater den several months ago. Looking at Jeremy in that T-shirt makes me think of the woman who died at the courthouse in my most recent raid. The one who, for the briefest moment, had reminded me of my friend Mia. A lump forms in my throat.

Olivia's killed so many people for something that's not even her reality. And she's used me to do it.

"You are pathetically slow," Olivia says through me.

Jeremy turns his head in my direction and gives me a dead smile. "This'll be over quickly."

I lift the padlock hanging from the ropes of chains on the door and begin picking it open with a rusty paper clip I find in the pocket of my shorts. "You say that every time we go out."

Jeremy reaches past me and wiggles the bent metal around until the lock comes undone in his large hands. He dangles it from his thumb and index finger before dropping it into my palm, his fingertips brushing my thumb. My heart hammers painfully in my chest, and chills slink across every inch of my skin.

This is the first time I've ever been spooked by Jeremy's touch.

He'd joined our group shortly after Mia. Back then I'd believed Jeremy was the most beautiful person I'd ever seen. Ridiculously tall, he has smooth olive skin, light brown eyes and a nose that hasn't been broken repeatedly like Ethan's.

Now that I know my life is a game, and I'm certain Jeremy and April and Ethan aren't at all who I believed them to be... Well, I'm not sure what I think. His eyes frighten me. I want to release a sigh of relief as Jeremy lets go of my hand and begins joking about my fondness for drawn-out raids.

I smile and nod, agreeing with everything he's saying.

But I want to vomit.

"...on Union's a good start," April is saying. Fat droplets of rain pelt her face. She doesn't blink.

"Right," I say. "Let me check—"

The accidental slide into Olivia's mind is less disquieting than before, now that I know what's going on, but it still manages to rock me. THE AFTERMATH is written at the top of the screen again. This time a gigantic map takes up the entirety of every display. I'm not interested in the way Olivia flicks her fingertips through the air to navigate our surroundings.

It's the miniature headshots with names typed beneath them that lure me in. Each name is highlighted either red or green, and underneath each green name is a neon-blue number.

What the hell does all this mean?

"Flesh-eaters on Union in one of the hotels," Olivia forces me to reply. "I refuse to deal with them today, so try again."

I study the screen Olivia is looking at painstakingly. My photo is there. So are Jeremy's and April's. Our names are written in bold green, capitalized font and our information is positioned right over the gold-colored rectangle labeled "Museum." My image is unsettling. Droopy eyes, as if I'm heavily medicated, and a giant smile on my face that shows my chipped canine. I practically lose my hold on Olivia's head.

I chipped my tooth not even a few weeks ago—this picture is that recent.

And I've no recollection of it being taken.

I do my best to push this thought out of my mind so I can concentrate on the task at hand. I want to see if I can find the spot where Olivia said the flesh-eaters were hiding.

It takes me a couple of minutes to locate Union Street because there are so many words and lines and shapes that signify the places we frequently raid. Finally, I find it in the upper-right-hand corner. I scan a row of gray squares—they're all labeled "Hotel." When I come to the one with three pictures lying over it, though, I freeze.

The names below those photos are all written in red.

And at the very top of the game screen is a small box that explains what all these colors mean. Neon blue for current points (updated within the last thirty seconds). Green for Survivors, for us. Crimson for flesh-eaters.

I look at the three red names on the gray square once again. Then I study my own spot on the game map. The number that must represent Olivia's points within the game—80,973. The green font beneath my photograph. And I realize something that makes me feel sick.

Olivia can see exactly where the people who want to kill me are.

I have been attacked and I've had the crap beaten out of me and Olivia can see the threat's precise location.

There's nothing I want more than to wrap my fingers around her neck and strangle her.

I hear my voice say, "Nothing on Demonbreun."

"Demonbreun Street it is, then," April replies. "Because Claudia Virtue is a boring wimp today."

I retreat from Olivia's thoughts as easily as I crept in. The map remains in my mind, reds and greens swirling together in a sickening tie-dye. Do all those photos represent people like me? Prisoners inside their own minds, people being used by other people in white rooms?

Are the cannibals pawns in this game, too? Being controlled by someone else who makes them attack and eat other humans?

And are any of these people—red or green, Survivor or flesh-eater—aware that the person dominating them can at any time force them onto the wrong street or into the wrong building?

Kill them in the flutter of an eye?

For the first time in my memory, I don't pay attention to my surroundings. I don't listen to what Jeremy and April are saying, or the way the rain drenches my clothes, weighing me down, as we take the long route to the crumbling buildings on Demonbreun Street.

I just focus on Olivia.

"Go right," she says through me, and I think of all the innuendos that I've ignored, all the strange things I've said that I chalked up to some neurological issue caused by the apocalypse and accepted with very few questions. Strange conversations. Lost time. The constant difference between my thoughts and what I say and do. Why we've never left this area, despite the hordes of cannibals. Why leave when food and supplies and enemy locations are only a screen away?

Why leave when the person on the screen isn't really you—and even if you do make a stupid decision, you won't be the one suffering for it?

There was no end of the world. There's only a game called The Aftermath, and I feel stupid for just now realizing this.

Back-alley ruins blur my vision. A liquor store sign swings from wires—it bangs the side of a building, making a noise like clacking teeth. A few feet away from it is an overturned garbage container that's so rusted there are holes bigger than my fists throughout it. A man sags against the front of the trash bin with eyes wide-open and his head turned to the side in an unnatural angle.

"Need to do a cleanup," April says.

I hear myself agree, but inside I am seething.

Because on Olivia's map, the man's name is green, just like mine. Unlike mine, it's flickering rapidly.

Olivia waits until we find a spot she determines is "perfect for shelter" before she mentions leaving again. I know what this means, and I'm prepared for it. Still, it's as though my breastbone and spine are slowly shrinking in on my heart, squeezing each beat out of it until it stops completely.

I don't want to go wherever it is I go when Olivia logs out. I don't want to wait for Olivia to go into her game room for the chance to think for myself again. I want to think now—because my brain is the only thing about myself that's partway mine.

We place empty water bottles in the alleyway so that we can gather rainwater for drinking and bathing, then start the process of securing the building. Out of all the ones we checked, it's the only structure with no broken windows and a somewhat decent bathroom and that's not attached to a half-dozen others. When Olivia finds the spot on her map, it's also the only one that's several minutes' walking distance from any other *character*.

Just thinking that word turns my stomach, and I wonder briefly if Olivia, in her safe little room, can feel everything I do.

"There's a box of food up here," Jeremy shouts from upstairs.

It probably belonged to someone with a green name, I think. Like that man against the trash bin. But I say, "Bring it on down."

April's behind the bar, sifting through partial bottles of liquor, and doesn't even flinch when Jeremy slams the box on the counter-top. "Anything good?" I say.

"Protein bars, water bottles—not sure if it's safe for drinking or if it's contaminated, though. And there's—" he grins at us, slowly pulling a handful of dusty black wrappers from the worn cardboard "—beef jerky."

April snorts, and I imagine her vacant blue eyes rolling. Glass clanks together behind the bar, and she asks, "Find The Save?"

My ears perk up. I still haven't discovered what The Save's purpose is within the game, but I'm determined to find out. I want to know everything about this manufactured world I live in.

"Upstairs," Jeremy says. "It's the only door on the right. Bed and everything—there's another privy inside of it, too."

I leave them talking about the room over the bar and what items they've found so I can check the alley door once again. Olivia has me jiggle the knob, bang hard on the dead bolt with the palm of my hand. It's secure.

Olivia talks to April and Jeremy as she steers me toward each window to take a look at the locks. "I'll be gone for a few days," I say. I'm used to whispering little conundrums like this and even more accustomed to being completely confused by what it means. Now I know exactly what it means—I'll be unconscious until whenever Olivia chooses to return. My stomach rolls.

"I hate that you'll be away," April says. Jeremy agrees with her.

My head bobs up and down. Olivia's likely doing the same thing. "Hey, do me a favor?" I call over my shoulder as I grab my bag and walk to the staircase. Resting my arm on the splintered banister, I turn to look at them with my other hand on my hip. "Lock up when you leave, okay?"

Jeremy nods quickly. "Mmm-hmm."

The stairway sounds as if it will collapse at any moment as I sprint up the steps, taking two at a time, sometimes three when I come to a stair that's too risky to test my weight on. I go into The Save and toss my bag onto the bed. Olivia makes me climb in next to it, maneuvering me into a lying position with my back against the wall.

It takes me a moment to comprehend that she has no plan to go with the others back to the museum. She's leaving me here, on this mattress that sags in the middle—in a bar with spray-painted windows and a floor that smells like cooking oil—with no way to defend myself. She will leave me motionless with a gun in my waistband, staring with unseeing eyes at a bag of food inches away.

Passive.

Dead, breathing.

The purpose of The Save is obvious to me now: it is here so gamers can leave their characters in a safe place while they're away from the game.

My head starts to buzz just as I hear the noisy click of the padlock on one of the doors downstairs. I stare up at the only window in this room, watch the rain splatter in places where the spray paint hasn't completely blocked the glass. I wait.

An eternity passes by with me sitting and staring, staring and waiting. What is Olivia doing? I don't understand why I haven't blacked out yet, and for a moment, I wonder if I have and this is me waking up again.

"Just do it already!"

These four words echo through the empty building, like hundreds of bullets going off all at once. I'm breathless when the silence returns. Are these my words? My whole body trembles at even the idea.

"My name is Claudia Virtue, and The Aftermath is not real," I whisper. "The Aftermath is just a game."

Years of conflicting thoughts and words, and the first ones that are truly mine are agitated, partially psychotic. I'll take it. Right now, I'm too afraid to try and move. I feel as though at any moment, Olivia will take over my body. Then she'll make me let this go.

When another several minutes pass and I am still looking up at the window, I move my right foot off the bed, then my left. I am hungry. I am thirsty.

I am free.

I raid the box of food Jeremy left on the counter downstairs. I eat a chocolate protein bar slowly, and then I think of the sustenance gauge—bright red with a disgustingly low percentage—on Olivia's screen and devour two more. I twirl around in dizzying circles on a ripped bar stool. Scream at the top of my lungs until my throat is raw and my chest heaves up and down.

And suddenly I have an idea. I grip the edges of the counter, place my forehead against the warm, grimy laminate, and I concentrate. I think of Olivia and everything I've learned about myself just recently. I imagine getting out of the game that's been my reality for so long.

I think of revenge.

When Olivia's mind sucks me in, I'm in her world. And despite the beautiful freedom I've tasted for mere seconds, I'd rather remain here, stuck inside her head. We are in the back of a car. But this is nothing like the one with the missing tires and shattered windows Ethan and I took shelter in a couple of years ago. For starters, this car must be self-driving, because there's nobody else in here with Olivia and me. The interior is immaculate, sleek black leather with gleaming metallic accents. There are flat monitors mounted on the backs of the headrests, one that's tuned to a ribbon cutting taking place in front of a gleaming glass building and the other on a loop of silent advertisements.

Olivia's used to seeing all this, so there are limits to what I'm able to observe since she's not paying very much attention to our surroundings. Intricate skyscrapers tower over the car. The path we're taking weaves between the buildings, and the car speeds effortlessly through traffic. When the car stops itself at a red light, my attention is drawn to the bus next to us. There are commercials playing on the side of this bus.

Once the current advertisement ends, a woman comes on the screen. Even from inside Olivia's car, I can hear what she's saying. "If you've received a diagnosis for the Warrior gene or AVD Type A or B and have received a physician's order, visit us at LanCorp International, where you can complete your treatment in as little as—"

I don't have a chance to wonder about what AVD Type A and B means because Olivia grumbles something under her breath and runs her fingertip across one of the monitors mounted to the headrest. She enters a series of numbers. Suddenly, all the windows darken until nothing on the outside is visible inside the car. There's no sound coming in now, either.

This is incredible.

With the push of a few buttons, Olivia can cancel out distractions. I've never seen anything so incredible, and I want to know what else she's capable of.

What else is this world capable of?

I'm still shaky when I unravel myself from her mind and drop back into The Aftermath. "She's not in her game room," I say, picturing Olivia's white room with its flashing red lights. "She's not there." I repeat this like a mantra through mouthfuls of food and water until I am sick to my stomach.

I crawl through a window, out into the rain. I'm standing in the center of the rows of bottles and jugs we set out here, with water dripping into my eyes and my clothes drenched, because I want to be here. Nobody forces me against my will.

After a few minutes of wandering through the storm, I climb back into the bar and bolt the window. Then I down a few more bottles of water and pick up my empty energy bar wrappers, until I hear the padlock move on one of the doors. I'm reluctant to go back into The Save—I don't want to huddle in a corner like I'm cowering from the world—but I do it anyway, unwilling to be caught. I close my eyes and tune out the people I've spent months, years, with.

I fall asleep—into a true sleep—so I don't listen in until much later, when April and Jeremy enter the room and I catch the end of their conversation.

"...has to be reaching the end of treatment. I've been in it for just about as long as she has, but Olivia's incredible. She has to have double the points I've got. Probably even more."

"You think she'll be deleted?" she asks. I open my eyes a bit. She sits on a plastic crate, staring at a torn beer poster on the wall. "She's pretty damaged."

Jeremy glances around, then shrugs. "I doubt it, even if she's been around awhile." He glances at me when he says this. "I mean, she's good and Virtue is a big deal. She'll stay in this game, even when Olivia finishes."

April turns her vacant blue eyes in my direction, too. "Olivia won't let anyone else take ownership of her. She'll find some way to have Claudia deleted before she does that—I guarantee it. Princess doesn't want anyone else's mind on her precious Virtue." Despite April's monotone voice, a ripple of dread squirms through me. She really hates me. Or Olivia. I'm not too sure if she's made the distinction or cares that there is one.

Jeremy shakes his head sadly. "Such a waste to just...get rid of her altogether."

"Why do you put up with her anyway?"

"Who? Olivia?" When April nods her head, he cocks his head to one side and says, "Because she's my friend. You all are."

I have to fight to stay in control and remain still, silent. Because I'm possibly in more danger dealing with Olivia than with the flesh-eaters I once feared more than anything.

I can be eliminated at any moment.

Then I realize something else, something that gives me hope.

If I can get into Olivia's head on purpose, then maybe I can gain control of myself.

And maybe—just maybe—I can escape The Aftermath.

CHAPTER SIX

The process to get into Olivia's mind is initially difficult. When I'm not being drawn into her head at random, I have to concentrate for long stretches of time, and the slightest noise or distraction quickly ruins my progress. I soon discover that squeezing my eyes shut and pressing my forehead against a hard surface gets me where I want to be much faster. Whatever there is inside my own head must be broken. Still, it's a malfunction I'm willing to accept in order to gain information about Olivia.

At first, I'm terrified that she'll realize what I'm able to do, so I flicker in and out, never staying in her head for longer than a minute or two. But after two days of doing this, I begin to relax and stick around for longer stretches of time.

I start to learn about the person who's been playing me for so long.

Today, she goes to the roof of the building she lives in. It's an enormous glassed-in dome with an amazing view of all the skyscrapers around it. On the far side of the roof, parked in front of a double garage door, is a sleek silver car that reminds me of a bullet. Other than the car and the small bench in the center of the dome, the rooftop is empty. Twenty feet above her, metal beams crisscross the top of the dome, making a pattern. A star. In the center of this hangs a light fixture—two curves facing each other that seem to be glowing even though the sun is out.

Olivia presses her hand to a sliver of glass by the door. A digital keypad appears on it and she punches a code in—117908. The lock pops. She starts to turn away but freezes, glaring straight ahead at the building directly across from this one. Sighing, she returns to the keypad and enters a string of codes. All the windows darken, like it is night outside, and the other buildings disappear from sight.

As she walks across the rooftop, a garden bathed in moonlight slowly appears.

Even though I know that the grass beneath her bare feet and the roses curling around an arched trellis are nothing but an illusion, I can't help but want to experience this for myself. There's nothing like this in The Aftermath. Olivia has the technology to bring about an artificial evening and exotic, colorful flowers.

I have dust and dying weeds and sunburn that won't go away.

Olivia stops in a courtyard located in the middle of the garden that looks out of place, ancient, in her world of glass and metal. She sits on a stone bench, clenching her fists in her lap, and breathes in and out, out and in. She does this for a few minutes, not saying a word, and I wonder if this is where she comes to get away from her worries.

Whatever those may be.

A shrill noise interrupts my thoughts. Olivia draws an electronic tablet from her bag and sits it down. To my surprise, when she enters her password on the device, a hologram pops up on the bench beside her—a full-size person to be precise. He's a tall, skinny boy with springy brown hair and tanned skin. He looks so real that I'd swear she could reach out and touch flesh.

She slides closer to him, until the only thing separating them is her tablet. Sighing, she peers down at her lap. "Didn't think you'd actually come," she murmurs, her voice quivering. It's strange to hear Olivia talking to someone and not using me to do it. When she glances up into the boy's eyes—the bluest I've ever seen—she says, "Landon, I've missed you."

Landon. The boy whose name I said while speaking to Ethan a few days ago. Is this the person who controls my friend? Is this boy the person who's really whispered sweet words to me, offered to die for me, for the past few years?

"I can't talk for long," Landon says. "But I wanted to keep my promise, see your face."

"I'm glad you did. Since you didn't make it the last time you promised."

"I have to be careful contacting you outside of the game—you know that. I mean, my parents can barely deal with me being in the same clan as you, so they'd freak out if they knew we were doing this. Mom heard me say your name the other night when I was supposed to meet you here, and she went ballistic."

So this is Ethan's gamer.

And this must be the reasoning behind us saying "Never break" so often. Landon and Olivia can't break character and call each other by their real names. That must be where Ethan and I come in. But why is it that they're not able to talk to each other in their world?

"Told you to stop saying it, didn't I?" Olivia snaps. He flushes, glancing down at his hands. When she speaks again, her voice softens. "Your parents still keeping track of these calls?"

He fights back a frown. Traces her lips with the tip of his finger. She shivers, and I wonder if she can feel anything since he's just a hologram. "You know they are. My mother's all over me every day about the points. She and Dad received my monthly point update on their AcuTabs a couple days ago and it wasn't pretty—72,528 points out of a prescribed 90,000. They wanted to know why I'm going on three years now with no end in sight. They just want me to finish my treatment and—"

"Come off the game so you can get away from me."

"The treatment is expensive and my parents—"

"Are acting like sympathizers," she says, scooting away from him until she's pressed to the far side of the bench. "I'm surprised they don't just go against the law and flat-out refuse to let you play!" The last words are almost shouted, and she grips the bench for support.

"They're my parents. And you know better than anyone how much my father did for LanCorp when the games were being designed. He practically built The Aftermath."

LanCorp. I'd heard that name before, in Olivia's car when I was in her head.

"Then tell your dad thanks for all the glitches early on in the game," Olivia says sarcastically. "And let him know what a hypocrite he is for not wanting you to receive the treatment he helped create."

There's a long moment of silence between them that gives me a chance to gather my bearings and try to sort out everything I've heard them say.

The game is a sort of therapy. Refusing to participate is a crime.

And even though Landon's father had a significant role in the creation of The Aftermath, now he's a possible sympathizer. I'm certain I've heard someone use that word before, but I can't remember when.

The sound of something crackling pulls Olivia's attention away from the flower she's staring at, a hybrid of a rose and an orchid. Landon's projection flashes several times, like a dying lightbulb. She snorts. "Your mother is disconnecting you."

"Olivia, I—"

"Goodbye, Landon," she says sharply, but he's already gone. After she restores the sunlight and noise to the rooftop, taking away the flowers and grass in the process, I jolt back into my own head.

And a memory hits me.

Someone carried me, jarring my body around. I could hear his breathing and feel his sweat running from his skin and onto mine. Pain shot from the tips of my toes to the top of my head as my left side collided with something flat and squishy. Then the harsh scent of mildew on vinyl filled my nostrils.

"Careful so you don't hurt her," a female voice had whispered. "You know who she is, don't you?"

"Don't be such a sympathizer. Because I promise you won't keep your job with the company for very long if you're speaking out against it. It doesn't matter who she was—what she is now is a criminal. Look at her—she's not even sentient. She doesn't even realize what's going on," a male replied, snorting. As if to demonstrate his point, he touched the center of my head, pressing into my flesh until I shrieked in pain.

He was wrong. I'd felt everything.

"She's still a human," the girl grumbled.

Who were they? I can't remember either of their faces, but I know this memory is real. Their voices are too alive for it to be anything else. And even though I've gained another small fragment of my past, I don't feel as if I've made any headway.

Because in order for me to understand why people are against The Aftermath, I need to know why the game was needed in the first place.

"We're going on a raid," I say to April and Jeremy the moment Olivia takes control of me again. "And you two are coming with me."

She's been away from The Aftermath approximately seventy-one hours and twenty-two minutes—I paid close attention to the time.

Just like I kept track of every bit of food and drink I had while the others were inactive and I was left free to roam the game.

"We'd be better off doing a rescue mission," April tells us. "That's where all the points are." But when Olivia maneuvers my gaze toward her, she doesn't say anything else. I wonder if the person playing April is afraid of Olivia. Or if she just loathes my gamer as much as I do.

Jeremy's expression is as deadpan as ever. "Of course I'll go, Claudia."

I feel myself nod. "I'll find a good spot, then." I am still turned toward April, and she gives me a tight-lipped smile.

I go into Olivia's head. It takes a few tries and a lot of concentration since she's playing me and I can't lay my head down, but I manage it.

Next time I do this, I'll gain access to her mind on the first try, I swear to myself.

Olivia checks the display with all my information first. Doesn't seem to notice that my sustenance level is at fifty-seven, not on forty like she left me three days ago. Next time, I'll have to be more careful and exert myself just a little more so she doesn't catch on to what I am able to do.

If there is a next time.

Olivia holds her palm out and moves it to the left, as if she's waving at someone. This drags another page onto the main screen—the long list of supplies.

"Anything in particular you want to find?" April asks.

"Not really. Well…I'd like to stock up on winter gear. I've got a source that says it's setting in soon. But you didn't hear that from me," I say, and Olivia changes the display again.

Summer is nearly over. But the days are still so hot they nearly char your flesh, and I usually return from our forays with blisters on my scalp and neck. How is it possible for winter to come soon? But then

I think of the snowstorm just a few months ago and how it had come right after a scorching hot day. I think of the 110-degree day we experienced last winter, in the middle of January. Maybe the change in the weather is just another element of the game.

Another way to torture unsuspecting characters, challenge our gamers.

"I hate the winter," Jeremy says, and I'm curious if the boy or girl behind his lifeless face is speaking as a character or from personal preference.

"West End," April says. "We haven't raided there in a while."

At last Olivia pulls up the game map. I've waited for this since I pushed myself into her thoughts, and I watch carefully. One flesh-eater is already on West End, but there are four Survivors surrounding him. Prey stalking the predator. Strength in numbers.

Less than a month ago, three flesh-eaters came after me as I was leaving a solo rescue mission at one of the record stores on Broadway. They'd cornered me behind the sales counter, backing me into rows of yellowed, autographed photos of smiling people wearing wide-brimmed hats. "Strength in numbers," one of them had said, leering at me as they began to close in.

I killed them all. One with the jagged neck of a guitar just after he smashed it in an attempt to knock me out, another with his own weapon and the last by wrapping my belt around her neck, pulling it taut until she stopped breathing. But the entire time I'd fought them off, and even as I took their belongings after they were dead, I'd wanted to run and hide.

I still want to do that.

I return my attention to Olivia. She spreads her thumb and index finger apart, then snaps them together in a swift flicking motion. The map expands, revealing hundreds, thousands of the little photos. Whatever is happening on West End no longer matters to me. I am more interested in the area to the left of the screen.

It's not like the rest of the map.

The space beneath my picture and surrounding it is a deep green color. It extends to the right, but even though the left of the screen is still in the shape of a landform, the green stops. And here, the land is shaded black. There are no photos with writing beneath them on this side of the map, nothing but a dark void. I'm not exactly sure how far away it is from my current location. Maybe fifty or so miles? I examine the map carefully, wanting to ensure I haven't missed any other dark areas, but the one to the left is it. Is there a possibility that it's the way out of the game?

I try to draw myself away from looking at the black spot, from the reckless thoughts that are suddenly popping into my mind, but it's impossible. The left of the map is different from everything else on the screen. I have to go there. I need to see for myself if the empty space is my way out. And I plan to make the trip at the first available opportunity.

"We'll wait until they're done, then follow them to see what they have," I hear myself say, and I know Olivia's talking about the four Survivors who have the flesh-eater surrounded on West End. All I can concentrate on is the black space.

"Any place else to go while we wait?" April asks. "You know, some way to actually earn points?"

Olivia zooms back in on the map, and green fills the display once again. I've seen plenty, though. Fifty miles, give or take a few. Northwest. Freedom. I want to leave now. I feel as if I could walk all fifty miles in one day and be out of The Aftermath by tomorrow morning.

"Lower-level flesh-eaters on Second Street. Pathetic, but they are usually good for something. Happy?"

"At the rate we're going, I'll never get my points," April whines so low I'm not sure Olivia can hear her, but I do, even with my mind set on running fifty miles.

Of course, my thoughts are wishful. Traveling that many miles in the course of one day in this heat would be dangerous, and, besides, I am not in control of my own body at the moment. I've no idea when Olivia will let me go, and even then, how much time I'll have without her coming back into the game.

But right now, that doesn't matter. Because I am almost certain I have figured the way out. The route that will get me to the world I saw through Olivia's eyes with its luminous buildings.

Finally, the red name on West End disappears, along with the picture above it, and Olivia closes the map. I don't need it anymore, though; while Olivia talked about strategy and raids and points—apparently earning them is an important part of playing the game—I committed it to memory.

Olivia plays me consistently for two days, waiting until my head splits from hunger and my stomach is about to cave in on itself to feed me. I use these forty-eight hours as an opportunity to practice getting in and out of her mind. I also have enough time to come up with various explanations for this ability I've gained that none of my friends seem to possess.

Brain tumors—her brain or mine.

Gamer–character telepathy.

A sudden blow to the head—one that came from a boy who was completely out of place in The Aftermath, at least if my faulty memory can be trusted. Despite my uncertainty about the boy, this is the theory that makes the most sense. Even though I'm still not entirely sure of all the events that took place afterward.

My chance at escape finally comes fifty-two hours after Olivia's return to the game, on a Wednesday afternoon. She's going on a trip with her father. She will be gone for five days. And she's convinced the others to take a break right along with her.

"I'm putting us on Group Save," she makes me tell everyone else as we huddle around in The Save. She has me standing in the middle of the room, with my hands on my hips. "So don't get any ideas about going ahead without me."

When April complains, Ethan and Jeremy come to Olivia's defense.

Jeremy shrugs his broad shoulders and then sits in the chair by the door. "It's not a big deal." He shifts his body so that he's sideways, draping his long legs over the armrest.

"He's right, April," Ethan says. I hear him moving behind me—his shoes make a scratching noise on the floor as he comes close. "It's five days, not forever. Besides, I have schoolwork to catch up on." He places his chin gently on the top of my head and circles his arms around me, locking my elbows in place by my sides. Suddenly, I'm dizzy.

Let go of me.

The pressure on my head—in the exact location I was recently injured—makes me nauseous. I can smell the acidic soap he used an hour ago when he washed up in the privy downstairs. Feel the tips of his fingers pressed into the flesh on either side of my belly button.

I'm not sure I want his hands on me anymore. Because nothing about the two of us is what I thought it to be. Our bodies are being used by Olivia and Landon.

Please, just let me go.

Olivia makes me turn slightly, smile up at him. She moves my hands so that they curl over his forearms. "That settles it. Group Save."

Olivia sets my character on something called Self-Sustain Mode. I watch through her eyes as she configures my Self-Sustain list. One protein bar a day. Two bottles of water. Enough food and fluid to keep me alive, but nothing more. Well, as far as she knows. But I don't plan on eating any more stale protein bars in the near future. Once I'm outside of the game, I hope I won't ever have to even look at a protein bar again.

She leaves me in the room over the bar with the others, cloaked in semidarkness, lying next to Ethan. I use whatever link I have to her brain to make sure she is completely away from the game before I consider moving. Then, just for good measure, I wait about another two hours, staring at Jeremy, who's motionless in the chair across from the bed. Finally, I unwrap myself from Ethan's arms and ease up from the flat mattress. I grab a flashlight from my bag.

My legs are numb from the position Olivia left me in. I shake them out and pace the small room a few times before kneeling down to look for April's holster of weapons. She's on the floor with her blue eyes open, lying on her side on one of the ripped plastic mats we brought from the jail. I find her knives in her backpack, which she's hugging to her chest.

"You'll get more," I whisper. But I still feel wrong for stealing them. Her arms tighten around my hands, and I let out a high-pitched shriek, sprawling backward to land on my bottom.

Slowly, April sits up. She presses her back to the wall and reaches into her bag. The tiny hairs on the back of my neck and arms stand on end, and my fingertips tighten around the Glock. Her blank eyes stare right at me. She starts to draw something from her satchel.

Her gamer is back. Her gamer has returned and she's found me out and I'll have no other choice but to defend myself.

But I shine the flashlight over the objects in her hand and realize she's not holding a weapon at all. She's just reached for food and water. I watch as she takes mechanical bites of her snack cake, a few sips of water. This continues for about five minutes. Then she wraps her forearms around her backpack again and resumes her position lying down.

What I just witnessed must be Self-Sustain in action.

We're like robots.

My stomach pitches violently, and I fight back nausea as I crawl back to April and take her knives from the bag. I drop the weapons into my own backpack and start to leave, but something stops me. My world may not be what I thought it was, but these are the people I had believed I cared about. That I still can't help caring about, even if everything they've ever said to me were someone else's words.

I have to try to wake them.

"April?" I touch her shoulder, shaking it softly. I bend until my face is close to hers and our eyes meet. "Do you... Are you in there?" She doesn't move. No blinking, not even a muscle twitch. She just continues to look straight ahead, clutching her bag like a child would her favorite toy.

I try the same thing with Ethan and Jeremy, but it's no use. They're just as unconscious as she is.

Shoulders slumped in defeat, I walk to the door and grab the knob. A sharp jolt of electricity streaks up my arm and through the rest of my body. I fall to my knees, screaming.

CHAPTER SEVEN

I'm on the floor facedown, convulsing and choking, for what seems like an eternity. When I finally work up enough strength to push myself onto my hands and knees, the current is still pinging its way through my bones. I squint up at the doorknob and rake my nails over my palms.

Why hasn't this ever happened before? I've gone in and out of this room plenty of times, and not once have I been shocked.

But I should have anticipated safeguards built into the game's system. The prospect of getting out of The Aftermath made me so giddy, I forgot caution. Never again. I get up carefully, trying to pretend I don't feel the pain or smell the stomach-churning odor of singed hair. Supporting myself against the wall, I look around the room and weigh my options.

There's the window. It's over the bed, but not so high up I won't be able to reach it. I could put the crate on the bed. Stand on it while I try to pry the window open. And then what?

I'm skinny, but not so thin I can squeeze through such a tiny space. And even if I could, I'm on the second floor. There's nothing in here I can use to climb to the ground. Attempting to walk fifty miles with a broken arm or leg is a death wish.

If I want to leave this building, I've no other choice but to use the door. I rip a large piece of cloth from the tattered hem of my jeans and wrap it around my hand before I grab the knob again. It does nothing to help me. The shock is just as horrible as before, but at least I know what to expect. I hurl the door open and stumble through the current and into the hallway, gripping the banister for support.

Hopefully this was the only surprise, and the front door won't set me on fire.

As I pack as many protein bars and bottles of water as I can into my bag, I start breathing heavily—an overwhelming surge of feeling is pulsing through me. Physical pain and anticipation and, most of all, absolute dread.

"I'm strong," I whisper, shrugging my arms through my backpack straps. I tighten them and groan at the weight. It has to be at least forty pounds. "I'm strong. I can do this by myself and survive."

But before I leave for good, I find myself upstairs, standing across from the electric door and gazing into The Save at the three people I've no other choice but to leave behind.

A couple of years ago, during one of our missions to a warehouse that was on the verge of collapsing, I discovered an old compass. It was bright orange, made of a thick, grainy plastic, with a broken lid. I've never used it—or rather, Olivia has never made me use it—but I've always carried it around in the front pocket of my backpack. Maybe… keeping it on me meant extra points for my gamer.

Whatever her reasons were, that compass quickly becomes my salvation, and I grip it in my hand as I walk, glancing down at the little arrows every few minutes.

I can't afford to make a mistake.

I am small enough to stay hidden and keep out of the way of other characters, so when daylight breaks and I realize that I'm at least fifteen miles into my trip, I decide to stop. It takes me another mile of stumbling through overgrown weeds and avoiding the holes in the ground—probably purposefully dug just large enough to catch someone's foot and result in a broken ankle—to find safe refuge. It's not a building or a house like I hope for but a crumbling underpass, nearly hidden from the world thanks to gutted and rusted cars and honeysuckle vines.

"Twenty minutes and then I have to leave. No more than that," I say as I sit next to my bag on the concrete. I take a careful sip of water, wincing at the way it burns my dry throat.

"What happens in twenty minutes?" a voice asks from the far end of the underpass, and I lose my breath.

As I scramble to my feet, the bottle of water I was trying to preserve falls over and liquid seeps into the hot, dry ground. I don't have time to try and save it, so I sling my backpack around my shoulders and prepare to run. But then a second voice—this one coming from the direction I planned to go in—stops me.

"Where are you going, girl?"

I dart my gaze between the two boys who've trapped me in. I had hoped this wouldn't happen, but I do my best to appear calm as they circle around me, their ragged shoes sliding dust and trash and scraps of glass and green metal from one of the cars about the concrete. They greedily eye my bag.

"What do you have in there?" the short, bone-thin one with the bright blue backpack asks. He looks ten years old but I'm guessing he's twelve or thirteen, judging by his squeaky voice. My body tenses as I remember awakening three years ago. It had been dark, very dark. The walls around me had been coated with blood splatters. And then

I'd noticed the shackles—rows of them extending from the baseboards and dangling from the ceiling.

I was thirteen then.

"Energy bars, water," I say. "Enough knives to make you wish you were dead. I've got a gun, too. Come too close and I'll show you how it works."

This is a partial lie. I've already decided that I refuse to kill anyone else. Still, if I'm threatened, I'm not above injuring someone.

"Where are you going?"

"Meeting up with my clan."

The taller one stares out toward the west at the miles of trees flanking either side of the underpass. "We just came from that way," he says, fingering the strap of my bag. I dart away from him. "Didn't see anyone."

"You didn't look hard enough."

"We need food," the short one says. "We ran out and our health levels…"

I don't feel any sympathy toward the gamer saying these words, but my stomach tangles into a million knots as I take in the boy who is slowly being destroyed by him. My arms tremble violently as I fumble through my backpack.

"Here," I say, shoving two protein bars and a bottle of water at each boy. I'll probably regret my decision later when I'm hungry and thirsty, but there's no way I can deny how gaunt and wrecked these boys—these characters—are.

"Take care of your characters." I zip my bag. "They look like they'll die at any moment."

When I take off again, this time through the woods, I hear the taller boy say, "Sympathizers make me want to hurl."

I take a short break every few hours. By the second evening, when

I have walked at least forty-five miles, I force myself to stop in the woods to rest. I take shelter on the forest floor on a bed of weeds I pray aren't poisonous. I remove my shoes, but my feet are so blistered they're hot to the touch, and I instantly regret taking them off. "Five more miles," I say. "Ten at the most. I have to do this."

When daylight appears again, I start walking. I don't even know why I bothered resting so long. I didn't get any real sleep—the kind of rest I'm just getting used to now that I have some freedom from Olivia. Every time a leaf crunched or the breeze ruffled a tree limb, I startled, coming to my aching feet with my gun drawn.

I am ready to rest without a weapon and not stare over my shoulder.

Four hours later, I am still walking, the sun rubbing viciously on the back of my neck and a heavy pain coiling in my stomach. I know I've traveled at least ten miles. Every muscle in my body feels as if it's been beaten to a pulp. My skin is on fire. And I'm still inside The Aftermath. Tears squeeze through my squinted eyes and spill down my dry cheeks like rain trickling through dirt. This is the first time in my memory that I've cried, and it hurts, both physically and emotionally. I slump against a tree, not caring that the rough wood chafes the skin on my sunburned back.

And then I see it.

Through the maze of trees, something glints in the sunlight. For the longest time, I gape at it. Breathe and stare. Swallow and breathe. The knots in my belly loosen and swift fluttering replaces them. "Please…" I whisper. I don't realize that I'm on my feet and running until I break through the trees and find myself on the road again.

Several hundred yards in the distance, a silver fence stretches across the landscape. The only intact fence I've ever seen in The Aftermath is the one around the recreation yard of the jail. Perhaps this fence will be the one that secures my freedom.

I don't care about the soles of my feet or my tired legs. I run as fast as my legs will carry me, pumping my arms and letting a hot breeze blow my hair from my forehead.

When I reach the gate, I curl my fingertips in the metal and fall against it. In the thirty-nine months of my life that I can remember, I cry for the second time.

Several minutes pass before I'm able to calm myself down enough to think rationally. I pace the fence, looking for a way out—a torn part to crawl under, a latch, anything. Twenty feet above me at the top are coils of razor wire. This puts scaling the fence out of the question.

I sift through the pack of weapons I took from April until I find a pair of rusted pliers. I run my fingertips along the bottom of the fence. I am about to start pulling at a corroded section of the metal when a male voice behind me says, "You do know escape is against the law, right?"

CHAPTER EIGHT

"That's what you're doing, right?" the boy continues.

I grip the fence so hard, it feels as if the thin links are making indentations on my bones. Silly, frightened character. That's what I am, because though he may not see it, I am shaking furiously, hoping against hope that his name appears on Olivia's map in green and not red.

Even then, that wouldn't mean that I'm safe.

"Well?"

What would Olivia say? Three years of her playing me and I have no idea how she'd respond. I loll my head back. Stare up at the rolls of barbed wire. Sweat drips between my shoulder blades, like lava drizzling down my flesh.

"I was curious," I say slowly. "And I wanted to see what was out here."

This isn't how Olivia would have me respond. No, not at all. Olivia would taunt him—ask him why he cared. Then she'd reach my hand for the Glock, even though his gun or knife is probably already trained on the back of my head. Maybe I'd win—I usually do when Olivia's in control—but as she made me shoot him down, I'd picture myself on the ground instead, and feel nothing but regret.

Now that I think about it, I'm glad I don't answer like Olivia. Olivia seems to enjoy putting my life in danger.

"You were curious?" I hear the sound of his feet shuffling in the dry grass for a few seconds, and then he says, "Okay, turn around."

The last time someone told me to turn around, that person died, tearing violently at the crown of her head. I hadn't understood why she would fuss over her head when the wound was on her chest. But now I know we're controlled by some technology that's been placed within our heads. Maybe she felt it as she were dying.

Will I be ripping at my skull today?

I swallow hard and turn. My fingers tangle in the metal behind me, and I hold on to it for comfort before I lift my gaze to his.

My heart leaps into my throat.

Gray eyes stare back at me. Dark gray eyes partially hidden by a messy mop of dark hair.

I know this boy. He is the reason I'm here right now and not un-responsive, trapped in a room over a bar with three other characters. He's the boy from the elevator.

"You," I breathe, but then I catch myself, biting into my bottom lip so I don't give myself away.

"You've got to be kidding me. Of all the…" Letting his weapon arm drop to his side, he tilts his head and gives me a challenging gaze. "What are you doing out here?"

Why is he still asking me questions? Shouldn't he be threatening to attack me again or trying to rob me or something, anything, other than simply staring at me? His lack of movement gives me an oppor-tunity to size him up. He doesn't look like any flesh-eater I've ever seen. Doesn't look like a Survivor, either. Though he's several inches taller than me, he's nowhere near Ethan's height. I try to remember ever seeing anyone in The Aftermath wearing clothes that didn't look like tattered rags, but this boy is the first person who comes to mind, in his black boots, cargo pants and black T-shirt that he fills out rather nicely.

I've also never met a Survivor, or a flesh-eater for that matter, with meat on his bones.

"Too scared to speak?" he taunts.

"Funny." I flash him my teeth in what I can only hope is a smile of confidence. "I'd almost think you were the one frightened of me."

But there are beads of sweat trickling from the tip of my nose and between my parted lips. I'm trembling so hard that I'm afraid I might vomit. Then he'll know I'm the one who's terrified. I'm the one who can barely stand up straight.

He regains his composure, narrowing his eyes. The corners of his lips pull up. For a moment, he lowers his long eyelashes against his slightly sunburned cheeks and looks down at the grass, like I've embarrassed him. I flinch when he lifts his head and weapon at the same time. "Please, you're as short and thin as a twelve-year-old. Now... why are you playing around at this?" He shakes his gun at the gate, drawing my attention to it.

His weapon is small and sleek and black. No surprise there. But the barrel is flat, and four metal probes extend from it. My gaze flicks from his hand to the fence. When I shift from the heat, he shakes his head, moving near me with both hands on his piece.

He is mere steps from where I stand. So close I can almost feel the probes sinking into the side of my neck.

"Careful now. You know what this is?" He jiggles the gun around, stares at it almost lovingly. When I don't acknowledge his question, he says, "Electroshock. Tech Arms Special Edition. Only a thousand were made in twenty eighty-three."

"Twenty eighty-three?"

He stares at me as if he's expecting me to continue, but when a long moment of silence passes between us, he lifts an eyebrow. "The year."

Coldness washes over me. The year 2083? It's 2039. My ID card says I was born in 2023, so it has to be 2039, right?

"And?" I ask. My voice is icy and hard. Good. Let him think he doesn't bother me, that I'm not frightened out of my sunburned skin.

"And I can control whether I hit you with fifty milliamps or five amps. It has a motion detector. You run, it finds you. But—" he waggles his thick eyebrows "—you run away from me and I'll probably just crank the full five amps into your skinny ass."

I glare at him. "Obviously I'm not running, but if you want to do it, go right ahead."

He grins. Squats down with his head cocked to one side as if I am a joke. I droop back against the fence and slide my body down the hot metal until I sit on the grass. It's rough and scratchy against the backs of my legs but much better than standing. I draw my knees up to my chest and stare at him. Part of me wants to test my luck and just run. I think that must be the sadistic portion of my subconscious still linked to Olivia.

"So you're going to electrocute and eat me? Or do you have some other plan? Because I've already had the hell shocked out of me. There's not much else that will surprise me."

His mouth quirks up—there's that sardonic expression again. "I'm not into you like that." Gray eyes skim my body, from the worn soles of my shoes to the bruises on my knees and finally to my green eyes. He's studying me with that confused expression again, and it makes the tiny hairs on my arms and legs stand on end.

I hug myself tighter. "Then why not let me go?" My voice is low, shaky.

"I will." He shifts the electroshock gun between his hands. "As soon as you tell me what you're doing here," he says.

"Strange request from someone whose name I don't even know."

"Declan. Satisfied—"

"Claudia."

"You're sneakier than I gave you credit for." He sneers. "Do we really have time for this? Just...confirm who you are already."

Sneaky? We've been in each other's company for less than fifteen minutes and he thinks he already has me pegged? "I just confirmed it for you," I say stubbornly.

"You're making my job really, *really* difficult, you know." He points his weapon at me. "Tech Arms. Fifty milliamps. Does that make it easier for you to remember?"

As if I could forget the power of his electroshock gun. My heart beats wildly, but I somehow manage to evenly reply, "I don't break, Declan. My name's Claudia Virtue."

"Come on, you're seriously going to pull that gamer crap when I'm holding a gun on your character? Why would you refuse to confirm who you are—who's playing this character—when I could so easily hurt her? Just tell me already."

But he has hurt me already—I'm just not going to mention that to him. If he isn't going to admit to seeing me before, I'm not bringing it up, either—maybe it'll be useful down the line.

When I refuse to say anything, focusing instead on a bald patch in the grass right by my left foot, he moves in closer. One step. Two more. His boots make a solid thud each time, and I swear it's in rhythm with my heart. He crouches down again—this time right in front of me. I have to fight to catch my breath.

"What's your Gamer ID?"

This is something I don't know. Up until just a moment ago, I wasn't even aware Olivia had a Gamer ID. All those times I witnessed her flipping through the multiple game screens and not once did I have the brains to look for something like what he's asking for. I was too concerned with the map and the location of flesh-eaters.

"117908." It's the code that Olivia had typed into her tablet. A lie that sounds so confident, I come close to believing it myself.

I gasp when he tucks his calloused index finger under my chin. I yank my arms away from my knees and pull myself farther into the metal gate, hoping I'll dissolve through it. Then I could take off running. Then I could be free of this boy and, maybe, this game.

Declan lifts my face, tilts it so far up that the uneven tips of my hair brush my sweaty shoulders. There's little space between our lips and noses and foreheads—just a few inches between my eyes and his. Gray eyes that are dangerous and mocking and something else.

Questioning.

Accusing.

"There are no Gamer IDs," he whispers. "Wait...you really are Claudia Virtue."

We stare at each other for a lifetime. He doesn't flinch. I don't breathe. This boy has me figured out after mere minutes, and I can't help but wonder if I was so obvious to the two kids I met on the way here.

"Of course I'm a character—this is a game."

"You know exactly what I mean," he says harshly. "Now, don't move."

And I listen. Stupid, really, because he pulls something navy blue from his bag and pushes a button on the bottom of it. Every muscle—every nerve—in my body tightens, leaving me as still as a corpse. I hold my breath. He swipes the flat, triangular-shaped tip of the object across the top of my head, and my skull tingles. I grit my teeth. At any moment, I'll likely be a corpse.

After about a minute of sliding the blue thing back and forth over my crown, he presses the button again and tosses it back into his bag. Air rushes out of my lungs in a low hiss. He's not going to kill me. At least not at the moment.

Declan sinks down in front of me on his knees. He's still too close for my taste.

"You're actually sentient," he says incredulously.

"You said that before."

"How?"

"I was...I was injured." There's no point lying to him—at least not completely—so I inhale a deep breath and add, "Something happened about a week and a half ago that woke me up."

If he recalls being the one who struck the blow that brought about my sudden ability to control myself, he doesn't show it. His expression is void of any emotion as he studies my face and head. "And your Cerebrum Chip is still linked." This is not a question, but I nod anyway.

There's a name for why my brain is so wrecked. And there is a boy sitting right in front of me who knows exactly what it is. "Who are you?"

"Declan," he says.

"You know what I mean. You're not a character, are you?"

"I'm...I'm a moderator."

"A *moderator*." The word sounds funny when I say it, and I narrow my eyes at him. I repeat the word a few more times as I wait for him to explain what it means.

"I make sure everything in The Aftermath goes exactly the way the game's creator envisioned it. I work for LanCorp."

If there were even the slightest chance of him letting me go, it's gone now. My heart breaks a little more. I've been chased by flesh-eaters and starved to the point of wishing for death, yet somehow this is the most hopeless I've ever felt.

"Oh," I say.

He laughs then. I gnash my teeth together as the sound of his voice rubs over me like sandpaper. He's making fun of me. And I hate him for it. I curl my hands into tight balls, hoping it will help control my violent trembling. "That's all you're going to say. Oh?" he asks.

I slam my fist into the center of his nose. He sprawls backward, clutching his face. "Why the hell did you do that?"

I stumble to my feet and kick out at him. My foot strikes his stomach hard, knocking the breath out of him. He rolls over on all fours, and I take off in a sprint. I hear him behind me, wheezing. Cursing. Threatening horrible things. "So you have something to remember me by when I'm dead," I say over my shoulder.

He tackles me before I make it fifty yards, pinning me facedown. I struggle wildly. This only makes him dig his knees deeper into my sides, and I scream in agony.

I feel his torso lower down on me. His weight numbs every part of my body. "Stop moving." His lips touch my right ear—the mutilated one—and I taste bile in the back of my throat.

I thrash harder, whipping my head until it catches him in the mouth, and he swears. If he's going to kill me, the least I can do is hurt him first. Suddenly, I feel the cold metal probes of his electro-shock gun press into my scalp.

"Quit. It. Claudia," he says between clenched teeth.

This can't be how it ends for me. I'm unsure if this makes me a coward or sensible, but I don't want to die today. My breath hitches, and suddenly I'm inhaling heavily. Sucking in rasping, broken breaths that shake my entire body.

The noises coming from me are so loud and pitiful, I almost miss what he says next.

"I'm not going to kill you, because I need your help. Do what I tell you to do, and I'll personally show you the border."

This from the boy who hurt me. This from a boy who will, without a doubt, hurt me again if I provoke him. This from a boy who works for the people who took away my ability to think for myself.

"And if I don't?" I ask, surprising myself by saying exactly what Olivia would say in this situation.

He laughs again, but this one isn't teasing like before. It's harsh. Serious. Lethal. "Don't, and I'll turn you in, and you'll die a horrible death. Decide now, Virtue."

CHAPTER NINE

Declan does not wish me dead.

At first, I do what he's asked me to do. I stop moving. I lay with the left side of my face against the ground and replay his words over and over in my head. *Do what I tell you to do, and I'll personally show you the border.* There's still a chance I'll get out of The Aftermath. A jolt of excitement rushes through my body, but it quickly turns toxic, squeezing my insides until I feel nauseous.

No, Declan does not want to kill me. Instead, this boy—this moderator—wants my help.

He wants to use me for something.

I dig my hands into the grass. "Turn me in to whom?" My voice is strained.

"Don't make this hard on yourself."

"Is that a threat?"

"No, that's common sense. It goes right along with the threat I made a couple minutes ago."

He shifts his body, and I moan as the bulk of his weight settles onto my lower back. I mumble something even I don't comprehend.

"I'm going to let you go now," he says in a tone that reminds me of an adult admonishing a small child. "Just because I've no plan to kill you doesn't mean I won't electrocute you if I have to. Understand?"

I grunt.

As he lifts his body from mine, I release a long breath and roll over onto my back. He juggles his precious electroshock gun from his left hand to the right. I lash my foot out at him, aiming at his kneecaps. With almost unbelievable grace, he steps out of the way, then stretches out a hand to help me up.

Glaring up at him, I knock his fingers out of my face and struggle to my feet. Tiny prickles annoy my legs from where they'd lain trapped beneath me for so long. When I finally steady myself, I whirl on him. "I'm not going to help you do anything."

"Why the hell not?"

Because I am inches away from the fence I'm positive will lead me to my freedom and I don't need his help getting through it. Because if I don't get out now, I may die in The Aftermath. I might be able to last another day or even another three years, but it's almost inevitable that this game will be the end of me.

Because I am tired of being used.

"I want to leave," I say. My throat is sore from my breakdown a few minutes ago, so I clear it a few times. "I'm one person. You could turn your back. You can pretend—"

"Nobody's ever escaped the game. Nobody's ever tried."

My voice finally collapses, and I sound like a lost child when I whisper, "But it's possible."

"Up until today I would've said no. Nobody escapes because nobody is sentient. Except you—you are wide-awake, and I want to know why. What went wrong with your chip to make you become self-aware on your own?"

"Why does it matter? Why do you care if I'm dead or alive? Sentient or not? Just let me go. I—"

"Stop mewling, Virtue, and catch your breath, will you?" Declan says, thrusting a metal canister under my lips. Liquid sloshes around inside. When I stare at it for a long time, he snaps, "Don't be such an elitist—just take it. This game is crawling with cannibals and you turn your nose up at filtered water?"

I turn my nose up at fresh water given to me by the people who are responsible for designing this twisted game, is what I want to say. Not to mention that I have no idea why he hasn't fessed up to being at the courthouse—meaning I can't trust him one bit. But Declan wiggles the canteen a few more times and eventually my thirst outweighs my better judgment. I take the container in both hands. The water doesn't taste like anything I've ever had. It's sweet and there's a hint of some type of flavoring. I finish drinking so fast I'm left coughing even more violently than before.

"Don't worry about me—I'm not thirsty," he says dryly as I thrust the empty canteen back at him. He fumbles it, dropping it to the ground. When he bends to retrieve it, I pull the Glock from its holster. Then I kick the electroshock gun out of his hand. It clinks against the metal gate four feet away from us. After a few seconds of silence, during which his only movement is his Adam's apple bobbing up and down, he cocks his head to the right. The corners of his mouth twitch. "What are you doing?" he asks calmly.

"I'm not helping you, Declan. Moderator. I'm getting out of this game today."

Sighing, he drops to a sitting position and shakes his head to each side. "Virtue, you—"

"Shut up," I say. I keep the gun positioned on his chest, right over his heart, as I walk backward. I grab his electroshock gun, then the pair of pliers I dropped earlier. Placing his weapon on the ground next to me, I stoop to the section of the fence I was trying to pry loose when he caught me and begin working on it again. One-handed. And with my eyes locked on him.

"If you weren't pointing that thing at me, I'd tell you I find multitasking attractive," he says. When I snort, he grins and adds, "So's your determination, but I'm faster than you, you know."

I picture him knocking me to the ground again. My ribs hurt just thinking about it. I tighten my grip on both the gun and the pliers. "Go ahead and try it." This sounds so much like something my gamer would say, a shudder races through my body. "But just so you know, I've killed before."

He doesn't need to know that I've never really been the person doing the killing, or that the act itself leaves me feeling numb for days afterward.

Declan doesn't respond. I almost think he plans to stand still and let me finish jiggling at the metal fence but then he begins to laugh. And he doesn't stop until I face him, hunched over and wheezing, with both hands on the gun.

"What's so funny?"

"You," he says. "And me. It's...let's just say I never saw this coming." When I give him a look that borders between disgusted and confused, he quickly adds in a cocky voice, "Look, I don't even know why we're going back and forth. We both know you're not going to shoot me, so you might as well put the gun up, Virtue. Look me in the eye and tell me that you honestly believe I feel threatened by you."

Spitefulness seems to be a common trait in the world Declan and Olivia belong to, and yet I'm still willing to do just about anything to find my way there. "Just shut your mouth before I shoot out your kneecaps."

I work in silence for a few minutes, pulling with all my might at the metal. Both of my arms hurt from the weight of the Glock and the constant jerking on the fence. The throbbing in my skull is back, along with erratic tremors that pulse through my whole body.

Apparently Declan notices, because he murmurs something under his breath and moves his left leg as if he plans to get up.

"Don't even think about it," I snap, swiping the back of the hand holding the pliers across my damp forehead.

"I've decided to cooperate."

"Well, then do what I say and just be quiet."

"No, I mean, I've decided to tell you this isn't the way out of The Aftermath," he says.

The tool nearly slips from my hand. "Stop it!"

"What? Trying to help you? You want to get out, fine by me, but at least listen to what I've got to say. You're wasting your time digging away at links and chains when your way out is—" he points to the east, the direction I traveled from "—that way."

He's wrong. He has to be. This is where I saw the change in the game map. This is where I found the fence with so much barbed wire. It's got to be here for something. "Don't lie to me."

Declan holds up both of his hands and shakes his head. "Let me ask you this. What would I gain by lying to you? You've got a gun—even if it's an antique that you may or may not be able to use properly—aimed at my heart. And you have my weapon. I'm at a disadvantage, Virtue."

But he doesn't feel threatened by me—he said so himself. "This has to be the way," I whisper.

He grunts. "The best way to die before sunset, yes. The way out of The Aftermath? Definitely not." When I draw in a deep breath and my shoulders sag a little, he adds, "The worst flesh-eaters in the game are outside that fence. Trust me—I was just out there searching for another character. You leave and I can almost guarantee you'll be over an open fire before the sun comes out."

I grind my teeth together. "They don't work like that. They don't kill their victims right away."

Declan lifts one of his shaggy eyebrows. Slowly, he stands up, his palms still lifted in front of him in submission. He turns to the fence, staring out at the flat landscape beyond it. "No, they don't. But their players are the ones making the rules, and out there, you've got a quick death sentence."

I want to scream at him. Call him a liar again. But there's something in his voice that makes me hesitate. Anger? Pity? And then I realize what it is: self-loathing. The same thing I heard in my own voice when I barely helped those two boys who begged for water and food.

What if he's telling the truth? What if I'm wrong and I've come all this way for nothing? What if—

"How do you get out of the game?" I croak. "Is it…even possible to get out?"

"I got in, didn't I? The way out is southeast of here."

Southeast?

Southeast.

He's saying I traveled sixty miles in the wrong direction.

"Prove it," I say.

With his hands still in the air, he moves toward his bag. I take a few steps closer, too. Kneeling beside the fence for such an extended period of time has made my legs useless, and when I move, it feels as if I'm waist-deep in sludge. I keep my face blank so he doesn't see how much pain I'm in, how easy it would be to overpower me.

"I need my tablet," he mutters, twitching his head down to his belongings. "Not much I can prove if you shoot me between the eyes the moment I—"

"Just get it," I growl.

Declan keeps his word. He grabs a tablet just like Olivia's and presses one of the icons, bringing up a holographic keypad. He spends a couple of minutes entering a succession of codes into it. Then he places the tablet on the ground between us and walks five, six, seven steps in reverse.

"Tap it once. I've disabled the touch recognition for the next ten minutes so you might want to hurry," he says when I pick up his device.

It takes me a few tries to get the tablet to work—I have trouble holding it and the gun and keeping an eye on Declan all at once. When it finally glows in my hand, a 3-D map of the area pops up in front of my face, rotating in a slow circle. I'm disappointed to see that it doesn't show any street names or character locations like Olivia's map. I search up and to the left of the image, yet there's nothing significant about the northwest, where I am right at this moment. But just over sixty miles southwest of Demonbreun—the street I left forty-eight hours ago—is a thin line slicing across the map. On the other side of the border is a yellow landform with two words written across it in bold black print: UNITED PROVINCES (U.P.)

I feel as though I'm choking.

"I'll just have to go southeast then," I say, keeping my voice as hard as possible.

"You're welcome to try, but you won't make it two miles in that direction."

"And why is that?"

"Because—" But then he pauses and drops his gaze to the grass for a moment. He clenches his hands by his sides before his dark eyes lock on to mine again. "Because I'll have the mods all over you before you lose sight of this fence," he says as he approaches me. He doesn't seem concerned that I still have my gun raised. All he seems to care about is coming close enough so that I'm within his reach. "I can promise you one more thing. You'll wish they just shocked you to death."

"And if I kill you before you can tell the other mods?"

"Then maybe you'll get out before they review the game records for the quarter. You have about—" he glances at his watch "—twenty-nine days before they check the footage, review your character stats and schedule you for maintenance. But even then, you're screwed if you manage to escape. You can't fake your identification in the U.P. Everything is done by fingerprint or retinal scan or biometric verification. Even the AcuTabs have touch recognition, and, trust me, you'll stick out like a sore thumb if you don't have one—they're linked to everything. And just because you go outside the border doesn't change the fact your brain is linked to someone else's head through your chips. Your gamer can just log in and march your ass back into the game. She'd probably just kill you, though."

I open my mouth to say something, but he interrupts me. "But I can make sure your chip is destroyed the moment you leave The Aftermath. No tracking. No gamer. Just you. I've got friends who can make you whoever you want to be in every national database in less than ten minutes, who'll make sure you have anything you need to survive in the Provinces. All you have to do is say yes."

Twenty-nine days is a long time to plan and execute an escape. And if I managed to make it this far so rapidly, I can do it again when the time is right. All I need is for Olivia to disappear one more time and then I can give it another go.

But if Declan is right—like he is about the border—I won't last in the world outside the game once I break free. It doesn't make sense to risk so much just so I can immediately stare death in the face. He's offering to fix me so she'll never use my head again.

If I say yes.

If I let him use me.

"What is it you need me to do?" I spit out.

He grins like someone who's won a major battle. This must be what a flesh-eater looks like right before snacking on his victim. Or, at least, what his gamer looks like behind his wall of screens.

"I've been sent into the game to retrieve a character with a glitch that's affecting the characters around him. His last known location was Nashville."

Another glitching character? "Where do I fit in?"

"The navigation on my AcuTab doesn't work in this game—too many firewalls—and all I have to go on is a general direction. You know the area. You can help me find him quickly, so I can get out of this place. This is a very sensitive and special assignment and I have a limited amount of time to get it done."

No, this is the most ridiculous thing I've ever heard. But I hear myself ask, "And you'll get me out, too, if I help?"

"I swear on my life."

"How long will it take?"

"A few days. Maybe a week at the most."

"Won't you get in trouble for helping me? Thirty minutes ago you told me escape is illegal."

He shrugs and gives me a smile that looks more like a grimace. "You said it yourself—you're only one person. My boss will never know I busted you out. I need to find this character, and I'm willing to break a few rules to do it."

This situation is wrong on so many levels. I'll have to go back to the bar on Demonbreun and allow Olivia to play me whenever she feels the urge to, which is much too frequently. And whatever Olivia free time I have will be spent with a boy who's just as shady as she is.

But he won't turn me in if I do this. And there's a chance—even though it feels much slighter than before—that I'll still escape.

My answer comes out in a whisper that's so soft, I barely even hear myself. "Yes, I'll help you."

CHAPTER TEN

We start our trip in bitter silence. I'm raging inside, terrified. I'm furious at myself for giving in to Declan, but also I don't know for sure if he'll follow through on his end of our bargain. What happens to me if he turns on me? I kick at loose crumbles of asphalt and grip the straps of my bag so tightly my knuckles turn white and my shoulders slump from the pressure.

But I think the worst part of this trip is the obvious: I'm going back the way I came.

My journey was a failure.

No matter how I look at my situation, I'm at a severe disadvantage.

Declan follows several paces behind me. When he'd suggested it, he'd sworn it was to protect me in case we were attacked from behind—this right after he had told me we were taking the highway instead of the woods for safety and the sake of efficiency. Yeah, sure. What he meant was he didn't want to deal with me attacking him. I haven't turned around to check, but I'm certain his electroshock gun is drawn, ready to send pain slicing through my body at the slightest provocation.

I can almost feel the electricity thrumming from the probes.

Breathing in deeply, I finally steal a glance over my shoulder. I was wrong. He doesn't have his weapon pointed at me. With his head down, his hands shoved into the pockets of his black pants and his lips drawn into a thin line, Declan looks deep in thought. I don't want to care what he's thinking about, don't want to waste my time and energy letting his pensive expression bother me, but I can't help it. Because even though he works for the people responsible for so many others' personal hells, he's the first person I've met in at least three years with life in his eyes and the ability to speak for himself.

So what is it he's not saying to me?

Does he congratulate himself for scaring me into submission? Wonder what I'm thinking about at this exact moment? Ask himself if I'll make a hasty, stupid decision and try to attack him again?

"Claudia." His voice is questioning as it interrupts my thoughts. I whip my head around to see he's no longer staring at the ground. Now his dark gray eyes are focused on me. "How long have you been sentient?"

Don't tell him, a warning voice screams in my head.

My sudden dry mouth has nothing to do with the fact that I've been conservative with the little water I have left. I flick my tongue over my lips, tasting fear. "As in?"

"Self-aware."

Three years. I've been partially self-aware for just over 150 weeks and completely cognizant for the past few. And it's all thanks to you.

I could tell him the truth, but I don't think honesty will ensure my safety. Not when the person questioning me is a game moderator. And I don't think being sentient in this game is a good thing, at least not from the outside looking in.

"Virtue?" Declan releases a deep sigh. When I choose to ignore him, he narrows his eyes at me. "You could at least give me a straight answer. After all, I'm the only person who can help you find your way out of this game."

Coming to a complete stop in the middle of the road, I spin to face him. He looks slightly stunned when I stalk toward him, so close I can see the tiny scar just above his lip, can count the three freckles that are nearly invisible on the bridge of his sunburned nose.

"A straight answer?" I ask. "You threaten to shock me to death, bullied me into helping you do your job and now you're demanding answers from me?" I jab the center of his chest with my knuckles, and he winces. He grabs my wrist in a quick motion that's not forceful, not harsh, but, nevertheless, it steals the breath from me.

"Look, all I care about is—"

"It should be doing your job so we can get out of this game. You shouldn't care how long I've been awake, just that I'm that way right now," I whisper.

His gray eyes harden. Standing there red-faced and strained, Declan seems to grow a few more inches. I refuse to let him get to me. Inside, I'm trembling and my head screams for me to back down, but I stare directly into his eyes, thrust my shoulders back and cross my arms over my chest.

"Trust me, I care about a lot more than just getting my job done." He twists me back around and nudges me forward. I stumble but quickly catch myself. "You, Claudia Virtue, are no good to me if you can't hold your own, if you have no idea what you're doing and I end up guarding your ass at every corner."

"You guarding *my* ass? How's your stomach feel?" I look back just in time to witness him cringe and drop his gaze to where I'd kicked him in the gut more than an hour ago.

"Maybe I stand corrected." Smirking, he jerks his head forward. "Let's go."

This time I walk beside him. The quietness is back, although I don't feel as though he'll shoot me now. Every few moments, he casts a sideways glance at me. And it makes me uncomfortable.

"Your reason for needing my help is kind of…ridiculous." I rub the back of my hand across my cheeks and forehead. My skin is so hot to the touch I just know the painful blisters will come soon. "You work for the game. So, how's it possible for you not to be able to find characters?"

"You've been aware of yourself for what—a few days—and you're telling me how to do my job?"

"No, I'm telling you your job doesn't make sense." I've spent too many years with everything around me an illogical mess not to ask questions now.

"There are literally hundreds of firewalls that prevent bringing any outside navigation devices into the game, even if it's a moderator trying to find a character. Our bosses would rather drop us off by aircraft onto the game board with a 'good luck' and some food than risk a rival company getting their hands on a valuable character."

"But—"

"It's complicated," he snaps.

Of course it is. Which is why asking about it means even more silence from Declan.

We take our first break after something in his bag starts beeping. Stopping in the street, he leans against the remains of a windowless seven-passenger van and pulls out his AcuTab. "Why's it making that sound?" I ask as he moves his fingers swiftly across the flat screen.

"I've got it set to monitor our food and water. It beeps—we rest. In the Provinces, though, we link them to our homes so that the central system installed in the house can just announce what it is we need."

Ingenious, but I don't tell him that as I focus all my strength on dragging myself from the highway and into the woods. Declan walks ahead of me, his steps energetic. Excited. Almost as if he's mocking my inability to keep up with his quick movements. I shake the idea from my head. Right now, thoughts like that will only make this trip worse for me.

I'll have plenty of time to loathe Declan while I'm helping him locate who he's looking for and letting Olivia take control of me in the meantime.

Gritting my teeth, I slide down beneath the shade of a willow tree, drop my head onto my lumpy backpack and curl into a tight ball. A few feet away, Declan rummages noisily through his bag. "It's impossible to get any rest with you doing that," I point out, opening one eye.

He pulls out two plastic packages and tosses one to me. It lands a couple of inches from my face. "You're welcome, Virtue."

I prop myself up on my elbow and pick it up. Small and rectangular, it's slightly bigger than a protein bar and in a similar wrapper. There's a picture of a creepy smiling boy on the front. He's holding his thumb up in approval; below him, there's large block writing: "CDS. Complete Nutrition in Every Pack!"

"Is this food?" I wiggle the packet. "You're not trying to drug me, are you?"

Declan cocks his head to one side and gives me a funny look. "It's a CDS. You know, Complete Daily Sustenance. They make them in the same factory as your nasty energy bars, except they taste a hundred times better and have triple the calories." When I continue to stare at him blankly, he adds, "You really don't know what it is?"

I shake my head. Am I supposed to?

He drops down beside me, brushing aside the willow leaves that fall into his face. "What all do you remember before becoming sentient?"

Flipping the CDS packet between my hands, I shrug. I don't remember anything other than The Aftermath, but I don't want to tell him that. And that's the thing about being sentient: I don't have to do anything I don't want to do.

At least when Olivia's not playing me I don't.

He snorts. "Okay, so you're not going to answer me. How about this one—what all do you remember about the day you woke up?"

I stick with silence for now. When he climbs to his knees, leans over my head and examines it with his eyes and hands, I cry out.

"You were hit recently." There's something different about his voice—a note of sudden apprehension—and I know without a doubt he realizes that he's the cause of this. The question is, will he tell me?

"You were hit hard recently," he continues.

Once again, yes...because of you.

"I don't remember what happened that day," I lie. "And I don't remember anything about who I was before all this."

Sighing, Declan sags against the tree trunk, tilting his head to one side to stare at me with his piercing gray eyes. "Your memories from before you were put into the game should come back sooner or later." There's relief in his voice.

Would it still be there if he knew I was already somewhat aware of myself well before that day in the courthouse? That I had no recollection of my life before The Aftermath even then? That I'm fully aware of what had happened with him?

I smile, despite the panic building in my chest. "You sound so sure."

"I am. And hopefully it'll happen before I take you to the border so you can find the people out there who love you."

There's nobody on the outside for me. I'm sure of that because if there were, nothing would stop me from remembering them. No, whatever happened to me must be too traumatic to recall. I bite the tip of my tongue and listen to him explain the tiny packet I'm holding. Apparently, the CDS will keep my belly full all day and then some.

But despite how delicious that first bite is—and it really is the best thing I've ever eaten—all I can think of are stale protein bars.

We don't stop again until after nightfall. Declan says we've gone twenty miles, but I swear it's more. Every muscle in my body feels like molten lava as I curl up with my backpack again. He pulls a cushiony sleeping sack out of his bag and rolls it onto the forest floor. Staring at him enviously, I hate that I didn't bring my own blankets from the shelter. Tonight is an anomaly, so cold it reminds me of midwinter— not the end of summer. It's a startling contrast from just a couple of hours ago, when the sun was so hot, the path ahead of us seemed to blur, and the asphalt burned the bottoms of my feet through my flimsy shoes.

Declan shines a flashlight over my face and gives me a half smile. "You're welcome to share."

I don't know if he's being sarcastic or just kind, but I don't budge. I purse my lips together and bring my knees as close to my chest as my muscles will allow. "I'm good, thanks."

"You know pride is man's number one downfall, right?"

I roll my eyes. I don't need a lecture from this boy. What I need is sleep—a few hours away from this world of cannibals and deceptive gamers—and away from him. Especially him.

"Funny, I thought my downfall was having my brain screwed with on a daily basis."

Shaking his head, he chuckles. I stare up at the night sky and hug myself tightly, clenching my teeth to keep them from chattering. Declan rustles around for a few minutes and then he's silent. I'm just about asleep when he whispers softly, "You're lucky."

I open my eyes. In the darkness, I can see the outline of his body through his sleeping bag. The soft glow of his tablet screen casts a bluish glow over his face. I wonder what he's looking at.

"Why's that?" I ask. "Why am I lucky?"

"You're sentient…you're getting out."

But I don't feel lucky. I feel beaten and bruised. Like there are so many obstacles standing in the way of me leaving this game that I may never reach the border Declan promises to escort me to.

No, I'm not lucky at all. Because even if I do break free, I'm self-ishly abandoning everyone I know. A little noise escapes from the back of my throat.

"The game is just going to get worse in the coming months," Declan says. "They're introducing something new and even more danger-ous than before. You'll be out before it takes over, though."

What he says sends a million questions pinging through my skull. What could be more dangerous than using humans as game pawns, fighting off cannibals daily? Will he tell me what he means?

But when I softly call out his name, he doesn't answer. I roll over onto my side, cold and even more lost than before.

I dream of cold metal tombs, of electroshock guns with fiery metal probes and moderators dressed all in black chasing after me. I wake up hot and sweaty, with sunlight burning through my eyelids. As I stand, my legs tangle up in thick fabric, and I nearly fall back down. Two rough hands grip my shoulders and steady me. I peel my eyes open to find Declan grinning down at me.

"You snore, Virtue," he says. "And I mean, loud, obnoxious snor-ing that's bad enough to—"

I knock his hands off my shoulders and hop backward. The sun catches his face—the flesh around his nose is bruised and purplish from where I hit him yesterday, and I feel a tiny swell of pride. That is, until I realize I'm wrapped in his sleeping bag. At some point during the night he must have put it on top of me. Something large and uncomfortable forms in my throat, but I fight it down.

"Thanks," I whisper. I disentangle myself and roll the bag into a tight bundle. When I place it on top of his rucksack he gives me a curt nod.

"You're a girl. And when it started snowing, you were shivering like a freezing puppy. I don't want you to die before we both do what we agreed on."

My head snaps up. "It snowed?" What was the deal with this ridiculous weather?

"For about an hour just after one." He begins stuffing the sleeping bag into his sack. "Don't think it really bothered you, though. You never stopped snoring."

I should be worried about snow in the middle of August. Or my current situation—being with a boy who epitomizes the word *enemy* for me. But I can't help smiling when I turn away to gather my belongings.

The walk today is more grueling than yesterday's. Every time I bring up what Declan said before falling asleep last night, he changes the subject. We talk about the sudden shift in the weather (it's well over one hundred degrees) and how long he's been a moderator (just over a year), but he refuses to discuss the new threat that's on its way to the game.

We stop to take a breather just after noon, at an abandoned convenience store off the side of the road. As we walk across the parking lot toward a row of gas pumps—some of which have been ripped from the concrete—he clears his throat. I glance over to see him holding my gun, and my mouth falls open as he holds the handle out to me.

"Are we having a duel, Declan?" I ask, and he rolls his gray eyes.

"You wish, Virtue, but no. I just want to make sure we don't have any unwanted guests that are going to sneak up on us. You're going to check out here while I look inside." Touching the faded credit card swipe of one of the few upright fuel dispensers, he leans in close to me. "We'll meet right here in five minutes, okay?"

The corner of my lip jerks up. "If I don't show up, then assume the worst, okay?" I start toward the back of the building only to stop and turn around when he says my name.

"Don't run away," he warns. "I'll be pissed and you'll be wasting both our time if I have to find you."

Creep.

But because I really have no choice but to stick with Declan at this point—after all, he knows the way out of The Aftermath—I don't venture away from the convenience store. It doesn't take me long to determine there's nobody lurking about who will massacre us. I'm just about to ignore his order to meet him at the fuel pump and go inside to join him when something familiar catches my eye.

Sagging against a graffitied sign advertising a soft drink is a bright blue backpack. My chest contracts as I force my feet toward it. I bend down, placing the Glock on the ground, and pick the satchel up, dangling it from the tips of my fingers. There's something in it. Even before I drag the zipper back, I know that I'll find protein bars and bottles of water.

So I don't finish unzipping the bag. I simply stare at the blood.

Tiny splotches cover the bottom of the blue bag. Even more—so much more—stains the ground a few inches from where I kneel. How far did those two boys make it before they were attacked?

Are they still alive?

"You okay, Virtue?"

I startle, dropping the bag. Spinning around, I punch Declan in the chest and shout, "Don't do that! Don't scare me like that."

He mouths a silent curse and rubs the spot where I hit him. "Next time you hit me, I swear I'll punch you back. And don't think for a second that I'll hold back just because you're a girl!" I don't answer, just return my gaze to the backpack. Hesitantly, he squats down next to me. "Hey, is everything okay? You look…funny."

"It's fine."

He flicks one of the straps on the bag with his thumb. "Does this belong to you?"

"No."

It belonged to two boys—kids who were only a few years younger than me—kids who are more than likely captured or even dead.

And I hurt for them.

CHAPTER ELEVEN

That evening, after Declan falls asleep a few feet away from me, his AcuTab lying facedown on his chest, I thrust myself into Olivia's mind. She's in a dining room with floor-to-ceiling windows. The ceiling is vaulted and, no surprise, windowed. Even though it's late at night where Declan and I are in the forest, the sun drenches Olivia's dining room in soft natural light. But I guess since there's a way to make her rooftop garden display the evening sky with a push of a few buttons, creating the illusion of daylight is possible, too.

Dragging my attention away from our surroundings, I focus on my gamer, who is in the middle of an argument with a woman sitting at the head of a white oval dining table, her blue-green eyes trained on Olivia as she paces in front of the table.

"I'm ready to go home. I'm sick of being stuck here if I can't do anything," Olivia says, her heels drumming harshly on the polished black floor, the staccato rhythm a perfect match for her angry breathing. When the older woman remains silent, Olivia leans down, digging her fingers into the back of her chair. She doesn't seem to notice the plate full of food inches beneath her nose. "Mom, please…" The desperation in her voice reminds me of myself a day ago, when I begged Declan to let me go.

How can Olivia be so fraught when she has so much?

Shaking her head, her mother races her hands through her immaculate short black hair. "Olivia, we've been over this. We're going home tomorrow morning. You can go back to that…game after academy. Now, sit down and eat your dinner."

"You don't understand, I—"

"A few missed days won't kill you. If anything, it might help you wean yourself off the gaming treatment." She clasps her hands in front of her on the table. "And honestly, Olivia, it's time you finished this once and for all. You're only making things more difficult dragging it out. You must see that?"

"My treatment isn't finished," Olivia mutters through gritted teeth. "What is it you don't understand about that?"

Her mother's face wrinkles into a deep frown. "Your goal is to hit one hundred thousand points and finish twelve missions. At the rate you were going when you first began, you should have fulfilled the obligations of your treatment months ago. I don't understand why you won't just make the damn points so we can end this. Don't you think it's time to put this obsession away? To move on with the rest of your life so that your father and I can move on, too?"

"Don't you mean so that your reputations can move on?" Olivia demands. "Let me ask you this. When that day comes—when I'm done with the game—are you sure you'll want to unleash me on society?"

"I believe you're purposely dragging this game on so that you can try—"

Olivia shakes her head furiously, strands of her dark brown hair flying into her eyes. "Dad doesn't believe that. He never has."

What doesn't Olivia's father believe? And what does her mother think she plans on trying to do?

Her mother's scowl morphs into a new expression that scares me.

On the surface, she looks calm, but beneath the facade, I can sense there's enough hatred to fill The Aftermath ten times. "Then you must have him fooled." She slams her palm down on the left side of her plate and the table lights up. A platform rises up in the center of it. She shoves the plate onto it along with Olivia's barely touched dish.

When it lowers a moment later, taking the dirty dishes with it, a monotone male voice announces, "AcuSystem records show that Olivia is at a severe nutrient deficiency in the following—"

"Ignore," Olivia and her mother both shout at the same time.

I guess Declan was telling the truth when he told me that the AcuTabs are linked to their homes. For a moment I'm dizzy with longing, ready to hold my own tablet, to hear a strange crisp voice tell me I haven't eaten enough nutrients. To simply have the opportunity to eat enough nutrients.

"Just forget I even said anything." Olivia turns to skulk away. The sound of a clearing throat stops her from leaving as the dining room doors slide open.

"End the game, Olivia. For all of us."

"When it's time."

"I know that Landon is still a part of your little clan."

And suddenly this conversation makes a little more sense. Her mother believes she's purposely dragging out the game to stay close to Landon, to Ethan.

Olivia's breath picks up and she drags her hands over her face, giving me a glimpse of her palms, which have notes written on them in messy ink. "So? His parents want him to get better. They don't think he has some ulterior motive." But she doesn't succeed at sounding nonchalant. Every other word her voice raises an octave.

"His parents are known sympathizers, so I'm curious to know what they think of you—of us. Olivia, they will force him to finish accumulating the points he needs, and then he'll be gone."

"Story of my life. Good night, Mother."

When I drop back into myself a couple of seconds later to the sound of Declan's snoring and the bitter cold night, I almost feel sorry for Olivia. I feel sorry she's forbidden to see the boy she loves and that she must use this violent game to be with him.

"But you use me to do it," I whisper aloud. Declan shifts, opening one of his eyes. Once he sees that I'm still in his sleeping bag, he rolls over to his side.

My pity for Olivia vanishes. If I'm to escape, I don't have time to feel pity for the girl who trapped me here in the first place.

Declan and I reach the pedestrian bridge that will take me back to the smelly bar on Demonbreun an hour after the sun comes up the next morning. In seven or eight hours, Olivia will be finished with school for the day and will log in to the game and take charge of me, but I linger on the bridge. She's the precise reason why I'm not ready to go home.

Declan waits for me at the end of the platform, watching as I sit on one of the concrete stools. There's an impatient look on his face. I don't think he understands how hard it is for me to return, despite his promise of eventually aiding in my escape. Maybe my journey west did take me the wrong way, and maybe I hadn't thought about what would happen once I broke free of the game, but for a few days I'd believed I was free. I had believed I'd escaped, that I'd never have to be my gamer's puppet ever again.

Even if I come right out and tell Declan that, I'm still not sure he'll understand.

So I dry the sweat from my face, wipe my hands down the front of my damp T-shirt and I get up. I walk through the enclosure of concrete and suspension wires and metal, and I join him, once again in the cage that is Nashville.

"It shouldn't take us long to find him," Declan says quietly as I lead him southwest, onto Third Avenue. "I promise—we'll find him so I can get you out of here, Virtue."

Every moment I have to spend in The Aftermath as a puppet seems like far too long. An enormous lump forms in my throat, and I don't dare look at him when I nod. "Good."

We pass a boy and a girl scavenging through a large garbage bin. Maybe they're on some sort of side quest, but more than likely their health gauges are just dangerously low. The girl looks up at us, eyes our giant bags and smiles. Two of her front teeth are chipped and rotten. I can't help but wonder what she looked like before the person playing her decided to let her forage for expired protein bars and stale water. Before she and the boy began to waste away.

Declan taps his fingertips on the Glock in my waist holster, and the girl's flat grin disappears. She lowers her head and starts sorting through the trash again. I want to ask why he didn't just show her his electroshock gun, since he has no problem threatening me with it, but he touches his finger to his lips and motions for me to keep walking.

"I told you," he says once we're out of earshot. Grabbing my upper arm, he pulls me away from a giant pothole in the sidewalk. "This is a sensitive assignment."

I roll my eyes. "And you really think a couple of Survivors who look like they'll die any day will interfere with your job?"

He stops walking for a moment to look back at me, tilting his head to one side. Like he's studying me. I don't like being scrutinized one bit. "No, the Survivors are shells. I'm more concerned about what their gamers might hear." He gives me a grave look. "You do know that when your gamer isn't on, you have to be careful, right?"

I poke my tongue into my cheek. Is he serious? "Do I look stupid enough to parade around as a sentient character? I already know I'll have to act as my gamer if I'm forced to interact with other characters."

"Never called you stupid, Virtue. Just want to make sure you know what you're doing."

Before I can respond, he's already walking. I steady myself, then pick up the pace until I'm several feet ahead of him. Fifteen minutes later, we stand in the lobby of the jail I once called home—the building that's right across from the courthouse where I initially met Declan. It's stifling in here, hotter than outside, and I shift awkwardly, cringing at how sore my body is.

"I'm surprised it wasn't that place." Declan gestures over his shoulder in the direction of the courthouse. "Prisons are always tricky with their self-locking doors and barriers."

The look on his face is expectant—like he's waiting for me to tell him that I remember what happened in the other building. I keep my expression perfectly still. "Then you'll have to be careful not to lock yourself in." I hug myself and rub my hands furiously over my upper arms. "I'll help you sweep the place for flesh-eaters, but I doubt we'll find anything. You're pretty safe with everything you have in that bag. And of course, I'll come back as soon as the coast is clear with locks and cha—"

"This isn't where you and your clan hole up?"

"Well, no— At least not anymore. But we stayed here for a few months and it's safe," I say. "We moved to a new location a couple weeks ago."

The muscles in Declan's shoulders tighten as he paces across the floor, stepping around the weeds that are growing through the cracks.

"I'm not staying here," he says, stopping behind a row of waiting chairs. He grips the back of one and leans in close. "It's not going to happen, Virtue."

"Well then, where do you expect to stay? Because The Aftermath isn't exactly bursting with luxury accommodations."

"With you."

"Excuse me?"

"I'm going to stay with you," he says.

"I live in a bar with three other people. And, just in case you haven't paid attention to anything I've told you the past couple days, they're not like me. Unless you tell them you're a moderator, you'll be just another target to them. A sitting duck," I say through gritted teeth.

And, besides, you're dangerous. Far too dangerous to stay with me.

"They'll never even know I'm there."

I release a harsh laugh. "They'll probably kill you and steal all your food and gear before you walk through the door. After you're dead, they'll call it an 'unmarked side quest.'"

"I'll show you how to hide me."

"Whatever. Like I said, you're not staying with me."

"And you'll stop me with what? Your menacing height? Your unbelievable strength?"

"Don't. Mock. Me."

"You can't stop me from following you. And you're better off hiding me than explaining to your clan how you met a moderator sixty miles west of here."

Moments ago he'd told me how I'd hide him from the people living with me and now he's threatening to expose that I'm an unsuccessful runaway. I drop my bag to the floor behind me. I move faster without it, and right now I'm thinking Declan will soon be gripping his face again in pain. His nose is still bruised from me hitting him two days ago.

"You won't do it." My voice is taunting and deliberate—so much like Olivia's that it makes my head spin. Whether I like it or not, my gamer exudes the cruel confidence that I need to deal with Declan. I curl my fingers into my palm and smile at him. I imagine it's the same look she'd give him.

"Why's that?"

"You said you need me."

"I do."

"And that means you won't all of the sudden decide to tell the other gamers and my own that I'm sentient. What good am I if I'm found out?" I ask.

I'll be deleted.

I still don't exactly know what all that entails, but I remember Jeremy and April's conversation and it sends a chill through my body.

"No good—you and I both know that. But think of it this way, if I'm with you, we can do what we need to do even faster. Don't you want to find out why you're here in the first place?"

I know that he's manipulating me, but I can't seem to make myself walk away. Declan probably figured out the moment he stopped me at the fence that I'd do just about anything to secure my freedom.

He's far more dangerous than I've given him credit for.

I turn my back to him and yank my bag from the floor. Stalking to the emergency exit, I call over my shoulder, "Are you coming or not?"

"Absolutely."

I swear I can hear the smirk in his voice.

The bar is smellier than I remember. But maybe that has something to do with the unbearable heat. I find two bottles of water in one of the cabinets behind the counter and hand both to Declan. "Sorry, if I take any more than this, they might notice." I jab my finger to the bent restroom sign dangling from the ceiling in the far corner of the bar. "The bathrooms are right over there."

Declan's intense gaze follows my finger, and when he turns to me again, the corners of his mouth pull up in amusement. "Aren't you an accommodating hostess."

I could argue with him. There's nothing I want more than to snap at him. But Olivia is probably coming back soon. I feel too drained from the past several days to try and get into her head, so I have no idea if that return will be thirty minutes or eight hours from now. All I know is that I need to get Declan into a hiding place and put myself where she left me, snuggled next to Ethan in the bed upstairs, before she logs in.

"We need to hide you before my gamer decides it's time we hunt for flesh-eaters and protein bars. Any ideas?" I turn in a slow circle, shaking my head at the lack of hidey-holes. "I can help you into a storage closet if you want."

He cocks an eyebrow. Sipping his water, he walks slowly around me, taking in the bar. He runs one of his fingers across a dusty vinyl stool, and then squats down to study the broken jukebox in one corner.

"I prefer we figure out what we're going to do quickly," I say.

He sighs and rises to his feet. "Sorry, I just find history…interesting. There's nothing like this in the U.P. Not anymore." He continues to stare at the machine for a moment, leaving me to wonder what's so historical about a broken jukebox.

"Why not?" I finally blurt out.

"Because this game represents an era from over half a century ago. The year 2036 was when the city we're standing in was actually vacated." He presses his palm over the jukebox's coin slot. "We

christened this new world The Aftermath. There are the cannibals—
flesh-eaters. And then there are—"

"And then there are people like myself. Survivors. We possess honor
and loyalty. We scavenge for food, not flesh. We're willing to die or
kill for the safety of our friends. And we choose our clans with care
because they must be prepared to do the same for us—one must be
so careful these days," I whisper in sync with Declan. When I close
my eyes, I can almost hear a woman's voice saying those words with
us in one of those dramatic, woe-is-me voices.

"Impressive and slightly creepy. You know the promotional log line
for The Aftermath." Declan lifts his shoulders. "If you ask me, Lan-
Corp could have done much better. The setting is perfect, though.
Authentic. Spooky."

"So this was once an actual place?"

"Before this state was condemned in 2036 after the war, yes. But
like I said, that was sixty-three years ago. It's 2099, Virtue." He scoops
his other bottle of water from the top of the bar and gestures to the
door leading to the basement. "Come on—let's set up my luxury accommodations."

We go down the narrow staircase. As he picks the lock, I ask him
about the game's point system. To my surprise, he explains without
an argument. "You've got to get a certain number of points and finish all twelve main missions to win. Main missions are the same for
every gamer and character and have to be done in order. After the
first mission, though, only team leaders can accept the big quests."

As he tells me this, I feel my hand move to the right side of my
face. Running my palm over the top of my ear, I tremble as I touch the
flesh that was mutilated three years back. Hearing that I was hurt in
a mission that hundreds of other characters must go through makes
me furious. How many of those people were injured, killed? All for

the sake of a game? "What about the side quests?" I hear myself ask in a tight, high-pitched voice.

"Way less points. And each moment in the game determines side quests. If the clan down the street is captured, then the system offers you and every other clan a mission to save them. Or LanCorp makes a modification to a main mission and you get a chance to find a character that'll give you a tip on it. Side quests are optional, but each gamer is required to do at least one a week. You get the most points for the ones where you help Survivors—'playing a saint' is what they call it in The Aftermath's gaming community. Robbing and taking out flesh-eaters gets you points, too, but usually not very many because most of those quests are unmarked."

Before I have a chance to ask my next question, he adds, "They're not listed on the mission menu, but if a gamer stumbles on one, he gets points. Like I said, they're not worth very much. The only good thing about them is they're like side quests—gamers don't have to complete them with their clan if they don't want to."

I shift and the back of my wrist skims his arm. I pretend I don't notice the way his muscles tighten. "So what do you have to do to lose points?" I ask softly.

"Isn't it obvious? Break the rules, just like with any other game. You screw over Survivors or your clan or yourself and, best-case scenario, you lose points." He leans in closer to the padlock and growls something under his breath. I consider pushing him aside so that I can unlock the door for him. Being in such a tight space with this boy makes me nervous.

I link my thumbs through my belt loops and press my back against the coarse brick wall. "How so?"

"I mean, the goal of the game is to off the bad guys and learn how to work together as a team, to learn how to be responsible and control your impulses. The game's philosophy is that if you're robbing or hurting Survivors, you're not learning any of those things. Whenever you raid the good guys or refuse to accept a mission to save a member of your team who's been captured, you lose points. And if you kill a Survivor—well, you start over from the beginning of the game, no matter where you are. You lose all your points and have to find a brand-new clan. Same thing goes if you get yourself killed. You say goodbye to your points and start over—with a new character."

Now Olivia's frequent Survivor raids make sense. She wants to lose points so that she can continue to play The Aftermath with Landon. I wonder if Jeremy's and April's gamers realize what Olivia and Landon are up to.

Finally, the lock opens and Declan turns the doorknob. I'm reluctant to go in first, but he nudges me inside and comes in after me, shutting the door. There's only one window in here, and I immediately start breathing heavily, even though I'm probably inhaling mildew. This reminds me of the bloody room I woke up in three years ago. It feels as though it's shrinking by the second, suffocating me.

I draw as much oxygen as possible into my lungs, but it's still not enough.

"Don't worry. I won't keep you long," he says. He sits his bag at the back of the small room and pulls a few things from it. Bundling them in his arms, he sweeps past me and kneels down by the door. I take a step closer as he sits the two small dome-shaped objects on either side of the entrance.

"I'm making a second save point in this building," he explains as he pulls out his tablet. He rapidly punches a succession of buttons until a bright green light emanates from the two things on the floor and washes over the room for a few seconds.

My heart skips a couple of beats. Part of me is curious and the other part expects the whole building to blow to pieces if I so much as sigh.

When the light dies down, Declan faces me. "It's a crude version of the technology used in the save points that protect characters when gamers log off. Except I've reconfigured this one to be active at all times. If anybody even touches that door, they'll be shocked, which will give me enough time to get out of here while they try to figure out what's going on."

That explains what happened when I first tried to open the door on the second floor after all the gamers left—someone must have changed the save settings. I run my fingertips over my wrist, recalling how the electricity spun painfully through my body as I pushed myself out the doorway. I don't tell him how impressed I am that he's managed to make his own safe room.

"What happens if they decide to come in anyway?"

"The current is twice as strong as a normal save point. Besides, only an idiot would keep picking himself up off the floor just so he can be shocked all over again."

Well, thanks.

"But," he says, "if that does happen, even if I don't get out in time, they'll see nothing but an empty room." At my wondering look, he adds, "Characters are expensive. LanCorp takes every precaution to protect their good name and reputation, so that means taking care of their gamers' investments."

I feel as if he's slapped me in the face. I'm an investment. The expensive belonging of a girl who lacks the decency to feed me enough food. The inner corners of my eyes burn and my vision blurs. I look away from him, at a dark smudge on the wall. At a centipede racing across the floor.

At anything other than Declan.

Taking a deep breath, I slide past him but pause before I try to open the door. I already know I'll be shocked when I return to the room upstairs. The last thing I want is for it to happen multiple times in the course of a few minutes. "Is it safe?"

The AcuTab beeps a few times. Then he says, "Now it is."

I go through the door and turn around to look at Declan. He leans against the doorway, rubbing his finger around the opening of his water bottle and staring closely at me. I fidget, tuck a stray strand of hair behind my left ear. "You'll come back as soon as it's safe?" he asks.

He knows I will. He knows I want out of this place more than anything. But I nod anyway.

"Be careful," he says as I walk slowly up the steps. "And be smart."

I clean myself up as much as possible in the privy on the first floor with a jug of water and some harsh soap that burns my chafed skin. I study myself in the grimy, shattered mirror. A red-faced girl with blond hair, green eyes. A recognizable stranger.

Three hours of rest is all I'm given in the room upstairs before Olivia returns. Much of that I spend staring directly across from me at Ethan's open-eyed, blank face and fighting off the tremors that still shake my body from the electric shock I received when I came in—apparently what Declan did downstairs to the basement door failed to disable the shock in this Save.

And the first thing Olivia has me say after she awkwardly manipulates my movements is, "Wake up—wake up. I want to go on a mission."

CHAPTER TWELVE

We're going on a rescue mission. From what I'm able to see when Olivia accepts the side quest on her mission screen, our objective is to save two captive Survivors from a flesh-eater den a couple of miles from here. We're supposed to speak to one of the cannibals—a boy named Reese—to obtain critical information about the final game mission. And we're supposed to leave him alive or forfeit all points from our last three side quests. My heart sinks as my clan plots the mission. More walking. More senseless violence. And more of me getting knocked around for no good reason.

Someone is bound to die today, and I hope I'm not on the giving or receiving end.

Jeremy pulls me aside as soon as I'm done speaking to the group. "I can't stay for long," he says quietly. "My family is hosting a party for my grandmother's birthday at—"

He stops speaking as Olivia shrugs me out of his grip. She turns my head in his direction, and I stare him down for a moment. Aside from his vacant brown eyes, he looks healthier than I've seen him in months. After he accidentally swallowed a mouthful of tainted water when we went on a mission to liberate a bunch of Survivors from the ruins of a showboat, he was nothing but skin and bone for nearly a year.

"Okay...how much of your time do you plan to grace us with?" Although my voice is steady, I've no doubt Olivia's tone is sharp enough to slice through metal.

"Two hours." Jeremy takes a cautious step closer. I press one of my hands to his chest and shake my head from side to side, pursing my lips together. There's too much force behind my touch, even if Jeremy does tower over me. I wish I could do something—tell him that his grandmother is more important than Olivia and this game. He gives me that shaky, out-of-place smile. "Maybe three or four. Or, I don't know, maybe I can just cancel. My parents might be upset at first, but they'll get over it."

Olivia maneuvers my lips into a grin and makes me say, "That's better."

My stomach twists into painful knots. I'm not sure if I should feel empathy toward a gamer, but I do. Whoever controls Jeremy is playing the game because he wants friends—he'd basically said as much the night he and April's gamer were discussing my fate in The Save. And Olivia will take that need and exploit it as much as possible.

Olivia plays the other gamers, her friends, just as often as she does me. My chest coils so tight I'm afraid it will rupture from the fury and panic coursing through me.

None of us mean anything to Olivia but entertainment.

"They've just recently moved in. We should get a move on. We've only got three hours to finish this mission," I hear myself say just as I'm drawn into Olivia's mind.

We're in her ten-sided gaming room again, but she's seated, not standing like usual. She's also not flicking her hands near as much. The only time she moves is when she swipes her fingers through the empty space in front of her to switch to a different menu or zoom in or out of the screen.

Despite her lack of motion, I know she has me busy preparing for the side quest inside The Aftermath. It's still stunning that she's able to move me about while I'm inside of her head, but then, I'm certain it doesn't matter what my mind is focused on—Olivia is in full control of my body.

On one of the screens, I'm pulling a few protein bars and a couple of bottles of water from the storage closet. My arms are mottled from the five days I spent in the blistering sun. It's so visible on the gigantic displays that I'm terrified she knows where I've been, what I planned to do, especially when she grips the armrests of her cushioned white seat and stares intently at the display. But then she moves her hand and changes the screen to look at my inventory. She lingers for a moment, studying the list, before returning to the view of the game.

Black text flashes across the bottom of the screen. Then twice more. This has never happened before and the words are blinking so rapidly that I'm unable to comprehend what they say until the fourth time.

The Aftermath
Mind Experience
Trial Version 1.2.0

On-screen, I whisper something to Ethan, brush a strand of his golden hair out of his hazel eyes and touch my lips to his. The entire time I'm doing this, Olivia remains as still and as quiet as a statue. A terrifying thought worms its way into my head. Maybe Olivia doesn't need to move any longer to control me. Maybe this trial version is a form of the game where her mind alone manipulates my body and words. A new level of power.

Something new and even more dangerous than before.

Is Trial Version 1.2.0 what Declan was talking about a few nights ago?

"Why do you have my things?" a voice demands angrily, launching me back into my own head as my gaze snaps toward April.

"What in the world are you talking about?"

She dangles her weapons in my face, and my heart skips a beat. Oh, no. Somehow, in my exhaustion and frustration, I'd forgotten to return the knives to her backpack, where they belonged.

"This was in your stuff. Why was it there?" she asks.

Somehow, Olivia makes me narrow my eyes into tight slits. "Why the hell were you going through my bag?" There's an edge to my voice that catches me off guard. Everything I say is typically dry and emotionless when I'm Olivia's puppet. But maybe Trial Version 1.2.0 changes all that, too.

April's blue eyes don't even blink as I rush at her. Buckling her belt, she says in the even voice I'm accustomed to, "My knives were gone. I needed them for the raid and—"

"Here's a suggestion, April." Olivia moves my hand so that it locks around April's throat, and I shove her against the wall so hard I hear the air being knocked out of her body. "Stay out of my belongings before you find yourself seeking a new clan. And I guarantee you'll be nowhere near as lucky."

Olivia doesn't give any further explanation. No denial. No wondering aloud about how April's knives ended up in my bag in the first place. Olivia offers absolutely nothing but a cold glare before having me loudly declare to everyone else, "That goes for the rest of you, too."

A million emotions run through me as I threaten the people around me with words I'd never use. Fear that Olivia will find out where I've been and punish me horribly. Fury because no matter how bad I want to make myself shut up, I can't do it, because she's stronger than me.

She has such a hold on me that I'm lost completely when she wraps her mind around mine.

And I also feel hope.

Hope that one day I'll meet Olivia face-to-face and I can tell her everything I'm dying to say—all the horrible words I've learned from her.

The flesh-eater den is underground, inside an enclosed parking garage. Exactly the type of building I hate because it reminds me of the one I woke up in years ago. Part of me feels as if I'm the same as I was then. Still unaware of everything that's happening. Still trapped. Still the loneliest person in the world. The little bit of safety and camaraderie I've allowed myself to feel over the past three years disappeared the moment I realized what my friends are.

What I am.

I give the orders as we huddle across the street from the entrance. April and Ethan will storm the cannibals outright, taking the elevator. It's the perfect distraction. Just enough for Jeremy and I to sneak in, release the captives and snag a bunch of supplies. "It's foolproof," I say confidently when I'm done explaining the plan, and everyone else agrees in unison.

This plan is anything but foolproof.

It's stupid. Someone's going to die. Some poor soul, some character who eats other humans just because she's linked to a sick, twisted player, is going to lose her life. Or maybe somebody in my own group.

Possibly even myself. Then Olivia will have to find a new Claudia Virtue.

Jeremy and I enter through the garage door at the back of the building. It's already cracked. I lie on the ground, crossing my arms over my chest. Carefully, I roll under the door. The sharp, rusted metal at the bottom scrapes my raw shoulders. I come out on the other side gracefully, but my body is on fire. Jeremy comes through next. When he stands up, there's a thin cut on the tip of his nose.

You're bleeding, I want to tell him, but Olivia has a different idea. "Come on—their gear is this way." She pushes me onward, farther into the flesh-eater den. It doesn't have the usual stench of decay and waste. It smells surprisingly clean. Like bleach.

A scent that terrifies me for some reason.

But no matter my fears, I continue on. After all, Olivia compels me to. The parking garage is like a junkyard. There's so much stuff. A few weeks ago, I'd have attributed the random couches and lamps, the gutted car, to years of people seeking shelter here. Now I wonder if moderators strategically placed the scrap throughout the place to make the game more exciting.

Jeremy and I crouch behind an armchair that's more stuffing than fabric. He places his hand on my shoulder, and grins down at me. "Have you started your research paper for history?"

"Shut up and stop breaking character."

"Sorry."

He's quiet as we wait for Ethan's signal to start the mission. My thighs hurt from the position Olivia's put me in. I try to flush out the pain by thinking about how long Olivia would last, hunkered down like this at such an awkward angle. Or how irritated Jeremy's gamer's family must be that he's shunning his grandmother's party in favor of playing The Aftermath.

Ethan's cue comes loud and clear. Two gunshots. Did he put them into a flesh-eater or just fire at the ceiling? I wish I could close my eyes to it all, but Jeremy and I slink quickly through the piles of junk, heading toward the reason why we've come here.

Two Survivors—a boy and a girl, both of them as young as the boys I met on my trip west—sit unguarded with their backs to either side of a pillar. Metal chains are wrapped around them. The girl glances up when I kneel in front of her, and if her face could show relief, I've no doubt it would.

"You're here." She sighs. "I thought we were done for. The last thing I want is to have to restart my treatments with a new character and have my points reset and—"

My hand claps over her mouth. "I'll reset your points myself if you don't keep your mouth shut," I say, and they both bob their heads. I let go of the girl's mouth. It takes a minute to pick the locks and two more to unravel the metal—quietly, so that the flesh-eaters don't hear us.

When I'm done, the pair hobbles to their feet and Jeremy tells them how to get out of the parking garage. The boy takes off, but the girl lingers behind, staring at me. I wonder if her gamer logged off. Or if there's a problem with her chip, too. But then she moves toward Jeremy and me.

"I hope to be as good as you one day," she says. "There's a whole gaming board about how your clan won the third main mission in less than half the time of any other clan. And you've done so many rescue quests that—"

Olivia shrugs my shoulders. "Can you stop the hero worship before I decide to chain you back up?"

The girl takes a step forward, shaking her head. "But—"

"Why are you still here? Me saving you doesn't make us friends. Now run along, before I decide to leave you here, after all."

The other character clenches her fists and takes another step closer to me, but Jeremy moves in her direction. He shakes his head menacingly. He could kill her with just his hands, I realize. And his character would make him do it if it meant protecting Olivia. His friend.

Luckily, it doesn't come to that. Without another word, the girl turns and leaves, making as much noise as possible.

"What an ungrateful little idiot," I hear myself say. "Come on—let's fill our bags so we can finish up here and get out of this dump."

This is one of those rare moments when I actually agree with my gamer.

These cannibals don't have a supply of packaged food, something that many other flesh-eaters keep. What they do have is a gratuitous amount of ammunition and medicine. Steel and opiates. A stupid reason to risk our lives, especially when the storage closet at the bar is overflowing with weapons. "Jackpot," I say.

I shrug the three empty bags I'm carrying off my arms and drop them on the floor in the middle of the stash. I start loading one of them with a group of knives hanging up in a steel closet. I can hear the erratic sound of gunshots echoing through the building. I should be used to this. It shouldn't bother me.

It does.

My fingertips flick across a curved blade that's caked with blood and something else, and my stomach heaves.

"Evening, ladies," a male voice says. I'm up on my feet with the Glock drawn before my brain even registers that Jeremy and I have been found out. The flesh-eater lifts his hands above his head in surrender. "Holy cra— Are you serious? You're Virtue. The guys in training won't believe this. I'm getting a chance at Claudia Virtue."

There are many things that I've not been able to explain about The Aftermath, but I do recall everyone I've encountered. And I've never met this guy. He's redheaded and freckled all over and at the most a couple of years older than me.

"There's no chance of that happening since I'm about to shoot you, love," I tease, pulling the Glock's slide back. It springs forward, and the boy just stares at it.

"Wow," he says. "This is epic."

I'm scared for so many reasons right now. Someone I swear I've never met knows me by name. But then again, hadn't the female Survivor mentioned how Olivia was well-known in some type of game boards? Claudia Virtue and Olivia are popular in the gaming community. Maybe that's all this is, some game-obsessed weirdo who follows my actions online?

"Good luck with your next job." I pause for a moment, not moving. Olivia must be looking at a different screen. "Reese. Try to last a little longer than a couple months."

What does she mean by job? I don't ponder on this for long, because Olivia has me inching closer and closer to the boy. She aims for me to kill him. This important part of our mission, the boy that we're not supposed to harm. I should have known this would happen; Olivia's itching to lose as many points as possible.

Just two months in this game and Reese will die today by my hand. I'm livid. His player seems so gleeful and ready to die. Why should Reese be the one who suffers?

I won't kill him; this is something I cannot do. So I concentrate. I tune out the noises in the background, and Jeremy's quiet voice urging me not to do anything that will affect the clan. The scene is too much like the day in the courthouse to my liking, but I have the chance here to change the outcome if I can just control my thoughts.

I feel my index finger starting to bend.

Don't do this. I can't do this. I can't kill Reese.

My fingertip touches the cold concave curve of the trigger.

You're not Olivia. You can control yourself because you're not a killer.

"Next time, shoot first," I say.

Do not kill him, Claudia!

My fingertip freezes in the most uncomfortable, painful and yet utterly welcome position possible.

"What the hell?" Olivia makes me ask.

Jeremy rushes forward. "Claudia, what's—"

"Stay back," Olivia growls.

I can feel her trying to move my finger. There's an uncomfortable itchy feeling in the center of my skull, and my head twitches to each side. A big grin stretches across Reese's face.

"And you're glitching. Awesome."

"You're wrong," I snap. Before I can stop her, Olivia makes me close my other hand around one of the knives. I hurl it across the room and it sinks into Reese's chest. He crumbles to the floor, still smiling.

I slide into Olivia's head just in time to see enormous red letters flashing across the central screen: Mission Failed.

CHAPTER THIRTEEN

Over the next day and a half, Olivia's game play is erratic. Five minutes here, an hour there—she makes it impossible for me to predict her movements and leave The Save. So I stay put. Watch through hazy eyes as the rest of the clan comes and goes. They play this horrible game like they're the ones fighting to survive. They treat the sorrow and death like it's nothing, even though they live in a world where I'm certain such violence doesn't exist.

Someday, and I hope that day is soon, I want to come face-to-face with a gamer, not his character, and ask him why. Why do you play this game? Why do you think death is a sport, a source of entertainment? And, most important, why do you make someone else challenge death for you—don't you know that we're real people?

Olivia's gone for the time being. She left me slumped low in the chair by The Save door, with my arms dangling over the sides. My back aches because the position is so awkward, and my arms feel as if they weigh a hundred pounds each. But I'm too scared to move. What happened with Reese in the parking garage may have blown my cover, so I have to be cautious.

I must be a broken rag doll.

An image of the flesh-eater's freckled face just before Olivia made me stab him flashes through my head. My nostrils flare. If I were stronger and knew how to block Olivia out of my head entirely, maybe Reese would still be alive.

I hear voices on the other side of the door, and I smooth my expression into a vacant mask.

Jeremy and April enter The Save. His hands are covered in blood, as is her chest. As far as I can tell, neither of them is injured, but there's so much red, and they smell like cold, wet pennies mixed with rusted iron and decay. Like death. I wonder what was so precious to their gamers, important enough to make them kill today.

I expect it won't be much.

"She hasn't been around." Jeremy nods at me as they begin unpacking their things. Out of the corner of my eye, I see him pull a second bag off his back. It's new and enormous, with dozens of compartments and padding. No doubt it's filled with the spoils from today's bloodbath.

"She ruined that side quest for us. If I were Olivia, I wouldn't show my face, either. Still, botched mission or not, Virtue glitched, and I wish I'd been there to see it. If she were my character, I'd have her game footage pulled immediately."

But I'm not yours, I want to say. I'm Olivia's. I'm *her* living, breathing game pawn. Instead, I continue to stare. Jeremy bends over me, placing one of his hands on my lap to support his weight. He's heavy, weighing at least a hundred pounds more than me. I smell his sweat intermingling with the stench of blood. Feel pain shooting through my legs from the pressure. And then, just when I'm sure it won't get any worse, he touches my face. Moves a loose tendril of hair away from my cheek.

Please get off me.

"Maybe the mods will come in after Claudia soon. And besides,

Olivia swore killing that flesh-eater was an accident. She just forgot the side quest instructions. I mean, it's an honest mistake."

Get off me, and stop *touching* me!

April snorts. Strange to hear this from a girl with such a passionless face. "Whatever. She's your friend, not mine, so believe what you want. And if I have to hear her brag one more time about the stupid game update…"

I drag my thumbnails over my fingertips, attempting to focus on something other than Jeremy's weight and odor.

"Don't be like that, April," Jeremy says. To my relief, he backs away from me, a creepy smile on his face. I sink my teeth deeper into my tongue. "She makes the game fun."

His reason for wanting Olivia around is nauseating. Fun. This is not fun—not for me anyway. I want to shake some sense into him. Scream at him that his idea of fun is my torture. Instead, I watch listlessly as he walks to the bed and lies on his side.

"If you call being held back fun," April says. "You don't think it's because of her being—"

"No," Jeremy says abruptly, cutting off whatever April was about to say, to my disappointment. He closes his eyes a second before my eye twitches. "Hopefully Claudia will be back soon. And maybe she'll surprise you and accept The Badlands." His entire body freezes, including his upturned lips. I shift my eyes to a splotch of blood on his T-shirt so I don't have to look at his face.

Something sharp digs into the flesh on my arm, and I grit my teeth to hold in the gasp of pain. April bends over in front of my face. She's smiling, just as Jeremy was, but I've a feeling that if her eyes held any real emotion, I'd find nothing but hatred there.

"If I could kill you myself, Virtue—Olivia—I would."

I realize there's someone else making her say this and that the anger is directed toward Olivia, but it doesn't stop the heat spreading through me like wildfire. First Jeremy touching my face, and now I'm being scratched and pinched. All I want to do is take out every bit of frustration I have with my fists.

My fingers spasm.

"But someone will do it for me eventually," April continues. Why eventually, I'm dying to say. What's stopping her from sabotaging me right now? What's stopping any of my clan from trying to kill me? April lies on the mat on the floor, turns toward the wall and then she's silent.

The girl she leaves behind doesn't know hate.

She doesn't even know me.

Since my movements are limited, I spend my time flicking in and out of Olivia's thoughts. She's furious. Probably because she thinks there's a glitch in the game, a glitch in me. Nearly every moment I witness through her eyes is spent fuming, and it's impossible for me to make sense of anything she says in her anger.

But I have questions, too. How was I able to block Olivia's commands? And when will she let me go long enough for me to see Declan? Now that she's suspicious, there's a nervous feeling in the pit of my belly, and I have a feeling it won't go away until I'm far away from the game.

I fall into her head again.

"The Mind Experience is a pathetic waste of time," she's saying. We're in a dark room that's so abstract it makes me feel drunk even from inside someone else's head. Dark tinted windows, spreading from wall to wall, slant in diagonal angles toward the ceiling. It reminds me of a black diamond.

Olivia sits at a six-sided table that's glossy, spotless. Every now and then, she covers her face with her hands, blocking my view of the room. I don't think she's had a good night's sleep in days. And I feel that, if I could see her now, she would look completely wrecked.

"This was a mistake," she murmurs against her palms. "It's not going to work. Why else would it take this long?"

"Olivia?"

At the sound of a man calling her name, she places her hands flat on the table. Lifting slightly out of her seat, she glares at the two people across from her. Sitting on the right is a man in a dark suit. He's brown-haired and middle-aged, with a thin mustache and a crescent-shaped scar beneath his left eye. His arms are crossed tightly over his chest and his lips pressed thin. He's just as frustrated as Olivia. I can tell by the way his brown eyes twitch every few seconds.

Next to him is a woman wearing a white lab coat with a LanCorp badge on the pocket. She taps away at her tablet's projection, nervously peeking up at Olivia.

I know her. This is the same person who fixed me after my run-in with Declan at the courthouse.

Dr. Coleman.

Olivia's having a meeting with the physician who might have something to do with why I'm not working properly. Have I been discovered? Does she know where I've been the past several days? If I were in my own head, my own body, I'm confident my heart would have already imploded.

Olivia bangs her fists on the table. "You saw the mods' reports about what happened. The new version doesn't work!"

Hunching forward, the man says through clenched teeth, "Not possible. The platform is virtually flawless."

"Flawless? Have you tested your own technology yet or are you going on the word of a bunch of idiots?" Olivia curls her index finger and tilts her head to one side, studying it. "Does this look flaw-less to you? Because my character's trigger finger froze just like this in the middle of a raid."

"Perhaps Claudia is broken," the man says. "She did nearly die re-cently. And don't say you weren't warned."

Olivia interlocks her fingers and presses them to her lips as if she's praying. I can hear the number of breaths she takes in gradually in-crease; I can see how violently her hands are shaking. If there were a knife nearby, I bet she'd hurl it across the table and into the man's chest, just like we did to Reese. Finally, Olivia drags her fingertips across a glass partition in front of her. A virtual image of my brain hovers over the middle of the table, rotating so everyone can see it. I hadn't noticed the implant the last time I saw a projection of my own head, but now that I know what to look for, it's obvious. A small square with rounded corners positioned in the top center of my head.

"You see that? Claudia isn't broken—she's perfectly normal. The mods took it upon themselves to check her stats and vitals for the last thirty days when they saw what happened the other day." When she gestures to the walls, I'm aware that there are images of me in the game playing on them, just like a video. Me freeing Survivors. Killing flesh-eaters. Arguing with April about her knives. None of Olivia breaking the rules and losing points. If I could hold my breath, I would. I'm ter-rified Declan's face will show up on the dark glass and then my facade will be over. They're all silent for another few seconds and then the clips fade. No Declan. And no images of me sentient.

"Version 1.2.0 is what's lacking. It's a waste of money—a horrible, expensive excuse for an update. That's why you let me test it, right? To tell you whether or not it worked," Olivia says.

Dr. Coleman lifts her hand, as if she's a student. Olivia turns our gaze toward her and she shrinks back into her seat until only her face is visible. "Well, guess what? The update is a bust. But Claudia Virtue—Claudia Virtue is just as functional as she was when we were first linked. Isn't she, Coleman?"

Dr. Coleman looks like a deer caught in the headlights. Obediently, she bobs her head up and down. Her lips stretch into such a taut smile, I'm afraid they'll start to bleed. Poor woman. She's just as intimidated by Olivia as everyone else.

I'm not sure I'll ever understand how Olivia has so much control over people. How it came to be that I'm the person she has the most power over.

The Aftermath is her obsession, and that scares me. Right now she doesn't believe it's possible for me to be sentient, but what if she digs deep enough to discover that I'm self-aware? What if she realizes that what she thinks is a glitch in the game was in reality me temporarily preventing her from playing?

Cautiously, I pull away from her and the angled room and the spinning projection of my brain to return to The Save. Olivia's argument is still going strong, giving me a little time to speak to Declan. Except for Jeremy, everybody is accounted for, but I'm not afraid of him catching me. All I have to do is threaten to kick him out of the clan and he'll do anything I ask.

Something bitter burns my throat and nose. I can't stand the thought of manipulating people—of acting like her.

I'm not electrocuted when I leave the save point. I've had plenty of time to think the past several hours, and I'm certain my getting shocked last time happened because Olivia changed the save setting to prevent the other characters from playing without her.

Thousands of other gamers and the one operating me had to be a sociopath with a power complex.

I race down to the basement. I'm careful not to touch the door

Declan rigged for fear of getting hurt. Banging the toe of my shoe against the wall, I whisper his name repeatedly until I hear the four beeps. The door creaks open and Declan stands in front of me. He leans against the doorway, grinning. Shirtless. Disheveled dark hair falling into his eyes.

"You look like hell, Virtue."

I barely give him enough time to move out of my way before I brush past him. The last time I was in here, I had almost freaked out. But today I'm determined to hold myself together, to ignore the fact that being in such a tiny space frightens me. Tightening my hands into fists, I focus on the first thing my gaze connects with: the mess.

CDS packets are strewn across the cellar floor, along with crunched water bottles. I sweep a section of garbage out of the way with my foot, then sit with my back to the wall. Crossing my feet at the ankles, I raise an eyebrow at Declan. I keep my eyes focused on his face because I don't want them to wander to his bare upper body. "Redecorating?"

He smirks. "Might as well make it my own." He comes to the middle of the room, where his rucksack is turned on its side, the contents spilling out onto the floor, and begins repacking his gadgets and food.

"What are you doing?"

"You don't think I'm going to leave this here while we search, do you?"

Of course that would be the first thing he brought up. Even though I haven't seen him since the day we arrived and my absence could have meant anything—capture or injury or even death. Nice of him to care. "We're not going out today," I say, shaking my head. "For all I know, we might not be going anywhere for a while."

He freezes, one hand on the strap of his bag and the other gripping the remote that operates the two small dome-shaped devices at the door. His smirk disappears, and his nose scrunches up. "Then why are you here?"

"I came to… Look, there might be a bit of a delay. My gamer has been playing The Aftermath more frequently."

"Why?"

Do I tell him about the past several hours and how Olivia has used me sporadically? Or about the short-lived moment where I defied my gamer's commands to hold my own? I trust this boy about as much as I do Olivia, but he knows the game. The Aftermath is his job, and even if I don't have much faith in him, he may be able to help me figure out what happened in the parking garage.

"I have a glitch," I say.

He stares at me as if I'm the biggest fool in the universe. "You function without your gamer—no crap you have a glitch."

The way he says it makes me sound like a robot. I throw an empty CDS wrapper at him. It lands a few inches between us after drifting quietly to the floor. He leans over and blows it back at me.

"No, that's not what I mean. When she was playing me—the day we came back—I was able to control myself for a minute. She wanted me to shoot some flesh-eater, and—"

"You blocked her?"

He's no longer interested in his bag. Instead, he drags it across the floor, drops it in front of me and then plops down on top of it. Everything inside it clacks together. I hope he hasn't broken anything we'll need.

"I just— Yeah, I guess I did."

He nods his head slowly, as if he's trying to digest what I've just told him. Cold fear slices through me, and suddenly I regret having told him what happened. How stupid can I be?

Bending his head close to mine, he pulls my hand into his and runs the pad of his thumb over my knuckles. I take in the sight of him—his narrowed gray eyes, clenched jaw, at the way he bites the center of his top lip. At his chest. I wish he'd put on a shirt already. I swallow hard, trying to force down the mass of uncertainty in the back of my throat.

"Why are you looking at me like that?" I ask in a small voice.

"Because you're an anomaly, Virtue. I don't understand why your chip malfunctioned like this. And I don't understand how LanCorp's scientists missed the malfunction. How—"

Scientists. That single word sends fear spiraling through me, ruining the moment between Declan and me. Whatever that moment was. I jump to my feet and head for the door, but he's on his feet, right behind me. He grabs my wrist, and my breath catches in my throat.

"Don't touch me," I whisper, though I'm not sure if I'm asking him to let me go out of fear or because his touch isn't so bad. Isn't nearly as dangerous as I'd convinced myself it was.

No, Declan's touch is something I didn't expect.

"Hey, wait. I didn't mean that as a bad thing, not really. I—" Cornering me against the wall, he stares down at me. "I've just never seen a character like you. Nobody…nobody with LanCorp has."

The tips of his fingers move over the scars on my wrists—painful little things that ache when it's cold outside. His hands trail up my forearms and finally stop on my shoulders. He bends his neck until our faces are centimeters apart and a lock of his black hair brushes the bridge of my nose.

I hear my breathing slow until it comes to a temporary stop. Feel my heart speed up—it's so rapid I'm afraid it will explode. His upper body presses against mine, and a scent that reminds me of clean garments drifts from his sunburned skin, filling my senses.

"You can't expect me to accept all of this at once," he says.

How does he think all of this makes me feel?

"Don't screw me over," I whisper once I catch my breath and the room stops turning. "Please."

But I expect him to. I only hope it's after he's helped me out of the game and not before. At least then I might stand a chance, if I run fast. "I'm not going to turn you in, if that's what you mean."

"Then don't mention LanCorp. Or scientists. Or anything else that'll lead me to believe you're ready to turn me over as soon as we reach the border," I say. "And take your hands off of me."

He's far too close, and too undressed, for my liking.

He finally releases me but doesn't step aside. "I'm...intrigued. Virtue, your head is..." It feels as if he's holding his words high above me, suspending them from a thread that's impossible for me to reach. I grit my teeth. Waiting for him to speak is almost as frustrating as not being able to control what I say. His face twitches and something close to a smile bursts across it.

"Your head is different from anything I've ever seen, glitch or no glitch. It's like your chip is on send and receive. And I can't help but want to know everything going on inside your mind—it keeps me up at night."

That's it?

There's some part of me that wishes he'd worded that differently. That he'd said thinking about me, not my head, keeps him up at night. But then I realize I'm probably not processing my thoughts clearly— I'm dehydrated from all the game play and I'm hungry, too. I swallow several times, trying to get rid of my sudden dry mouth. "What do you mean by send and receive?"

His eyebrows pull together as if he's remembering something. At last, he says, "Characters and gamers both have the chip. Gamers are on send, characters set to receive. Your chip— Well, it's like you're on both." He presses his thumb and forefinger together and flicks them back and forth as he would a light switch. "Your gamer can send you a signal, but from what you just said, you're able to send one back. That's not normal, Virtue.

"You're everything LanCorp is afraid of," he adds, almost as if he's talking to himself. "If they even thought this was possible. Smart. Resilient. Self-aware. And now you can block your girl out? Put you in a gaming room and you'd be able to play her."

"What do you mean?"

He backs away from me.

"Well?" I ask.

"Aren't you listening, Virtue? If your chip is sending and receiving information, there's little stopping you from controlling your gamer. You go in a gaming room where you can see what she's seeing, you could do the same thing she does with you."

I forget how to breathe. When I finally glance up, Declan is examining my face.

"You okay?"

I shrug as indifferently as possible and say, "Yes." He doesn't seem to notice the tremor in my voice. He's too busy pacing from corner to corner, warning me about the dangers of coming to see him if I'm not ready to leave for a search.

"Don't block her. Don't ruin your chance to get out of this game because you want revenge," he says, a little too sharply. He gives me a wild, desperate look. "Suck it up, Virtue. Let her do with you what she will."

I agree with him. But as he continues to speak, my mind zeroes in on what he said before. *Put you in a gaming room where you can see what she's seeing and you could play her.*

He doesn't realize that I don't need a special room to see what

139

Olivia's doing. That just about any hour of the day, I can slip into her head and know if she's asleep or awake. I can witness her conversations and, in doing so, determine whether she's livid or appeased.

"Let me out," I say. "I'd better get back before she returns." Or before I run into Jeremy. My head is such a mess right now, I'm not in the mood to talk, much less concoct a lie.

He disables the save point, then slides the rectangular controller into the pocket of his black pants. "You're going to get tired of hearing this, Virtue, but be careful. You're much too valuable to me— I don't want you doing anything stupid that'll ruin everything."

I don't think I'll ever get tired of someone showing concern for me. Declan is the first person in three years who's been genuinely worried about my safety, not the well-being of a costly toy. I appreciate that, even if his motivation is selfish.

"I'll stay out of trouble."

When he closes the door, my shoulders sag. I drag my feet up the concrete steps slowly. I don't want to go back into The Save. Doing so will only give me more time to think, to let the questions eating away at my brain repeat on a loop until I do something irresponsible, like testing Declan's theory on my gamer.

I go in the bar and lean my forehead against the unstable wooden door as I secure the locks. I try to shove the thoughts of manipulating Olivia out of my head. They won't budge.

Frustrated, I turn around to walk upstairs. And I collide into a soft human wall. I swallow down a gasp, a scream. Fight the urge to stumble backward. Calmly, I brush my short blond hair out of my face. I lift my chin until my eyes meet blank hazel ones.

Ethan.

No, Landon.

I'm done for.

CHAPTER FOURTEEN

"You're on early," Ethan says. I'm suddenly aware of the shotgun cradled between his hands. I shift my gaze between him and it. This can't be happening to me. Not now. I wish there were emotion on his face. Hell, right about now I'd be happy with natural body language. Then I could gauge whether or not he's figured me out.

Slow down, I silently beg my heart. I have to keep calm, make sure he doesn't suspect I'm not Olivia. I need to get myself out of this situation without getting shot in the face.

"No, I'm not," I reply, my voice steady.

"But you said you weren't coming on until later."

"Things change."

Blinking, he tightens his hold on his weapon. Does Landon plan to make Ethan hurt me? A month ago that thought would never have crossed my mind, but now I'm wary. Of him and the others. All the people I believed to be my friends.

Ethan slides forward. Now I'm completely pinned between him and the closed door. I draw myself to my full height, mostly because my body seizes up from panic, and even then I'm so short and he's so tall, it barely makes any difference. I curl my fingers into my palms.

He's weak on his right side. Several months ago he was cut on a raid—a deep X-shaped wound on his back, under his shoulder.

If this goes badly, I'm prepared to use his injury to my advantage, to hit him with all my might. I won't kill him, though.

Not in a million years, no matter who he really is. I've grown too attached.

"No, things don't change—not for you, at least. You never log on spontaneously."

Has he not noticed how random Olivia's been since the last raid? She's a terrifying combination of calculating and impulsive.

"I needed to come here," I say. "To...get away from my mother."

Because that's what The Aftermath is to Olivia. An escape. She lives in a perfect world, but the only time she's happy is when she pretends to be me. When she pretends she's submerged in chaos and violence.

From what I saw the last time I visited her mind, she spends a large portion of her time away from the game teetering on the edge of insanity.

"Olivia, you never—"

"And that's another thing," I say through gnashed teeth. I try to keep my face under control, lifeless, but it's hard. "Remember our rule not to break? You're doing it right now, so stop. Stop bringing Olivia into this game."

I expect him to argue. Or call me out as being an imposter—but he drops his chin. Then, to my relief, he relaxes his grip on the shotgun. "You're right, if your dad had the mod files reviewed, we'd be..." He shudders. "Look, I'm sorry, Claudia. Do you want to go on a side quest with me?"

Another mission. Everything is about raids or quests to these people. The monotony and violence of it all makes me sick to my stomach, but I guess that's the purpose of the game. Raid and kill flesh-eaters. Save the Survivors, the good guys. Take over a building and make it our new shelter. I push Ethan backward and walk away from him. Keeping my back turned, I try to catch my breath. After it slows to normal, I look over my shoulder at him.

"I have to log off for a little while to do schoolwork," I lie. This is not how Olivia would respond—she's always game for good, bloody chaos, for any opportunity to be with him, with Landon—but leaving the bar to go on a raid right now is impossible. If she logs back in and finds me anywhere other than the armchair inside The Save, I'm most certainly finished.

"But you just said—"

"Let's play a game, Landon," I say. "You take me for my word and stop questioning me. I have no issue with kicking you out of this clan if you can't do that. Or maybe I'll just go off on my own."

"You don't mean that."

"Try me. In case you haven't noticed, there are small children with better game strategy than you."

There's a sharp pang in the middle of my chest because my words are so cutting. But he doesn't say anything else. He cares too much about Olivia to risk making a big issue out of this. Even if I have to stay in The Aftermath for another six months, or ten more years, I'll never get used to knowing that Ethan, the boy I believed to be my closest companion, isn't the least bit concerned about me.

He only cares about Olivia.

"You know I won't."

"Then stop asking me questions. I'll be back later, like I said before, and then we'll go—" I fight to hide my shudder "—on a mission."

He nods and turns his attention to the basement door. I nearly lunge forward to stop him from opening it, but I steady myself, clear my throat. Ethan looks over his shoulder at me, and I grab his hand, pulling him all the way around. I bring his lips down to mine. Our kiss is long and robotic, and I can taste the vanilla from an energy bar on his lips. But I use this moment as an opportunity to coax him into moving away from the door. I try not to let my thoughts wander to the boy on the other side of it. When Ethan draws away, he's smiling. How can his gamer enjoy something that another boy is actually experiencing?

"I'm going to check inventory before we go," he says.

My eyes dart over to the area behind the bar where our water bottles are stored, and I nod. "That's probably a good idea."

"Promise you'll be back?"

"Of course. And, Ethan? Don't forget what I said. No more breaking. It's—" I pause. "It's not good for *us* to do it."

My heart beats wildly as we kiss again and I force myself to return the gesture. I go back to The Save and resume my spot in the chair, but there's a suffocating weight holding me down. All it would take for everything to unravel into a million frayed pieces is for Ethan to bring up what just happened to Olivia.

I've a feeling she'd kill me if she were to find out.

When Olivia returns a few hours later, she's more relaxed than I've seen her in days. Almost as if she's heavily medicated. I slip into her mind for the briefest moment and discover the reason why: she's playing the old version of the game, the one where she's standing and flicking her hands every other second.

I pause for a moment before spiraling back into my own mind. I could try to take over right here. Right now. I could make her do something small—bend a finger, move her hand a fraction more in one direction. I could try to make her hit herself. But then I admonish myself. She believes all is well at the moment. If I try to control her and she realizes it, she won't let go of me until she finds answers. If I'm ever going to get out of The Aftermath alive, I'll have to be more disciplined than she is, control my impulses.

I'm back in the bar, inside my own head, just in time to accept an invitation from Ethan to go on a side quest. Wonderful. But he's not as interested in the mission to find and return a lost Survivor kid to her clan as he is in talking.

After we find our objective's location on Olivia's game map, we skulk through the alleyways, his body so close to mine our arms rub. At first we compare inventory. We discuss how many weapons we have and what we hope to find on our next few raids. But then he stops me beneath a faded blue awning. Behind him is a neon sign for a blues club, dangling from its hinges. It looks as though it's about to fall and shatter into a million pieces.

"Oli—Claudia—I can't do this much longer."

"Do what?"

"The game. And I know you hate it when I break character, but this is important. I don't want you to come back one day and see that I'm just missing without an explanation."

Olivia spins me around so abruptly that I nearly slam into a brick building. I rest my back against it so that Ethan and I are face-to-face. "What do you mean by missing?"

"My parents are making me quit."

"Don't joke with me like that."

"No...I swear. They don't want me playing The Aftermath or any of the other games."

This is the first time I've heard about other games. How many are there? Are they all like The Aftermath? Suddenly I'm so cold, I feel as if I'm standing naked beneath a deluge of freezing rain instead of a fiery, relentless sun.

"Your parents are idiots," she makes me say.

He reaches out to cup my face, but I knock his hand aside. I'm back to limited expression again, but I can only imagine Olivia's face right now. Not too pleasant.

"When?" I demand.

He shrugs. The movement is so slight I wouldn't be able to see it if I weren't standing so close to him in the alley. "Mom contacted The Aftermath's chief mod and requested that all my game footage be pulled so they can recount my points. Sympathizers or not, they still have influence."

"So by the end of next month?" I ask, pulling back from him.

"Yes. They plan to challenge the results. Then they'll practically stand over me while I do the final missions."

"There's got to be some way to slow them down. There's always… something." But she's unable to make me finish the sentence. This is exactly what her mom warned her about. I wonder if she's thinking that, too.

"What will you do with—" She pauses. Flicks my hand out until I'm touching Ethan's forearm. "Landon, what will happen after you're finished? What are your parents planning to do with this character?"

This character? It sounds as if she's speaking about an object instead of a human being. I feel the muscles in my neck tighten and my toes curl.

Ethan is not a thing; he's a person.

"They'll do everything they can, but he's got too many flaws. Too many injuries." Landon doesn't mention that Olivia just broke character. Instead, he makes Ethan pull my hands into his. "You know better than anyone how the contract with LanCorp works. If he's not picked up within a few days of my leaving the game—"

"He'll go up for deletion," I say, and he nods.

I ping back into Olivia's room. She's on the floor with her legs folded over each other. Her pale fingers are clasped together, and she's rubbing them up and down over her nose and between her eyes.

"Funny, your mom and dad swear they're character advocates, but they're willing to have yours deleted so you won't have to be around me. Make sure you tell them what wonderful people they are."

"Olivia…"

"My father can talk to them," she pleads, her childish voice broken and raspy. She twists her fingers through each other as she waits for a response, and I wait, too, staring impatiently through her eyes at the screen. Ethan smiles down at her. His face is as sad as an emotionless shell can be.

"Your father won't even let me talk to you."

"I don't want to play this game without you."

"Then don't do it. Let's get our points. Be normal. We'll…figure out another way to see each other."

She shakes her head. "No. I can't. I've already told you that. This treatment is the only thing that helps me. I *have* to stay until everything is right with me." She stands up. Moves her hands around wildly until I've grabbed Ethan's fingers in mine and we're walking again. I untangle from her head. The rush into my own is cold and dark.

"Do whatever your mom and dad tell you to do, but don't use my feelings to try and make me do the same. If they make you complete the final main missions, then you'll be doing it without me," I say. "If we can't see each other, then I guess it wasn't meant to work out."

Months ago—hell, a few weeks ago—I thought Ethan and I had something special. But now I know the slight touches, the teasing, was simply Olivia and Landon. Their star-crossed relationship played out between two gaunt teenagers inside a game.

It's sick and twisted and, in a way, romantic.

It makes me want to hurl.

But I put aside my disgust and complete the mission. We find the missing Survivor girl hiding under a table at a restaurant with no windows and half its roof missing. Ethan and I help her back to her clan's home base—a tornado shelter located under a garage floor. Then, just as I think Olivia's over trying to lose points, she makes me rob their clan.

Ethan and I score an entire backpack full of energy bars and beef sticks, as well as a few bottles of water. He holds both of our guns on them while I bag their belongings. Right in front of their faces. They're stone-faced and skinnier than we are. They remind me of the two boys fifteen miles from here with the bright blue bag.

These people will probably die soon, too.

"Good looking out for your own kind," one of the boys says. He must be referring to all of us being Survivors. Olivia has me wiggle a packet of jerky in front of the boy's face, taunting him. "Hope she chokes to death on that," he adds.

Tilting my head to the side, I grin at him. "I doubt it. She's pretty good at surviving. And he's—" I gesture over my shoulder at Ethan "—about to be deleted. Learn better game play and you won't be captured or robbed."

The boy says something else softly but I manage to make out "die" and "Virtue." Olivia doesn't seem to care that she's stealing a group's only source of food when we still have plenty of crumbly bars left from the last raid. She only cares about the twelve hundred points that disappear from beneath her name on the map when she and Landon are finished raiding the clan. And although she was upset about Landon's news just minutes ago, now it's a joke to her.

She can make light of Ethan getting deleted to make herself feel better.

But it's not a joke to me. And until I know what will happen, I'll get little rest.

Deleted.

Today is only the second time I've heard that word, but I fear it. A million images filter through my head—an eraser dragging across words, making them as if they never existed. Declan getting rid of information on his AcuTab.

And regardless of the exact details of deletion, I know it's not something good. Some part of Ethan will be taken away.

Like it never existed.

That night when everyone is situated around The Save—eyes blank and bodies immobile—I go see Declan.

"Didn't I tell you not to come here? It's too dangerous," he says. But he lets me in anyway.

His AcuTab is the only source of light in the cellar. It sits in the middle of the floor, on top of his sleeping bag, casting a metallic glow on the walls that's so eerie, I'd be less creeped out if we were in total blackness. He crouches in the shadows, head down and forearms resting between his thighs. Black curls fall over his forehead, around his face. He yawns, stretching his arms above his head. I forget my fear for a moment, forget everything that's happened the past several days, and watch him.

No, no, no.

I cannot think about him in any way that's not conducive to our mission.

He's my way out, nothing more.

I'll pretend he's not the only boy I've ever met whose eyes are alive.

"They're all…asleep."

Snorting, he shrugs his shoulders. "Can you really call it that?"

No. I guess I can't. But I refuse to say what they really are: shells. Corpses who breathe and move but can't think or act for themselves. Even if I couldn't control myself a few weeks ago and I spent all my time wondering why—at least I had my thoughts.

Most of the time.

"No," I say.

"What are you doing here? Do you know their habits well enough to predict them? For all you know, midnight is when they want to unwind with a little chaos. And I wouldn't want your boyfriend sneaking up on us again."

There's something off about his voice, but I can't put my finger on it. "You know about that?" My voice is tinny. He nods. Of course he knows. I wouldn't put it past him to have some high-tech machine in his bag of tricks that lets him hear and see everything I'm doing while he waits for me.

I shift uncomfortably at the thought.

"If it's so dangerous, why'd you answer the door before I made it down the steps? How'd you know it was me?"

His head pops up. That sardonic look is back—the one that extends from his half smile to his gray eyes. "Your smell. Like soap that's not been sold in the Provinces in years, decades," he replies. I cross my arms tightly over my chest.

"What happens when you're deleted?" I blurt out. "I need to know."

Something disturbing happens to his features, like something's wiping them clean. "One of the characters in your girl's clan getting deleted?"

He must know I hate it when he calls Olivia "my girl," but I don't mention it. "Yes, I— It's Ethan. Landon, his gamer, plans on deleting him."

I almost expect Declan to mock Ethan again. He doesn't. His eyebrows knit together and he pushes himself to his feet. He paces the length of the cellar—back and forth, forward and back—until I'm dizzy and must lean against the wall to wait for his answer.

"Well?"

"His cerebrum link—it'll be broken."

If not for the tremor in his voice, I might believe a broken link is a good thing. That maybe Ethan will be freed and get a chance to thrive away from the game. Except Declan's voice is shaking and he's pinching the spot between his eyes as if he's in pain.

"He'll die," I say.

Declan slides his fingers up and down his nose and starts pacing again. I watch him, with my heart lodged so far into my throat, I feel as if I'm suffocating. Finally, he looks at me. I never expected to see much of anything besides cynicism in his eyes, especially not pity and grief.

"Yeah," he says. "Ethan'll die."

"How?" I whisper.

"Later, Virtue. I'll explain later."

I won't accept that. Not after he just told me Ethan may not live past next month. He can't possibly expect me to let it go until later. "No," I say. "I need to know now."

He squints at me. He looks so tired that I'm not surprised when he says, "I can't tonight. I can't until you—"

"Why can't you? Because you're tired? Exhausted? What exactly do you do all day while I'm out on raids and missions, wanting to puke because I'm so hot and tired? While I'm forced to kiss a boy I don't

151

even know, simply because our gamers are in love with each other?"
I tremble. "I don't understand your world."

"Neither do I," he says.

Sliding my back down the wall, I bite my lip, then hug myself as
hard as I can. "What happened to make it like this?"

And then he tells me. He won't explain deletion, but what he does
say will haunt me for days, weeks, years. "There were two wars," he
says. "One that began in 2034, where this state and another called
Texas rebelled, and then a second war in 2041 started by three different states."

I learn that after each war, the government condemned the states
that initially started the conflicts and all the residents were evacuated. "Why do away with them completely?"

He lifts his shoulders. "Because they started the problem, I guess.
Here, let me show you something." After bringing up the menu on his
tablet, he taps the image of a book. He scans through a long list before
selecting text near the very bottom entitled "United Province History."

A holograph of a man emerges between us. "Thank you for access-
ing the AcuTab history library. Please select a topic."

"The Reconstruction Initiative," Declan says, enunciating every
syllable.

"Launched in 2052 following the end of the United States' third
civil war, the Reconstruction Initiative was a project spearheaded by
President Callaway to eliminate the feeling of dissent throughout
the nation. Over the next two years, the forty-five remaining states
were zoned into seven provinces and renamed the United Provinces.
Officials were elected to each province, and, according to U.P. law,
would serve no more than a single two-year term to prevent political
corruption and give citizens a choice. These first officials were given

the harrowing task of rebuilding the areas of the nation that were affected by the wars.

"First on the agenda was employing U.P. civilians and establishing a twenty-hour workweek that left ample time for rest, recreation and family. Under new mandates, voted on by U.P. civilians, laws were put in place to manage the ever-growing population with the child cap—a maximum number of children based on income and projected job availability. Space-efficient housing was also introduced, along with new methods of travel."

Digging my nails into my palms, I lean in closer to the projection.

"With the political system and social programs in place, the United Provinces embraced an era of prosperity and peace, but our young nation also faced its biggest hurdle of all—preventing another war."

The man disappears and it takes me a moment to realize Declan's tightly gripping his AcuTab.

"So where do the games come in?" I demand.

"The Reconstruction Initiative hired a team of scientists to research ways to avoid violence. The theory was—is—that if you do away with violence, you don't have crime or war."

"But you can't do away with violence," I say.

"Exactly. But this one scientist, Natalie Lancaster, claimed giving people a violent channel was the cure. It took over twenty-five years to perfect the treatment and it was—" Scraping a hand through his messy hair, he points his gaze behind me, at the room's exit. "It was Lancaster's son who did it, but the games seem to work. Real crime is unheard of in the Provinces."

"So violent people play the game and earn points that count toward their treatment." I've already basically figured this out just from spying on Olivia, but it doesn't make the brick in my stomach feel any lighter.

Nodding, Declan drags in a wobbly breath and then says, "They test for the violence gene. They say it's a disease. They treat the affected to save the world. If you've been diagnosed, you can't get a job unless you have documentation that you're in an approved treatment program. And treatment— Well, it's expensive. If you're well-off enough to afford the therapy—"

"You buy a character," I finish for him. "But if you don't have the money? What then?"

"Then you're the character the wealthy people buy. Homeless people, orphans—they're the ones who go into the games. If you can't find work because of the gene, then there's no other choice but to sign a contract with LanCorp. You agree to let someone play you, to go into Rehabilitation, until you beat the illness."

I shake my head because what he's saying doesn't make a bit of sense to me. "But I don't understand. If the Provinces are so prosperous, then why the hell would there be destitute people to begin with?"

Unable—or maybe even unwilling—to answer me, Declan glances down at his boots. I don't even have the strength to ask him what Rehabilitation is, not tonight. "Guess there'll always be people who get the short end of the stick," he finally says.

"You know a lot about this."

He sneers. "History is an important part of anyone's job."

Then I remember what Landon made Ethan say about the other games. "How many are there? How many games?"

"Four. LanCorp bought the condemned states and turned them into the gaming locations. The game that someone's assigned to depends on which mutation of the violence gene they have. Your gamer has— I can almost guarantee your gamer has Violence Gene B."

"What does that mean?"

"That she's a premeditated psycho. Because The Aftermath? It's the worst game of them all."

CHAPTER FIFTEEN

Two days later, I drop in on Olivia while she's at school. Though I've heard plenty about it, this is the first time I've seen the academy, and I'm stunned by it. There are dozens of school campuses in the game and even colleges, but they all look the same. Red brick and hundreds of grimy four-paned windows and classroom doors falling off the hinges.

Olivia's academy is high-tech and sleek. The only thing I see when looking up at the several stories of see-through walls is sunlight and clear skies. Olivia steps onto what looks like an escalator without actual steps, talking softly to a short, overweight boy in a dark school uniform that's too tight around his middle. While he looks up at her like she hung the moon, I drink in the surroundings.

A girl is quietly arguing with another girl a couple of feet away about leaving class to go to something called an airbus exhibition.

"Well, I'm going—" the first girl begins, but the rest of her sentence is cut off when the machine stops on the sixth floor and my gamer steps off. Olivia and the boy walk to a stainless-steel podium in the center of a courtyard and stand in line behind other students. When it's Olivia's turn, she stops directly in front of the podium and a red light encircles her, scanning her body before fading. A screen appears with a message "Thank You for Signing Into Fourth District Academy, Olivia" and the date "Monday, August 19, 2099."

A biometric scan. Just like Declan had mentioned.

Did I ever go to an academy like this? A school with moving ramps instead of stairs and a biometric scan roll call?

Even if I did, will I ever remember any of it? The fear I've tried hardest to push away finally surfaces—that I may spend the rest of my life with no memories of my childhood, no memories at all apart from what I've seen in The Aftermath. Memories that halfway belong to another girl.

"I'm going to cut out early today and go to the Calwas Province," she tells the boy after he finishes signing in to school. Her voice is calm, happy, nothing like the last times I checked on her where she was either raging about the game or wishing death on Landon's parents.

They duck into an open, rounded classroom. Inside, compact white desks are arranged in circular rows around a stage in the center of the room. There's a shimmer of glass on the stage, and I'm certain it's there for a hologram.

The boy waits until they're seated in two chairs farthest from the platform to ask, "What are you going to Calwas for?"

"I'm going to meet my father. He's sending an exclusive aircraft for me. And nobody else from the academy is invited," she brags. "So don't expect me to come back to the game until tomorrow morning at the earliest."

No wonder April's gamer despises her. But if she's offended the boy, he doesn't say anything. He places his hands flat on something in front of his seat. It takes me a few seconds to see that it's a transparent desktop. Olivia waits for him to respond for another moment, and then she pulls her AcuTab from her bag. When she places it down, the desk illuminates and a bunch of words and pictures appear.

"What did you do yours on?" the boy asks.

"Population control—you?"

When he doesn't answer her, she leans over and looks down at his desk. Most of the type is too small for me to make it out, but the heading is clear.

Visionaries of the Twenty-First Century: Natalie Lancaster
    HIS 117: U.P. Society and Culture (2034 to Present)

Natalie Lancaster. The scientist Declan told me about who came up with the theory that started the games in the first place. The mother of the games' creator.

Olivia stares up and looks at the boy for a long time. "There'll be at least five more papers like this, you know?" When the professor appears via hologram in the middle of the stage, she drops her voice to a whisper and says, "Your parents mad about you skipping out on your grandma's birthday?"

This is when I leave her. My eyes catch Jeremy's dark, blank ones across the room, and I'm aware that I was with both of our gamers just moments before. I'm aware of something else, too. Olivia's plans for the rest of the day will give Declan and me our first chance to search the city for his assignment.

I'm almost ecstatic, walking on air, when I go and retrieve him. When we step out of the bar and into the heat, though, my excitement starts to fade. It's at least 115 degrees. So muggy I can see condensation on a bit of unpainted glass when I turn around to make sure the doors are locked.

"You sure you're safe?" Declan says once I turn to face him. I roll my eyes—this is the third or fourth time he's asked the same question. He motions for me to turn around, and I comply. He adjusts the straps of my bag so the weight doesn't strain my shoulders. His fingertips brush my rib cage as he draws his hands back.

I suck in a quick breath and say, "We're fine for the next several hours."

Declan comes around to walk beside me and presses something crinkly into my hand. A CDS package. "Eat, Virtue. You look like you've lost five pounds since we met."

"But—"

"There's enough in my bag to last three months. Besides, I don't want you fainting on me. I'd hate to carry you back here."

I jerk the packet from his outstretched palm hastily. He laughs, then follows me to the side of the building, where I sit on the steps beneath the side door. I shake the pack a few times by knocking it against the inside of my wrist, like he showed me before, then open it. I rip the smiling boy on the front into two pieces.

"What's the plan?" I ask between bites.

"His last known location was a shopping mall on—" Declan takes out his AcuTab. I click my fingernails against the concrete. I'm starting to wonder if he can function without that tablet. Once he finds what he's looking for, he gives me the name of the shopping center and a pleading look. "Please tell me you have any idea how—"

"It shouldn't take too long."

"What?"

I crumple up the empty wrapper and stuff it between a couple of loose bricks behind me. "We better get going. It's a few hours from here, two if we're fast."

"You don't even have to think about it?" he asks as I walk to the corner of the alley.

I smile a little. "Nope," I say. How can I possibly tell him that I've been to that area of town so many times I've lost count? Some of our earliest missions had taken place across from the mall, inside the concert hall overgrown with foliage. When Olivia had accessed her completed missions a day ago, I'd found that particular one. It had been a main mission—the only one we've finished out of the three required to complete the last levels of the game.

I wish I could tell Declan all of this, share just a few of my memories, but I can't. Doing so will reveal my lie—that I've been somewhat sentient far longer than two weeks. That my glitch is far more complex than he ever imagined.

"You coming?" I ask.

He blows his dark hair out of his eyes and nods.

At first, we travel quietly. Unlike the last time we did this, we're not irritated with one another; this time, we go back and forth, making small talk. I'm just about to ask him about the deletion process again when his AcuTab beeps and we take a quick water break outside a crumbling vinyl-sided building. When I finally do broach the subject, his face clouds over and he refuses to talk about it. The same thing happened a couple of nights ago. He dropped a bomb on me when he said Ethan would die, and then he refused to explain. And thirty seconds after he told me about the history of the Provinces, he asked me to leave.

No, that's not right—he told me to get the hell out before he physically carried me back to The Save.

"Then tell me why LanCorp sent you into the game to retrieve a character," I say. Because I'm having a hard time understanding why a company with such intricate technology can't fix a glitch from outside the game. Unless, of course, Declan is lying and the character we're looking for is just like me. Sentient. When I ask if we're searching for a self-aware character, though, he shoots me a harsh look and shakes his head curtly.

"I told you already—you're the only one I've ever met who's like that."

"Then what's the matter with this character?"

He cocks his head to one side. At first, I don't think he'll answer because he walks away, leaving me behind. But then he sighs, glances at me over one of his shoulders and says, "My assignment was given to someone new, but he was still picking up signals from his previous player. When LanCorp shut him down manually, they didn't realize his old player had changed his location. Nobody was able to get in touch with this guy, but my boss pulled enough game footage to determine he's in a flesh-eater save point...but we aren't sure which one. My job is to find him and take him back to the Provinces so that his chip can be synced to his new player. Happy now?"

Absolutely not. Because now I'm very afraid for this character who has had not one, but two players controlling his mind, making dangerous moves that could result in his death. "And there's not a faster way of tracking him down?" I ask, catching up to Declan. The left side of my body brushes against his. His gray eyes dart over me—his expression is frightening. I veer to the right to put some distance between us.

"LanCorp promises an authentic gaming experience. Sending a huge team in to retrieve a single character would irritate gamers," he says. "Now can you drop this? Your questions give me a headache, and I'm about twenty seconds away from electrocuting you."

"Don't be an ass," I say. Even though I don't like the idea of ending our conversation, I change the subject. "Tell me about Rehabilitation."

He parts his lips to say something. Then he pauses. "There's not much to tell." When I frown, he shakes his head and releases a low whistle. "But since you're asking—why don't you explain it to me. You're the one who was there up until two weeks ago."

And now I want to kick myself. I've put myself in a corner where I can either tell the truth—at least partially—or remain ill-informed. He must notice I'm conflicted, because he slides closer to me and gently touches his fingers to my left shoulder. I try to keep walking, but he stops me. He grasps my other shoulder and stares into my eyes.

"According to LanCorp, it's the simulation characters' brains go to while they're being played. Where they're rehabilitated—taught how to be nonviolent members of society. But that's just what LanCorp tells the press." Declan snorts. "There's no real simulation. Just the character being trapped inside of his own mind—nightmares, nothingness, insecurities—while he's completely unaware of what's being done to his body."

"That's awful," I hiss.

Declan doesn't confirm or deny this. "Do you remember any of it, Virtue?"

No, I don't. I remember the real nightmares. Pursing my lips together, I say, "No, but I'm sure it's the glitch."

I'm starting to hate saying that word.

"Just so you know, your memory is a disaster."

Frustrated, I shrug myself out of his hands and stalk past him. "Yeah, I know."

The theater and mall are still standing. Both look the exact same as they did three months ago when Ethan and I came to this part of town to steal weapons from a clan living in a restaurant a few blocks away. One of the women had been pregnant, and I remember feeling so remorseful for taking their only method of defending themselves. It was the same feeling I'd had a couple of days ago when Ethan and

I had raided the Survivors after completing the quest to help them—like I was scum.

Now, thinking back to that pregnant woman, I have a better understanding of what I saw and it makes me feel queasy and light-headed. The gamers controlling our bodies can make us do whatever they please, most of the time without our knowing it. They can make us mate with one another, or shoot ourselves in the head, and the only thing they face for breaking the rules is losing points or having to restart the game with a brand-new character that they can ruin all over again.

Part of me wishes I had the luxury of not knowing what's going on—but then I shake that thought from my mind. Desiring ignorance—no matter how blissful it might be—is silly and weak.

I nearly pass out when Declan covers my mouth with his hand and drags me with him behind a crushed sign. There's glass everywhere, but he's careful to avoid it. I tilt my head back until our eyes meet and silently question him. His rough fingertips slide from my lips and down the side of my face.

Touching the back of my neck, he guides my head to the right. My eyes bug. At the entrance of the shopping mall is a small group of characters ranging in age from early teens to late twenties. And they're flesh-eaters. I can tell by their blood-caked clothing and the way they're acting—feral, shoving each other around and teasing. I'm so used to Olivia steering me everywhere that I've forgotten how to get around undetected.

"Pay attention, Virtue. Keep your mind off your boyfriend before you get yourself killed," he growls in my ear. "And don't think I'll save you if it comes down to between the two of us."

My nostrils flare. He's punishing me for what I told him about Ethan two nights ago, and it twists my stomach into knots. I won't let him know that his words bother me. If I do, he'll never let it go. "Nice to know you plan to just let me die," I say angrily.

"Only if it comes between me and my assignment," he says, laughing; although part of me is sure he means it. Warm breath fans the back of my neck and shoulder blades, ruffling thin strands of my hair. I hope he doesn't notice the sharp jerk of my body or feel my heartbeat pick up. He's so close, though. And when I look back at him, he's wearing that cocky partial smile again.

Stupid, stupid girl. Use him and get the hell away.

"And you're sure this is his last known location?" I say, turning my eyes back to the mall entrance.

He chuckles. The sound vibrates in my ear. "It's not."

"You're such a liar."

"But it made you feel better, didn't it?"

For about half a second.

I ease from his arms and twist around to face him. We spend a few minutes kneeling down like this, almost touching but not quite, running through our plans. I suggest finding out if there's a way into the mall through the sewage system. It might take some time, but at least it would reduce our chances of getting caught by flesh-eaters and tortured to death.

"That's stupid," he says. "And disgusting."

My face burns. "Okay, you're the moderator. Tell me how we're going to get in."

"I'm going to jam their signal," he says at last.

"What?"

He draws a black box from his pocket. It's as big as my hand and square. Three shiny tubes extend from one end of it, and the tube in the middle has a green blinking light.

Blink, blink. Pause. Blink, blink, blink. Pause. The box looks as if it will explode at any moment. I cover my head.

"Signal jammer, meet Virtue. Virtue, meet my way in. Press the button on the side—" he wiggles the device in front of my face so I can see the small black knob; I push his hand away "—and everyone with an active chip stays down for about forty-five minutes. Completely idle while I look around."

I lift an eyebrow. I don't like the look on his face. He won't meet my eyes. And then I get it. He didn't say we'd look around—he said the signal jammer is his way in, meaning he plans on searching by himself. Because I'll be idle just like everyone else.

"No," I say.

This plan is stupid. Utterly flawed. I'd rather wade around in garbage and filth and whatever else we may find in the sewers any day rather than allow him to leave me helpless for nearly an hour.

"It's the only way, and I promise nothing will happen to you."

"You're lying. Besides, won't their players know something's wrong when they suddenly go off-line? Aren't you setting us up for failure?"

"That's the glory of the jammer." He grins, rubbing his fingers over the metal cylinders. They spring back and forth rapidly. "It takes them all down—every character in the vicinity—so it looks like a problem within the game. And just so you know, flesh-eaters aren't played by gamers. They're operated by LanCorp employees. Come on, Virtue, what kind of treatment would eating people be?"

This is new, but it makes sense. It explains what Olivia said to the flesh-eater she killed in the parking garage. "Good luck with your next job, Reese. Try to last a little longer than a couple months," she'd teased.

My stomach turns. So this is the type of job that keeps 99 percent of the Provinces' inhabitants employed? Playing an unaware human inside a game that's made him into a cannibal? No wonder Declan's assignment has a new player—his former player probably quit his job. And maybe once he realized he was still able to control his character, he'd decided to play a cruel game with LanCorp. Hide-and-seek with a helpless boy who has no idea what's really going on.

I press my lips together. "You're not disabling me."

"It's a good plan. I've got it figured out," Declan says.

Of course he's got it all figured out. Everything down to abandoning me after I help him. I feel the blood rush to my neck and face and ears. If he knew that his assignment was here the entire time, why did he blackmail me into coming with him and letting him stay in my shelter?

"Do you trust me?" he asks, rising to his feet. His knuckles are white from clutching the jammer.

He's asked me this before, but my head is so foggy right now, I can't remember when. He's going to deactivate me. Then he plans to leave me in a pit of flesh-eaters, and I don't know if he'll come back for me. I'll wake up to a flesh-eater mauling the side of my face, just like my first day in The Aftermath—except this time, I'll already have three years of horrible memories, and nobody will be there to save me. I shake my head.

"What do you think?" I snarl.

"You should. I made a promise. Now sit tight."

I tackle him as he presses the button. I pound on his chest hard with both hands, and there's a mixture of discomfort and astonishment on his face that's instantly gratifying. Then I pause. Over his shoulder, the flesh-eaters begin to drop one by one where they stand, like dominoes falling down. He looks behind us, then back at me, eyes wide. "You're kidding me?" He waves his hand in front of my face.

"Stop that."

I expect him to make a disparaging comment or tease me. Instead, he rubs the tips of his fingers over the spot where my chip is implanted. Tilts my head from side to side. Touches the middle of my forehead so hard I wince. Pulling his gaze away from mine, he mutters, "Come on before they wake up."

CHAPTER SIXTEEN

For just over half an hour, we search the mall frantically. We race from store to store. When we find someone, I stand a couple of steps behind him, helpless, while Declan studies his face under the sunlight shimmering through the open roof. "It's not him," he says so many times I lose count and optimism and part of my mind. And even though we don't find who he's been sent into the game to look for, I discover something in one of the last stores that stops my heart: Survivors. Seven of them in all, chained to the walls in various stages of despair. Hooking my fingers into the sharp steel of the security gate separating me from them, I stare at the youngest one—a skinny girl no bigger than myself—for a long time.

"I'm letting them go," I say. As I bend down to open the gate, Declan's hand closes around my arm. He gives it a squeeze, shaking his head, but I pull out of his grip. "Don't screw with me."

I pull on the security door with all my might. It creeps up a couple of feet; then I roll beneath it.

Declan doesn't help as I pick the locks with my knife. He sits outside the gate on top of a headless mannequin that's dressed in lingerie. Every few moments he clears his throat and rubs his fingers back and forth over his nose. The noise grates on my nerves.

"Stop it," I say.

"What do you think you're accomplishing by letting them loose?" he demands.

I've no intention of answering him—he doesn't deserve it. He was going to disable me. And he didn't care that I was afraid or against it. He didn't even ask me how I felt about his plans beforehand. I jab the knife into another lock. It skims the edge of the flimsy metal, slicing across the palm of my other hand. I ignore the pain.

"All you'll manage to do is hurt yourself."

I'll pretend I don't hear him. I'll pretend as if the area between my shoulders doesn't hurt, pretend I don't want to turn the weapon on him, send it flying into his chest just as Olivia did to the redheaded boy a few days ago.

But I glance behind me, take him in, before I tackle the final two bolts.

It's much too difficult to ignore him.

"And now what?" he asks when the last lock clicks open. "We have five minutes left until the flesh-eaters are all over us. Are you going to drag each of them to safety?"

Pressing my lips together in a tight line, I stand and slip the knife back into its sheath. "At least they can run now. Their gamers can try to get them out of here. They can—"

"Do you think their gamers are going to magically log in the moment we leave here?"

When I turn my back to him, keeping silent, he continues, "They're not. So it doesn't matter if they're released. These characters will just lie here, bodies wasting away, until their gamers come back to let them get tortured a little more or wait for some point-happy Survivor to come along and save them. Now, we have four minutes. You can stay here, but I'd rather you be with me. We still have a lot of work to do."

"You were going to use the signal jammer on me," I say, my voice breaking.

He sighs. I hear the gate jangle—he must be pulling on it or banging his head against the metal in frustration. "No, I was going to use it on them. You were a temporary casualty, and I promised I would come back for you. I wasn't going to leave you. I never break my word."

A temporary casualty. I should be irritated that he's calling me that, but for some reason, I'm not. I'm sure I've been called much worse. "I don't want to leave them." I look around me, at the seven lifeless characters—no, humans—surrounded by chains and their own blood. "They'll die."

"No, eventually someone will accept this mission and free them. But you'll die if you stay. Two minutes, Virtue."

I'd forgotten that the slightest change in this game results in new side quests. That someone's captivity eventually means more points for another gamer. But even knowing that some clan could sweep through here to play saints as soon as Declan and I leave doesn't take away the burning around my eyes. I blink away the tears. For thirty seconds, I count quietly in my head. I punch the wall, grit my teeth together. Then I roll under the gate, keeping my eyes off the people on the other side. I don't care that my knuckles burn or that I bite the tip of my tongue so hard it bleeds. "Do the gamers know that we're real people?" I know that Olivia does, but what about everyone else playing LanCorp's games?

"Yes."

"Why do they do this?" My voice sounds different, like something that's been beaten halfway to death. Declan can explain the Provinces' violence solution to me a million times—tell me how the games are a way to fix both the gamers' and the characters' disease—but I'm not sure I'll truly understand it.

"If you're diagnosed with the gene, treatment is mandatory. It's against the law to refuse it. But LanCorp always gives everyone with the gene a choice—pay the money to play the game or go into Rehabilitation, become a character," he says, sounding as if he's quoting that directly from a prompt he studied in moderator training. He pulls me away from the gate and guides me toward the mall's main entrance. Our eyes meet. The shame in his startles me.

"But if you had the financial resources, would you really want someone else controlling you when you could be the one in power?" Declan asks.

It takes us a while to get home, an extra hour to be exact. After what happened in the mall, I feel powerless. That hopelessness screams through me, making me little more than dead weight.

To my surprise, Declan doesn't complain. He walks next to me, although there's at least two feet between us. He avoids my eyes, his mouth twisted into a grimace. I want to know what he's thinking, but maybe asking outright is not a good idea. So I keep quiet.

When we reach the bar, he steps in front of me, blocking my way in. I sigh—a drawn-out noise that's so full of defeat it physically hurts. I'm exhausted. I don't want to deal with Declan's games. I open my mouth to tell him this, but he cuts me off, covering my lips with his index finger.

"I'm sorry, Virtue," he says. "For making you think I'd go traitor on you."

We're standing out in the open, where any player can see us, and he chooses to apologize? Crazy, strange, gorgeous Declan. I feel a little surge of joy in my chest, though. "No harm done," I say. My words are muffled because his finger is still over my mouth.

He smiles and moves a little closer to me. I notice how flushed his cheeks are, how strands of black hair cling to the sweat on his fore-head. How heavily he's breathing. "Do you still want to know about deletion?"

"Yes."

He drops his hands to his side. "It's not pretty."

"Nothing about LanCorp is," I point out. "You've already said he'll die. I can't imagine death being anything but ugly. And I've seen so many people die it's pathetic. I can handle whatever you tell me."

"Virtue..."

"Don't Virtue me. Don't lie to me, either. You never break your promises, remember?"

His smile wavers, then fades completely into a frown. He's usually so calm under pressure, and everything about today has caught me off guard. He places his hands on either side of my shoulders, bends until we're eye level.

"Why do you need to know this?"

"I'm not immune like you are, Declan. Every moment I'm with you and not out of this game I'm at risk of my gamer finding out what I can do. Don't tell me you don't think she'll have me deleted in a heartbeat?"

But in the back of my mind, I'm curious. Maybe I am invulnerable to deletion. If Olivia tries to do away with me by severing my connection, would the result be the same as Declan's signal jammer? Back at the mall he was so sure I'd go idle with the rest of the characters, but it didn't happen. What other LanCorp technology do my head and the chip inside it challenge?

"I'll protect you from her," he says, interrupting my thoughts. "She's not going to hurt you."

"Please tell me the truth."

He entwines his fingers with mine. Static rushes through my arm, and I suppress a gasp. He doesn't seem to notice as he leads me away from the building. The sun is setting. Over the dry vegetation springing up out of the sidewalk and street and the broken buildings, it's lovely. Heartbreakingly beautiful.

I shiver and he looks down at me. "I am being honest, Virtue. Nobody will hurt you when you're with me."

For some reason, this time, I believe him.

Flesh-eaters don't frequent this area. I've paid close attention to Olivia's map, and the only names nearby are highlighted in green. Still, I fumble around to make sure my gun and knife are easily accessible.

We don't go far—to a child's playground a few blocks from the shelter. It's a pointless landmark in this game. Only an idiot would use it for shelter and the few younger children in The Aftermath who aren't quickly killed by flesh-eaters are too busy running for their lives to find any enjoyment in it.

Yet, here I am, next to Declan, on corroded swings that creak as they sway back and forth.

"Reminds me of being a kid," he says, squinting up at the sky.

"Deletion," I prompt him.

He looks down at a patch of dirt and rakes his boot through it. The corners of his mouth lift just as his shoulders sag. "They'll take him to a deletion facility."

"A deletion facility. Like a special place just to kill characters?" I ask. He nods, and I almost shout, "Why not just shoot them or electrocute them to death?"

"Who knows? That's just the way LanCorp does it."

"And once the character reaches the deletion facility?"

"They're operated on by a physician."

I listen to the squeaking of the swing and close my eyes. Deletion is done by a doctor. In an actual facility using a method that requires

physical contact. I suddenly see myself, lying inside a coffin, unconscious, with my face swollen and dozens of clear tubes running into
my body. I swallow hard.

"And they do something to their head, huh?"

He nods. "Total deactivation. They break the link between character and gamer or player. Fry the Cerebrum Chip." He reaches over and
taps the top of my head. I duck, push his hand away. "The character
is brain-dead in thirty seconds, a minute max. LanCorp doesn't want
their technology duplicated, but deletion doesn't happen that often.
Usually characters are picked up by contractors after their gamer's
done with treatment or decides to buy another character. Then they're
put back into the games as villains with hired workers playing them.
Like the flesh-eaters. In order to be deleted, you have to be so damaged, the effort and cost to fix you isn't worth it."

The image of me in the machine evaporates from my mind. It's
replaced by another memory—the woman who reminded me of Mia
in the courthouse grabbing at her head and screaming for me to get
something out of her. I tighten my grip on the gritty metal links.
"But what if a character finishes LanCorp's sham of a Rehabilitation? What then?"

When he shoots me a look out of the corner of his eye, I immediately know that no character has ever gotten through Rehabilitation
and it's very likely that no character ever will. I breathe in deeply to
calm myself. "And you're okay working for someone who does this to
other humans? Who offers people jobs to play flesh-eaters?" I demand.

"Virtue—"

But he doesn't finish. We just sit there, swaying, people watching. Character watching. Only a few pass by, and none of them pay
us any attention. Someday, any of these people might regain control
of themselves only minutes before their brain explodes.

"Do you think they feel what's happening when they're being deleted? The characters, I mean?" I ask.

He exhales sharply. "Yes, sometimes."

"Then...can it be stopped?" When he raises one of his eyebrows, I continue, "Can the games be destroyed and deletion be stopped? If there's the technology to jam several chip signals, isn't there something that could—I don't know—free a mass of characters at once?"

And then what? Return their minds to the right place just to make them fight to survive?

Declan looks down at the ground. "It's possible." Then he snorts. "One of LanCorp's rivals is probably already on it."

"I hope they are." And I hope it's in time to save Ethan. I don't realize I say his name aloud until Declan clears his throat. I glance over in time to see him roll his eyes. "What?"

"Why do you care what happens to him?"

"Because he's a boy who might die because some asshole has the right to just discard him." Because there's an enormous part of me that's emotionally attached to Ethan's voice and his kind face.

And to Landon's personality.

Declan stops swinging and shakes his head to each side. "He could be completely unlikable, you know. The real Ethan could be a killer or neurotic. He could kick puppies."

"I could be any of those things, too," I point out.

He inches closer. The swing makes a grating noise that causes me to shudder. "You're none of those things."

"I've killed," I say. "Many times."

"You killed because somebody else made you do it. You're not her, Virtue." But even he doesn't sound entirely convinced.

"It still feels like me, especially when it's my finger pulling the trigger." I release a choked noise from the back of my throat. "I can try all I want to pretend like it's not, but it doesn't change anything."

He tilts his head to the side and stares at me for a few seconds. I feel like I'm a bug under a magnifying glass, and I bite my lip and look away.

"What?" I ask.

"You're going to tear yourself to pieces with all that guilt, Virtue. Do me a favor and just relax for a minute. Here, close your eyes."

"Why do I—"

"Just do it. Close them and go someplace else. Anywhere but The Aftermath."

I grumble, but then I do it. I squeeze my eyes shut. And the moment that I do, a memory hits me.

I'm standing on a ledge, between two windows, with my back pressed against a limestone building. This isn't anywhere I've ever been inside The Aftermath, but it's familiar. I can taste the fear. Feel my damp palms slide against the glass on either side of me. Hear my heart pounding in my ears. There is nothing but havoc all around me—the other buildings are up in flames, and people are fighting in the streets ten stories below me.

I slide open one of the windows and climb in carefully. Just when I think I'm safe, I grab a gun propped against the wall. It's a sniper rifle, though I'm unsure how I know that. Leaning against the window, I lift the gun and look through the telescopic sight. Then I fire all ten rounds perfectly at people on the street.

Reload.

Repeat.

Reload.

Chest shot, head shot, chest.

When I finish, I close the window. The breeze ruffles my hair—

it's twice as long as I ever remember it being, and dark brown. I push it back from my face. Tuck it behind my right ear. I realize there's not a chunk of it missing. But when I open my mouth to mention this, I'm unable to speak. And when I try to touch my skin again, my hand won't move.

"See, I told you I could handle it," Olivia had made me say. "I'm the only one who can play her."

When my eyes fly open, I discover Declan leaning over me. He grips the seat of my swing, holding it still, his hands brushing my legs. "You look terrified—I thought I told you not to think of the game."

But I didn't, I want to say. I thought of a different game where I was a different type of gamer. And worst of all, I'm not sure where the memory came from or if I'm simply imagining even more violence.

And the craziest thing of all is that I hope that's it—that it's my imagination, that I'm going off the deep end; that there isn't more blood on my hands.

CHAPTER SEVENTEEN

We barely make it to the bar in time. Declan questions me the entire way home about what I saw when I closed my eyes, but I run too fast to reply. I go as fast as my legs will carry me, as fast as I can without my heart exploding. I run away from the images of burning buildings and bodies hitting the ground. And I don't care that he's left without answers. It'll give him something to think about while I'm away. Approximately ten minutes after I position myself the way Olivia left me, in the chair by the door, she logs in. She's early—hadn't she told Jeremy's gamer she wouldn't return until tomorrow morning? Next time I leave, I'll check in with her more often, I promise myself. Next time, I won't let my emotions or Declan cloud my judgment.

And next time he tells me to think of something other than The Aftermath, I won't listen, because every time I close my eyes now, I see people falling from the bullets I shoot at them.

During the following day and a half, I don't regain control of myself for longer than an hour or two. But then Olivia has me corner Ethan while he's checking his inventory behind the bar. "I'm going back to Calwas until tomorrow afternoon," I tell him. "You'll stay away with me, right?"

As I wait for him to answer, my breath hitches. Besides Olivia,

Ethan's my only real obstacle when it comes to navigating The Aftermath on my own. He's the sole member of my clan who keeps track of Olivia's schedule, the only one who will ask questions if I up and disappear. If they're both gone, there's so much I can accomplish. She forces me to rest my forearms on the counter. I cross my fingers for luck, but then I realize what I'm doing—controlling my body while Olivia's playing me. I pray she doesn't notice.

"Yes," Ethan agrees. I wish he'd question why she's going there—I'm curious—but at least she's releasing me for twenty-four hours. Once she's gone, I'll use the glitch to my advantage; go inside her mind to figure out what's so important she'll abandon the game for a day. Ethan counts the last of his jerky and water. Then we return to The Save, hands clasped and smiling at each other.

"See you tomorrow," I say. "Four o clock."

"I'll be here."

"And, Ethan," she makes me say. "I—I'll miss you."

Then I feel the hold on my head disappear. I sink in and out of her head for the next hour and a half, waiting for something to indicate she has no plan to come back to The Aftermath. At last, I drop in on her and her mother; they're boarding a small silver jet. It's parked on the roof of one of the skyscrapers. As Olivia sits down and takes out her tablet, the pilot's voice booms over a loudspeaker.

"Thank you for traveling Province Air today. Please fasten your safety belts and review the travel data sent to your AcuTabs. Today's trip to Calwas—1,749 miles—will be concluded in approximately three hours and nineteen minutes."

Nearly two thousand miles in just over three hours. The thought of going just about anywhere I could imagine in the time it takes me to walk five or six miles leaves me breathless with envy.

Olivia turns away from her mother. As the aircraft takes off, she closes her eyes, cutting off my view of her world.

Not that it matters to me right now.

The rest of this day and a portion of tomorrow belong to me.

Jeremy and April are on a side quest helping another clan defend their base from flesh-eaters. Since they left an hour ago, I have to rush if I'm to make it out of the building before they return. I gather my things from the corner. Glock. Ammunition. Knife. Backpack. Although they're just as threadbare, I change into a different T-shirt and another pair of torn jeans after I wash off in the bathroom. I don't have many clothes, and often Olivia makes me wear the same ones for days at a time, but at least these are clean. I stuff the dirty garments in my bag—I'll wash them the best I can when Declan and I come home—then I leave The Save.

The back of my hand brushes Ethan's shoulder as I drift past him.

Declan is already waiting for me. He sits at a table in the bar, sipping water from his canteen. When he sees me, he grins. So much time alone in the cellar is probably making him half-senile because he looks pleased. "Looks like you're all mine until tomorrow."

He sounds much too excited for my liking, and I glare over my shoulder at him as I drop a few bottles of water into my bag. "Guess you were listening in." I don't bother pointing out how he's breaking his own rule by being so blatantly out in the open. What if one of the other members of my clan returns early? Or all of them at once—then what will we do?

Then again, what does it matter if they do barge in on us? He has an electroshock gun that will prevent them from moving more than two steps in his direction.

I shiver, dropping a plastic bottle to the floor. It rolls across the hardwood, but Declan stops it with the toe of his shoe. I bend over to pick it up, pausing for several seconds when our eyes lock.

"I hear just about everything that goes on in here," he says, breaking the silence.

Way to make me uncomfortable.

"Before we go anywhere, we've got to move him," he says, pointing up toward The Save. He gestures downstairs. "To the cellar."

"But why—"

He waggles his eyebrows suggestively. "The other gamers won't ask any questions if you two disappear together."

Olivia and Landon. Sleeping together. And using us, their characters, to do it. My mouth quivers, and I feel as if there's acid in my stomach. Declan tucks his finger under my chin. "Come on, Virtue."

Ethan's body is heavier than I imagined. I carry the trunk end of him. Every five or six steps, I stumble, bumping his arms into the wall or against the handrail.

"Try not to kill him, Virtue," Declan teases.

I glare down at him as he wiggles the doorknob to his hideout. "Then next time do this by yourself."

We lay Ethan on the floor, on top of a sleeping bag. Before we leave, Declan reactivates the save point. He holds his AcuTab high in the air, punching the hologram passcode deliberately, like he's mocking me. I grind my teeth back and forth. Link my thumbs together behind my back so I won't smash his device to the floor. "You'll cry the whole time if you're not sure he's safe." I can't help but notice the growl in his voice.

"I rarely cry," I say, but he rolls his eyes.

"You've been self-aware for less than a month. You rarely do anything."

I bite my tongue until I taste blood—it's the only thing keeping me from telling him off. Or hitting him. After a minute, I close my eyes and give him a strained smile. "Where to?"

When he asks me to take him to all the places where I've encountered flesh-eaters since becoming sentient, I don't flinch. I'll personally escort him to each and every flesh-eater within a twenty-mile radius if it gets me out of this game any faster. I lead him to the closest location first—the courthouse where I met him. The electricity is no longer working. The building is shrouded in darkness and sticky heat. I carry the Glock. Declan doesn't seem to be worried about what's lurking behind the doors or wooden stands, since he only totes his AcuTab, using it as a guiding light.

"What exactly is the point of this?" I ask as we creep past the elevator on the third floor. A fly lands on the back of my neck. I swat at it, and a vivid picture shoves itself into my head. It's as if the double doors swing open and the object in Declan's hands flies at me all over again. The center of my skull throbs just imagining it.

He shrugs. "Maybe we'll find some type of clue. Something he left behind."

Wouldn't he have noticed that here before since he's been here more than once?

"How do you know he's not dead? Hell, he could've been the boy I killed last week," I say. I can't mistake the way Declan's shoulders instantly tense up. "His name was Reese. Is that your assignment's name?"

"No."

"Then what is it?"

Declan shakes his head, his disheveled curls falling around his dark eyes. "Does it matter? He's not dead, okay?"

"I don't understand why you're being so secretive about who we're looking for. In case you haven't noticed, I'm as much a part of this as you are." The bottoms of my shoes scuff across something sticky on the floor, and I hold back a shudder. It's dried blood. This is the exact spot where I shot the flesh-eater a few weeks ago. Swallowing hard, I maneuver around the stain and move closer to Declan. "How long are we going to walk in circles, searching for someone who may not even be in this area? If you tell me his name I can—"

"What, Virtue? Track him down with the navigation system in your head? Sentient or not, you are still a character."

"There's always the map."

"The map?"

"Yes. You know, the giant grid of the area. It tells where all the characters are at any given time."

"And how do you propose we get a copy of this?"

"Don't you have one?"

"Of course not. If I did, we wouldn't be in here, would we?" he demands. "I've already told you I'm not able to access it in here. There're too many firewalls."

"So it would help."

"Why does it matter if it would?"

I take a couple tentative steps toward him, and he shines his AcuTab on my face. "Because I'm able to see it…in my head."

Declan's eyebrows furrow together. Pressing his lips into a thin line, he says, "Stop wasting my time so we can finish up here. I want to hit as many locations as possible by sunset."

When he turns to stalk off to the stairs, I grab a handful of his black shirt. He twists back around with his eyes narrowed, seething. I press closer. Our bodies touch.

I will not let some game moderator bully me.

"Why would I lie about something so small? Why else would I have even risked my life by traveling west? It looked different on the map, so I automatically assumed that was my way out." *Maybe if I looked harder, thought things out instead of running at the first opportunity, I would have gone southeast first. Then I wouldn't be standing here arguing about wasted time with you,* I add silently.

"Okay, what does it look like?"

I consider ignoring this question. He's implying that I'm making this up, and it doesn't sit well with me. But a dribble of perspiration runs into my right eye, and I realize I want to get out of this hot building as soon as possible before I melt. "A bunch of red-and-green writing and pictures. Kind of dizzying, but it shows everyone's first name and whether they're Survivor or flesh-eater."

I don't tell him I'm able to see Survivors' points, too.

Declan pulls on the hem of his shirt and wipes sweat from his forehead. His knuckles are white. "How did you get it?"

I bite my bottom lip. I haven't considered what explanation I should offer for having access to the map. It's not as though I can tell him I jump into Olivia's head and, every now and then, I'm fortunate enough to see the map. So I pretend like this is normal. "Sometimes I see images of it when I sleep. Like a dream, I guess. My glitch, maybe?"

If I blame everything on the glitch, then I'll be fine.

"I should've guessed," he mutters. Resting his forehead against his hand, he draws in a harsh breath. "Do you know how insanely valuable that map is?"

Something in his tone startles me. It's strained, shaky. Fearful and yet excited. "Doesn't everyone have access to it?"

"No, Claudia. I've never heard of a gamer who does."

When I don't speak, just sink down on the tile floor and rock back and forth, he joins me. "Another anomaly," I say at last.

"Don't get me wrong. There's a map each gamer is able to access.

It's basic and shows names of towns and monuments. But what you're talking about is cheating."

It's so strange to hear that word in reference to The Aftermath that I laugh. Tremulous, partially deranged laughter. I don't stop until he shoots me a dark look, and even then I hiccup every few seconds.

"What kind of game would it be if everyone had a map like that?" he says. "Wouldn't be worth playing, would it? Your gamer would just breeze through the game because she'd know where everything is. What she has is rare—what's in your *head* is rare."

Rare. I'm sick of hearing that word. For once, I want to be the norm. "So my gamer has something she shouldn't have?"

Declan backs away from me, and I can't help feeling disappointed that our bodies no longer touch. Keeping his eyes off mine, he rubs his hand over his face. "I don't know. I mean, that type of map is usually available only to game developers, high-level moderators."

It takes me a moment to digest this information. "So she's a moderator?" Olivia might be like him. A cruel, high-ranking, female version of Declan.

"Maybe, maybe not. But she's dangerous either way, so we have to be even more careful." Drawing his eyebrows together, he takes a tentative step closer to me. "Is there anything else you know about her?"

Another opportunity to come right out and tell him about my ability to see what she's seeing. I stare at his profile, wondering what he'll say. Then I decide against it. There's something—and I'm not quite sure what it is just yet—screaming at me, telling me how dangerous it is to say anything and it's not just because I'll be revealing that I remember what happened between us here in this building.

Don't tell him, that familiar warning voice in my head shouts at me. It's distorted and fuzzy, but I know it's important that I listen.

"No," I say.

Declan glares at me for a long moment as if he's mentally processing my bluff. "His name is Wesley," he finally says.

"Wesley."

"He's a flesh-eater."

"I've gathered as much," I say. "I'll keep an eye out."

I don't find Wesley for the first couple of days after Olivia resumes her game play. Part of this is my fault—excruciating headaches keep me from staying in her head any longer than a half an hour at a time before I have to break away. Although he doesn't complain to me, it's obvious that Declan is frustrated and angry it's taking me so long to find his assignment. I hear it in his voice when I tell him I was unsuccessful again, see it in the way his eyes lower to the cellar floor and his cheeks flush.

He doesn't think I'm trying hard enough, so I tell him about The Badlands. We make a plan to take the trip into the mass of flesh-eaters at the first given opportunity.

But on the third day when Olivia zooms out on the game map and I'm able to easily locate Wesley, I realize the other reason why I couldn't find him. He's twenty miles away from here. No longer in Nashville like Declan believed him to be, but on the outskirts of town. And to my relief, his location is nowhere near The Badlands.

I can't make out his picture, because his face is downcast, but he's the only Wesley I've found and he's in an obvious flesh-eater den. I can tell because that tiny spot on the map is so overrun by names in red it looks like a bloody palm print.

As soon as Declan and I get the chance, we're leaving to find him. Then he's taking me over the border.

Another week passes—no, it crawls at a snail's pace. Olivia plays The Aftermath a few hours every day, but only when Ethan is around.

She comes into the game late one evening while everyone sits around the bar comparing weapons they've stolen from the latest raid. She steers me out of The Save and down the steps, parking me nonchalantly on one of the bar stools. And she makes an announcement that gives me my way out.

"I'm going with my father to Calwas for a week as of tomorrow," she says. "And you're all going on Group Save."

I hear them agree, see them nod, and my heart pumps a little harder. A little happier. But then April says, "That's ridiculous. Don't be such a selfish, greedy bitch, Olivia. I paid for the game, same as anyone else, so I get to play whenever I want."

Tapping my fingertips on the counter, I look at Ethan. He smiles at me and shrugs. Then I say, "It's not open for debate. Don't like the rules, leave."

April rises up from her spot on the floor by Jeremy. I expect her to argue with me, then disappear into The Save. Instead, she plants her palms on either side of my chest and shoves me down.

I fall off the stool backward and onto my hands. The old hardwood scrapes my palms raw. For a moment, Olivia doesn't have me do anything. I don't move. I don't blink. This might be a test—Olivia might be attempting to see if I'll react when threatened—and I'm smart enough to pretend like I'm not at all here. But then April rushes at me again, her fingers curled, flame-red hair flying around her face.

Olivia propels me to my feet. My vision blurs and my head spins, like a wobbling merry-go-round. I catch April's fist just as it comes toward my face. Twisting her wrist, I kick her feet out from under her. She drops to the floor, and I straddle her waist, jabbing my knees into her sides. I can hear the others behind us—all of them admonishing April. Olivia forces me to repeatedly slam April's face with her own fist.

I jump into her mind for a split second. She's punching at her screens calmly—crisp, systematic movements that make me feel cold inside. When I return to my own head, I find myself kneeling over April. I wipe the blood—hers—that's dripping down the back of my right hand onto her T-shirt and glower at her.

"As I said before, we're going on a Group Save tomorrow. And if I were you, I'd look for a new clan while I'm away. Wouldn't want to return to find your character deleted and all your points gone, would you? From what I hear, you might not be able to get a new one. It would be a shame for you to have to become a character yourself."

My heart skips a beat.

Is it possible for Olivia to have someone else's character deleted?

Does she hold that much power over the other gamers, and The Aftermath itself?

I walk away as poised as Olivia was in her gaming room, but my insides are pulled into tight, fraying knots. It's not until I return upstairs later that I realize my own palms are bleeding.

CHAPTER EIGHTEEN

The next afternoon, I stare around The Save for the last time. I am elated, breathless, but I'm also sad. I sit on the corner of the bed where Ethan lies. Landon left him flat on his back, staring up at the ceiling. I slide my hand into his. There's a silly part of me that expects it to be cold, like a corpse, but it's not.

"I'll figure out a way to get you out of here, too," I whisper, although I know he can't hear me. Just like I know that even if I find a way to free him from the game, he won't be the person I thought was my friend. He might even hate me. But at least he'd be able to make that decision for himself.

Declan stands in the doorway, his bulging bag high on his back. The corners of his lips twitch. I can't decide if he looks as though he's about to smile or frown. Then he says, "Heart-to-heart talks with a comatose person are a waste of your time. And that means you're wasting my time."

"Don't be so insensitive."

"I'm just saying," he says. "The person you're talking to is somewhere else right now—and if that person were awake, he wouldn't even know who you are."

"You know, for someone who works for LanCorp, you sure as hell sound an awful lot like a sympathizer."

"I'm just speaking the truth. Besides, I never said I liked my job."

"Then quit."

"After this assignment," he promises. "Then I'm letting go of Lan-Corp. Now, say your goodbyes so we can get out of here."

But why is this particular job so important? Why did he ever start working for a company he loathes in the first place? I imagine his assignment has to do with money. Declan will leave The Aftermath with an enormous paycheck, I'm sure of it.

"Kiss your boyfriend so we can go, Virtue," he says.

Before I can respond, he's gone. I hear his heavy footsteps on the stairs, then a bunch of slamming noises on the first floor. Rolling my eyes, I turn back to Ethan. I touch a hand to his cheek.

"If you're in there—in Rehabilitation or wherever—just know I'm breaking you all out." My eyes dart around the room. At Jeremy and his dark good looks. And April, whose face is bruised and blood-stained from our gamers' fight last night. Will she even still be here if I manage to come back for her?

When I head downstairs, Declan is pacing in front of the side door. He holds out my backpack, and I sigh. It's heavy. Full of weapons and bottles of water. Another day of travel, lugging around a bag that weighs as much as I do. Lucky for me, this is the beginning of the end. I pull the bag onto my back and follow him out of the bar. Away from the life I know.

Away from the game.

We make the trip in seven hours and arrive during that part of the day when the heat makes everything seem as if it's moving in slow motion. The flesh-eater den is inside an antebellum home. In my opinion, it's a strange place for a group of cannibals to hole up. The home is strangely beautiful, majestic, for a pseudoapocalypse—two stories, rows of windows and at least a dozen columns. There's a balcony, too. It wraps around the second story of the house, and I can imagine stepping out on it, gazing up at the cold night sky.

I imagine Declan with me, our bodies close, our mouths touching.

I breathe deeply. Where did that come from? Heat burns through my body, and I try to avoid making eye contact with him as we sneak past the flesh-eater den.

Use him and get away, I remind myself.

Instead of barging right in, we set up camp across the street in a two-room shack. Declan lays all his gear out on the threadbare carpet while I take inventory of our water. There are sixteen bottles left—eight for each of us. Hopefully, we'll bag more when we go in to get Wesley.

"How are we doing this?" I ask once I'm done. I twirl his electroshock gun between my fingers. He looks up at me and freezes.

"Don't play with weapons, Virtue."

I slide it toward him. It rolls two times, then snags on a piece of the carpet. "Scared I'll shock you?"

"Scared you'll shock yourself," replies Declan. He goes to the window and peeks out the dusty blinds. "They probably won't log off for another five or six hours at least. There are two guarding the front, two more in the back. Organized. Kind of impressive, if you ask me—usually the people who get these jobs are pretty low on smarts."

I don't care much about the flesh-eaters' organizational skills—not when Declan has a signal jammer in his bag. "Why can't you just interrupt their signal like before? We go in, get him out and then we can head for the border."

"Not this time. We already know he's in there, so we're better off waiting until their shift ends and they log off the game. Sometime this evening." Placing his head against the window frame, he winds the looped shade strings around two of his fingers.

"Seems like a lot of work for one character."

He shrugs. "It's my last job. Have to go out with a bang. You understand, right?"

I nod, but I don't comprehend. Not completely anyway. I join him at the window.

"You didn't mention the dead bodies on the front porch," I say, lifting one of my eyebrows.

"Didn't think you wanted to know."

My shoulder brushes his upper arm, and he smiles down at me. Touching Declan leaves me blinded, electrocuted—but in a good way that also makes me confused and out of breath.

I try and convince myself it's not him I'm attracted to. I'm enticed by the fact he's not a character and has the ability to tell me what he's really thinking. Even if it's usually something sardonic and irritating.

Yes, that's it.

"What are you grinning like that for?" he asks.

I didn't realize I was. Rubbing my lips together, I turn away to hide the warmth rising to my cheeks. And then I catch a glimpse of a familiar face standing guard in front of the mansion.

Mia.

Mia is less than five hundred yards away from where I stand.

Mia, my best friend. The girl who left our clan behind.

Why is she here, living with a group of flesh-eaters?

I somehow manage to keep calm. Declan suggests we move away from the window, and I nod, not really hearing him. We eat CDS meals on a makeshift table—our backpacks shoved together in the middle of the room—and share a bottle of water. The entire time we eat, I'm silent. He thinks I don't notice, but I can tell he's staring at me from beneath his long eyelashes.

"Are you okay?" he says at last.

I frown and look behind me, toward the window. "No. I mean, yes. It's just that—that girl, the one on the front lawn—she reminds me of someone I've seen before."

"In the past few weeks?"

So much longer than that. But I say, "Yes. She was a Survivor then on the map. Guess her gamer finished her treatment, huh?"

"Maybe, or her gamer may have just had to buy a new character. Remember, it's one of the punishments when a gamer has to restart the game after breaking one of the big rules."

I feel my chest tighten. Mia disappeared after she was stabbed in the abdomen during a rescue mission in The Badlands. Back then I worried, though of course, I didn't voice that concern aloud. She'd left no note, no explanation as to why she was going, and nobody else seemed to find it strange that she'd disappeared in the middle of the night during a snowstorm. And now...I swallow the last mouthful of water. My throat is so tight I have trouble forcing it down.

Now she's a flesh-eater who's being played by a LanCorp employee in a world supposedly free from violence.

"It seems like a bad dream. All of it. And you know what really makes me sick?" I say. He shrugs and gestures for me to tell him. "I don't know what I would be if I weren't in this game. Would I be a sympathizer? Or am I truly violent— Would I be one of these people who live and breathe a bloody fantasy?"

Declan scoots closer to me and takes my hands into his. "You wouldn't," he says. His hard fingertips close around my wrists. I inhale. Exhale. Suddenly, I can't remember how to breathe. "They hacked you up pretty good," he whispers. "Sensors—they're supposed to be discreet but yours…"

He rubs his thumbs across the puckered scars, his touch a static current. The hair on the back of my neck and arms stand on end, and it leaves me wanting so much more.

If I'm not careful, his touch will be my downfall.

"Sensors," I repeat.

He lifts my arms until the slivers of light filtering through the blinds hit the scars. "I keep forgetting—your memory. The sensors transmit your vitals to LanCorp. They're a little like our AcuTabs except these are internal. Every character has them. Here." He runs his hands down my body and touches the insides of my ankles. I shiver. Then he presses his fingertips over my heart. "And here, too."

There are more crude scars in all the places he touched.

"Do you remember any of it? The procedures, I mean?" he says.

The only procedure I have a complete memory of is the one with Dr. Coleman, when I was outside my body and in Olivia's head. I wish I could trust Declan enough to talk about it. About the Regenerator that looked exactly like a casket and the cold mechanical arms restoring my features. About how I woke up unable to scream because my lungs refused to expand or contract.

About a new memory forming in my head right now—one where I am screaming because there are several physicians installing sensors in my body, sticking sharp needles into my skin. Speaking quickly, excitedly the whole time.

"…have to prepare her fast."

"He said she's going into the game tonight, and—"

"Heard she shined last night in War. Ten kills in less than three minutes. Olivia and Claudia will be an incredible force."

I'm grinding my teeth when my thoughts return to the present. No,

I can't tell Declan about any of those things. Because this boy works for the company that messed with my head and body in the first place.

I pull away from him, coming to my knees, and stuff my hands into my back pockets. Lift my head until I'm staring into his dark gray eyes. "None of it," I say. "Why's it matter?"

"Because I'm starting to think I'm losing my way."

"Why?"

"Because of you."

But what about me? "It's hard to be around one of us who has the scars to prove how corrupt LanCorp is, isn't it?" My reply comes out harsher than I intend. I realize I'm trembling. "Hard to be around someone who thinks for herself?"

"I wouldn't be able to stand you if you didn't think for yourself—if you were her."

I don't like this feeling, like my mind is being scrambled. I've spent too much time with no explanation for the things I know and don't know. And now that everything is starting to make sense, it's all falling apart again.

I want to hate Declan for tearing that logic to shreds.

He returns to the window, this time with a pair of binoculars we stole from my clan's supply stockpile. "Won't be long now."

Declan's right. At any moment this will all be over. Then I'll be free and he'll leave.

When we rest, I dream of Mia.

We're standing on the roof of the theater we used to live in. I'm on the edge, watching for flesh-eaters across the street, and she's behind me, talking. Laughing.

At me.

"You won't ever get out," she says. I hear her shuffle closer—her boots skid on the hard surface.

My shoulder blades involuntarily jerk together, and I squint at a tiny speck in the distance. "Don't say that."

"Don't kid yourself, then. You'll die if you leave."

I shake my head. I can't afford to believe that—even if this is a nightmare. "No, I'll die if I stay." At last, I turn to look at her. She's an arm's length away from me now, wearing one of those emotionless smiles I've started to despise. Blood coats her chin and neck, like a thick circular layer of drying red paint.

But it's her eyes that give me reason to pause. They aren't empty. Her eyes are mad and gleaming. Hungry.

My breath catches, and I take a tiny step backward. My heel slides along the edge of the roof. I clutch at the air to balance myself. She doesn't help me—she just stands there, with her hands clasped in front of her.

"I'm going to figure out a way to save you all," I say once I'm upright.

She laughs. "Don't—we're better off in here. I'm starving, Claudia. I'm so hungry I can't think straight." She takes another step toward me, and her metallic odor burns my nose and throat. "You know how this goes."

I just want it to end.

Her teeth rip into the right side of my face, my ear, as we tumble from the roof. And right before we crash to the ground, I wonder if there's anything I could have done to change things.

CHAPTER NINETEEN

When I awaken, panting and covered in sweat despite the fact it's freezing inside the shack, I shoot straight up. My forehead collides with something hard in the dark. Declan mutters a few curse words and shines the screen from his tablet in my face. Once my eyes adjust to the bright blue light, I notice that his nose is red.

"Sorry," I mutter but he shrugs it off. Apparently, he's gotten used to me hitting him in the face.

"It's time to go," he says.

I don't realize I'm holding my ear until he helps me to my feet.

"Are you ready?"

Don't kid yourself. You'll die if you leave.

Pursing my lips together, I ignore Mia's words and grab my bag. All the water bottles have fallen to the bottom, and they knock hard against my lower back. I grunt and look down at the toe of Declan's boot so he doesn't see how agitated I am.

"To go into a flesh-eater den? Always," I say.

"Because if you're not, I can leave you here. I don't want you going in there and ruining my assignment. Not after we've come this far."

I narrow my eyes at him. He's as obsessed with his assignment as Olivia is with the game. Annoyed, I bite the inside of my jaw. I yank the door open and walk outside. "I'm twice as qualified to do this, so don't start with me tonight."

He laughs and comes outside in the cold with me. Even though he mutters it under his breath, I feel my face grow hot when he says, "You're cute when you're bossy."

We run across the path to the mansion. Now that I see it up close, it's not so beautiful. Several of the windows are smashed and the house looks more gray than white, probably from years of decay. There's blood splatter on the columns, but then why would I expect anything different? This is The Aftermath.

"It shouldn't take too long," Declan says as he digs through his bag. He pulls out an armful of devices and a utility belt. He organizes his gear and puts the belt on. It fits him snugly, and I think of April, with her stained weapons holster drooping around her pointy hips.

I drag my backpack and his to the side of the house. I take a knife, a flashlight and my Glock from mine; then I hide both bags behind a shrub.

"Here," he says. He presses something cold and heavy into my hand. I squint down at it. His electroshock gun.

"I'm touched," I say. I glance up at him "You'd give me your Special Edition Tech…"

"Tech Arms. And I'm not giving it to you— I'm just letting you borrow it. I won't need it." Before I can stop him, he comes up behind me, pressing his body close to mine. He lifts my arms together and positions my hands on either side of the gun. "Quick tutorial," he whispers.

I can barely breathe, much less concentrate, but I manage to get the gist of his instructions. Release safety catch. Wait for the target light to blink. Pull trigger—it will hit my target regardless of whether or not he moves. Don't touch the amp setting. Right now, it's set to where it will knock someone out without killing them.

"And we don't want any of these characters dead," Declan warns. He draws away from me, turning slightly to adjust his tools one last time. I find myself gravitating closer to him, but I stop myself. I focus on the electroshock gun.

"I know," I whisper.

"They're still people."

"I understand," I snap. Nobody understands that as clearly as I do, especially not a game moderator.

I pick the lock on the front door. A gutted character sits on one side of it, his head flopping to his chest. I glare harder at the bolt so I don't have to see the blood. I imagine there's plenty more inside. The lock releases and I step forward to walk in, but Declan catches the hem of my T-shirt and yanks me back.

"Wha—"

"We don't know if they set the entire house as a save point or just one room. I'd hate for you to get your arms and legs fried before we even make it inside."

I feel a mixture of gratitude and irritation. Gratitude because he cares enough to stop me from getting electrocuted. Irritation because he's wrong—the current won't fry my arms and legs. I should know, since I've already experienced it twice.

He tosses a coin through the doorway. When nothing happens, he steps inside and motions his head for me to follow. Shining the light from his AcuTab and my small flashlight, we walk through the hallways, opening doors as we pass them. There's a horrible smell emanating throughout the house, and I try my best not to take too many breaths.

We come to a staircase. It's long and winding. I'm dizzy just staring up at it. Gripping the smooth black banister tightly, I climb up first. Every other step makes me feel as if I'll fall over the side and come crashing down. Declan nudges me forward until we reach the top.

There's a hallway with four doors on either side.

"You check the right," I say to him, as I fling open the first door on the left.

I'm at the third door when he says to me, "Found it."

Cocking the Glock, I join him. He glances at me, at the gun in my hand and the electroshock gun in my waistband, but doesn't say anything. He must know it's habit and not murderous intentions. At least, I hope he realizes that.

The save point is a ballroom with white walls and elaborate molding around the ceiling. In the center of the room is a large chandelier. I shine my light on it. With its broken, jagged crystals that are covered in a thick layer of dust, it reminds me of human bones suspended in midair.

After Declan disables the electric barrier protecting the characters, I stand beneath the lighting fixture, looking around the room at the flesh-eaters and their victims. My eyes locate Mia swiftly. She's beneath an archway, her arm wrapped around a male flesh-eater's waist, her head sagging against his shoulder.

Just seeing this makes my chest tighten. I push away all the horrible thoughts trying to make their way into my head. I don't want to think about what the LanCorp employee playing her has made her do.

I turn away from them and walk over to Declan. He kneels over a flesh-eater lying down on a brocade settee. This must be Wesley. He touches the boy's throat to check for a pulse, and when he does this, Wesley's head lolls forward so that his face is visible under my light.

A hundred years could have passed, a thousand even, and I'd have recognized that face. A narrow nose, thick, dark eyebrows and a small brown birthmark under his right cheek. My ear tingles as I drop the flashlight and lift the Glock so that it's pointed at the middle of the boy's head. I press the barrel to his skin.

"He attacked me," I say.

Three years ago. In a dark parking garage. And I was completely helpless.

But now I'm not.

"Claudia," Declan says, inching closer to me. He rarely ever uses my first name. It stuns me, makes the waves churning in my head crash even harder. He holds his hands out and nods toward the Glock. "Give me the gun, okay?"

"He attacked me. Bit me." I turn my face just slightly so he can see my ear. "He tried to kill me."

Declan swallows and shakes his head. He's so close now that the tips of his fingers hover right over my hand. "No, the LanCorp employee operating him attacked you. And your gamer let him. He had no control over what he was doing. Just like you."

I touch my ear. Rub my fingers over the uneven skin at the top of it. It hasn't hurt in nearly three years, but right now it burns as badly as it had in the minutes after Wesley lunged at me. "Decla—"

"I know. And I'm sorry for what happened. But he's not the one who hurt you—he never was. Be angry at the person who collects a paycheck for making him into—" he swallows again and drops his eyes to the dark-haired boy on the couch, staring sideways with un-seeing eyes "—this."

This is my dilemma. It's so difficult not to rage at the person in front of me, in the flesh, instead of someone I'll likely never meet. And the voice of reason in this scenario? The person who works for the company that made me suffer so much in the first place—and another boy who's hurt me, even if he doesn't realize I remember it.

"Claudia?" Declan says, pulling me toward him and gently removing the weapon from my hand.

"You're right," I whisper into his chest. And, as much as I hate to admit it, he is.

He places the Glock back in my hand. "You hold on to this." He steps away from me, but I still can't move because I can't take my eyes off Wesley. Declan turns back to me, lifts my chin. He gives me a tight smile that is so far from his usual smirk it makes my chest hurt. "This will be over soon."

Stop reminding me.

"I know," I say. I pick my flashlight up and shine it onto Wesley's face. His pupil's contract, but he doesn't blink. "So...we're carrying him out of here?"

It's funny, all this time we spent talking about finding this person and not once have I asked Declan what would happen once we did. I cringe at the thought of having to help carry him along with my bag. I remember moving Ethan through the bar, banging his arms against doors and walls. Wesley is taller by a couple of inches, probably heavier, too.

Declan shakes his head, drops to his knees and pulls off his utility belt. He bends over it, rummaging around. Finally he pulls out a stainless-steel device that I've not seen him use before.

But it's familiar anyway.

It looks exactly like the tool Dr. Coleman used on my head after it was injured a few weeks ago.

I take a few steps backward, thudding into a piano. It makes a horrible screeching noise, and we both startle. "Why do you have that thing?"

"To get him out of here."

"You're going to torture him?"

"Of course not, what the hell is wr—"

"Don't lie to me!"

His eyebrows knit together as he slides the belt against the wall beside the couch. He comes toward me, but I stumble out of the way. "I thought you said you were okay."

"That thing in your hand…"

"Is going to permanently disrupt his chip. It's a Triple C—Cerebrum Chip configurator."

I dig my fingernails into my palm to keep from grasping at my own head. The details of what happened with Dr. Coleman are still fuzzy, but what I do recall is the pain. Searing, vomit-inducing agony, starting the moment I found myself inside my body. And it certainly didn't block Olivia from playing me.

"You brought me here to help you kill him," I whisper.

Declan's mouth drops open and he stares at me, long and hard. Every moment that passes by without words makes me angrier, until I'm shaking. I should run. I should shoot him in the head right now and run, because once he's done with Wesley, he'll break his promise. Turn on me, or give me to his moderator friends who will do God knows what to me.

He might even turn me over to Olivia.

"If I wanted him dead, I would've let you put a bullet in his head five minutes ago. I'm interrupting his chip, breaking the link to his player. That way Wesley the person, not the character, can walk out of this game with us. Carrying him forty miles isn't my idea of a good time."

Oh. Heat rushes through my body, and I turn my back to him so he can't see my red face. Assuming the worst of Declan has caused me nothing but embarrassment. I ball a handful of my shirt in my free hand and contemplate apologizing. I wish he'd stop proving me wrong so I could stop saying sorry.

"It's all right, you know," he says. "To ask questions. To worry about other people. It just shows this game hasn't completely screwed you up."

I wish he'd stop accurately reading my emotions, too.

I wait until my face has cooled to face him again. He's positioned his AcuTab on an end table so that its flashlight function beams right over Wesley's head. Holding his thumb and forefinger about an inch apart, Declan carefully measures from his forehead to his crown. "Cerebrum Chips are…difficult. I have to find the exact spot to disrupt the signal or this will go over just like a deletion."

I stand at the opposite end of the settee, studying Declan's precise movements. "This thing you're using—it's the same tool used to delete a character?"

"No, but it can be used for a quick deletion," he says. Our eyes meet. "But those don't happen often, and they're messy."

My throat constricts. I don't have the stomach to ask what he means by a messy deletion. Not right now while we're standing in the middle of a cannibal den.

"What else is it for?"

"Resetting a chip. Deactivate, delete, reset. Triple C—and before you ask, I know none of those things begin with a *C*, Virtue."

But I'm not worried over the reasoning behind the device's name. Was this what Dr. Coleman did to me? Reset my Cerebrum Chip? "Does it hurt?"

He raises his head and squints at me. "I'm not sure."

I take an uncertain step forward; feel my hand on top of my own head although I didn't even realize I lifted it. "Can you do this to me?"

"No," he says, concentrating. When I tense up and open my mouth to speak, he wrinkles his nose in frustration and holds up a hand. "I'll tell you why when I'm done."

My heart feels as though it's jumped into my throat. It stays there as he continues working. He presses the flat end of the Triple C to Wesley's crown. There are beads of sweat on Declan's top lip. His shoulders tense up as he pulls a button on the tool up with his thumb. He holds it as Wesley begins to twitch violently. Even when the other boy trembles off the couch, Declan doesn't release the trigger. I can see his lips move, silently counting.

"Done," he says when he reaches forty seconds. He scoots back on his hands and bottom and sits against the wall, next to the rest of his gear.

Wesley lies on the floor in a twisted heap. If not for the slight rise and fall of his chest, I'd think he was dead. "Is he going to live?"

"He'll come to in a few minutes."

I nod, then move next to Declan, supporting my back on a portion of the wall that is not bathed in blood. We're quiet for a very long time before he starts talking. "Your chip is different. Your link is different."

"What do you mean by different?"

"Exactly what I just said. I've known that since the moment we met," he says. I close my eyes and picture him probing my head with the blue device at the fence. "The structure of your chip is different from other characters. Ten times more complex. My chip reader couldn't even read it. The only thing it was able to tell me was that you were an active character."

"You're just teasing me." He has to be. There can't possibly be something else wrong with me.

"No, I'm serious. I'll have to wait until we're out to try to work on yours."

He doesn't plan to just disappear once we leave the game. I want to feel some relief over this, but it's impossible when he's sitting beside me telling me my chip is an anomaly.

I'm an anomaly.

"I want to go back, Declan," I say. "If I'd known you had a way to deactivate the chips, I'd have made you free my friends back in the bar."

His mouth hardens. "They're not your friends. You've never even really met them. And don't tell me you've grown attached to the gamers inside their heads."

I hate him a little for saying that, but I continue, "Still, you have what it takes to get them out of this game."

He snorts. "Going back there is suicide. Once Wesley comes to, we have forty-eight hours, tops, to get out of the game before we're found out. The sooner the better."

This is new information. And even though nothing shocks me about Declan anymore, I suddenly have a million questions. "Why do we have to get out? You're a moderator. You work for the game. You—"

"Save your questions for later, Virtue."

There's an uneasy sensation slinking its way through my body. But I don't get a chance to tell him how I feel—tell him how selfish he is for not informing me about his ability to break links or the time constraints we now face—because Wesley moves.

Declan stumbles to his feet. I have no time to react before he's by the boy's side. I cup my ear protectively, shrink as close to the wall as possible. I have no idea what will happen next.

Wesley rolls over on his back and stares up at Declan. His chest heaves up and down. He's...laughing. "You got chubby," he says hoarsely.

Declan grins and shakes his head. Shrugging his shoulders, he replies, "So what? You look like a corpse."

I watch in horror as this flesh-eating character, Wesley, moves shakily into a sitting position. They're staring at each other. Why hasn't Declan restrained him or made a move to make sure he's not dangerous? Why the hell are they both grinning?

This boy is an assignment. He's Declan's last assignment before he quits LanCorp. I repeat this over and over in my head, holding my breath and praying this whole situation will start making sense soon.

Wesley glances over at me and gives me a half smile that chills me to the bone. Not because of who he is and how he attacked me three years ago, but because I've seen that grin many times over the past few weeks. It's cocky and self-assured, even for someone who looks an inch away from death.

It's Declan's smile.

I expect that up close, his eyes are the same shade of gray, too.

"Leave it to you to bring a girl to a prison break, little brother," Wesley says.

CHAPTER TWENTY

They want to leave immediately—Declan and his older brother—but I refuse to budge. Gritting my teeth, I train my eyes on Mia, who's sitting across the room from me.

Declan kneels in front of me and blocks my view. He touches my hand, but I jerk away from him. When I don't meet his gaze, he gently touches my chin to turn my head. His gray eyes look up at me apologetically. "Claudia, I—"

"Save it," I say.

He bares his teeth and scratches both hands at the back of his neck. "He's my brother." He makes it sound as if he's trying to convince me.

I already understand. If there were a member of my family in The Aftermath, I would do anything to free them, even if that meant sabotaging my job or my life. But still, I'm furious. And there are other things that Declan is keeping from me that I'm bent on making him reveal. Right now.

"You were a character, weren't you?" I demand. His head pops up and his eyes widen. He can lie to me if he wants to, but his expression tells me everything I want to know. Declan is not a moderator. "Did you escape?" I ask.

"I told you already—nobody's ever escaped the games."

"Then how'd you get out?"

His shoulders tense up. After a long moment, he takes a deep breath and squeezes his eyes shut. "Why does it matter?"

"Because you've been lying to me for weeks. Because I deserve to know the truth." I wish he had just told me what was going on from the beginning. If he had, I wouldn't feel like such a pathetic fool right now.

But I'm a liar, too. And there's a part of me that knows that I should tell him everything, that desperately wants to tell him just in case he knows something that might help me.

I shake that thought from my head. No, that guilty part of myself will just have to wait.

"I didn't escape the game. I was just outside of it, being taken to a deletion facility, when I broke free. Some sympathizers found me, took me in, and we started coming up with every possible way to save my brother. Took us about six months to find which game he was in. Another four to figure out how to infiltrate the system, gather all the gear I'd need to complete the mission. And one more to find my key into The Aftermath. Meeting you was the best thing that ever happened to me, because I'd honestly planned to walk around in circles 'til I found Wes— I didn't know the area, this game, at all. Happy?"

My face burns, and I silently admonish myself for being so weak. I shouldn't feel anything. I've known all along that he was using me. Still, having him come right out and tell me that makes my chest hurt. "How can you ask me that?"

He jumps to his feet and whirls on me, but I stand, too. I cross my arms over my chest and count down from fifty in my head to control my breathing. "I did what I had to do to save myself. And I'll do whatever it takes to get my brother out of here alive."

"What about me? Or am I just along for the ride in case you need to throw the mods off your scent?"

"How can you ask me that?" he demands.

I draw myself so close to him that our shoulders brush. He's glaring at me, but I won't back down. As long as he tells me the truth, I can take whatever it is he has to say. "Well, am I?" I ask.

"Absolutely not. I promised to keep you safe and get you out of here." He rocks back and forth on his heels. "Please, Virtue...just work with me, okay? I'm sorry for lying, but we have to go now."

There's so much more I want to ask him. What game was he in? Does he remember anything at all about it? Why was he put up for deletion anyway—he doesn't look damaged to me. But all those questions can wait for later, when we're not on the run from a deranged company.

"I want you to use the Triple C on the rest of them first," I say.

He groans. Out of the corner of my eye, I see him shake his head slowly. "That's impossible, Virtue."

I know it is. I know what he's doing is illegal, but it doesn't make me feel any less vulnerable. When we leave here, I'll know that I left so many behind that we could have helped.

How am I supposed to live with myself, knowing I could have given someone their freedom?

"They'll catch us quickly if you do." My words are more of a statement than a question, but he nods anyway. "At least let her go," I say, using his shoulder to climb to my feet. I gesture to Mia.

"Why?" he whispers, squinting up at me.

"Because you got Wesley. I deserve her."

I expect him to argue with me. I expect him to come up with some kind of excuse for why we can't take her. But instead he touches the side of my face, brushing the tip of his thumb gently over my bad ear.

209

"All right."

He finishes severing Mia's link quickly. She lies a few inches from the boy she held when we came in, and I sit beside her, waiting for her to awaken. Hoping she's not too damaged.

I slide my hand into hers.

Declan and Wesley work on installing a signal jammer. There's already a tear in one of the walls, so Declan programs the device and they slowly lower it into the hole. The entire time they do this, I watch Wesley carefully. If he turns on us, I'll shoot him in the ankles.

My breath hitches. I'm disgusted with myself for letting that thought enter my head for even a split second.

Mia's fingernails clamp down on my hand, and I jerk away from her. She inhales so deeply it sounds as if she's choking. I scramble up and lift her head. I watch as she opens her eyes.

"Listen to me," I whisper. "I don't care if you remember me or not. You were—are—my best friend. And I'm getting you out of this game."

She screams.

Declan rushes past me. "She's in shock." He picks her up as if she's as light as his rucksack and carries her from the ballroom. Wesley and I follow him, and I can't help but keep a couple of steps behind him, with one hand on the Glock and the other on the electroshock gun.

"It wasn't me who hurt you, you know," Wesley says, looking backward as he runs down the spiral staircase. I take each step hesitantly. Between the vertigo and the smell clinging to the air and all that's happened, I'm worried the CDS I ate earlier will come up.

He stands on the bottom stair, looking up at me. I move to the left. He blocks me. The same thing happens three times. Declan and Mia are already outside, and I feel trapped. I lift the Glock. Shove the barrel into his flesh. It clinks against bone and my teeth chatter.

"Move," I say.

"Declan told me what happened to you. It wasn't me." But he steps aside. I jump down and hurry past him, wondering if Declan also told him about knocking me unconscious the first time we met. Had that been a part of his plan to find Wesley, too?

"It's fine," I say.

He grabs my arm, whirling me around and I point the gun at him again—this time at his belly. "Do you think I wanted to be like this? I wanted in this game about as much as you did." He pushes the Glock down and toward me. "We have the same goal. Save your trigger finger for Thomas Lancaster."

Lancaster. He must be the person behind LanCorp—the creator of my living nightmare. The son of that Natalie Lancaster. Thomas Lancaster is the reason why I'm so broken.

Wesley leaves me standing there, cradling my gun to myself. I'm shaking so violently that I can barely keep hold of it. I'm furious. At Wesley and Declan. At myself. I kick a spot on the wall where the wallpaper is falling loose and I scream as loud as I can, until my chest hurts and my face is on fire and I find myself unintentionally slipping in and out of Olivia's head.

She's talking to what looks to be two physicians—Dr. Coleman and a younger man—in a room with blinding lights. This catches my interest and I push aside my frustration to focus in on what they're saying.

"You should be well enough to play the game by next week," Dr. Coleman tells her soothingly.

"Do you think it will work?" Olivia asks.

"It should."

As I lean over to catch my breath, I wonder aloud what's wrong with my gamer. She hadn't seemed different before she left for Calwas. Maybe she's gotten sick since arriving. Hearing Dr. Coleman tell her she wouldn't be able to play The Aftermath until next week makes me feel a little better—I don't need a week to get out of the game; I only need a few more days.

"Stay sick, Olivia," I say.

Then I put the Glock back into its holster and join the rest of my new clan—two former flesh-eaters and a fake game moderator—outside.

Mia stays near me—so close our shoulders rub as we walk—but she doesn't say anything for a few miles. When she does speak, her words are so shaky I don't understand her at first.

I move closer to her. She backs up, her foot snagging on a branch, but I catch her hand. Dried blood stains her palm and fingertips. A massive weight drops onto my chest.

"Have I— Was I asleep for long?" she whispers. She looks closely at her hand, then shivers and slides it into her back pocket. Staring at the ground, she inhales several times, then releases it in one big breath. "It feels like I was there for only a day or two, but…"

Three years. Mia's been stuck in Rehabilitation for at least three years. She joined up with Ethan and me a day after we met. Now I'm sure our gamers planned it all—they were probably friends—but at the time, I was drawn to her personality. She's strong and brave.

At least, she *was* strong and brave.

The real Mia seems as if she'll have a heart attack if I even yell at her. Before I can stop myself, I pull her into my arms, wrap her up. I think this surprises her. She stands still for a moment, with her arms half raised as if she's not sure what to do with them. Then she buries her face into my shoulder and lets out a soft sob.

This whole emotion thing—it's new for me, too.

"How long?" she asks again. I feel her tears on my shoulder. They drip down my chest and back, like scalding water. I grit my teeth, hating LanCorp and Thomas Lancaster a little more each second.

"Not long," I lie.

She steps backward, pressing her fingers to the corners of her eyes. "Thank you," she whispers. "For picking me. Out of all those people back there…"

It was never a choice, I want to say, but instead I smile. A tight and painful smile, one that rips me into thousands of tiny shreds. I hear soft laughter up ahead, then the sound of a zipper coming undone. "Come on," I say. "Let's not waste rest time."

We eat dinner—or breakfast, I suppose, because the sky is already starting to lighten—between two oak trees. I try my best to eat my CDS and drink my bottle of water, but it's impossible. Every time I look at Wesley or Mia, I think of the things they've likely been forced to do while under the LanCorp workers' control.

It turns my stomach.

And an annoying voice in the back of my head whispers to me, *You're no better.*

Trembling, I bite into the CDS.

"How far are we from the border?" Wesley asks. He balls up one CDS wrapper, then opens another. I almost want to point out that only one is necessary, but then he shifts, and I see his rib cage through his dirty shirt. I stare down at my own empty packet, wishing absurdly that I could have given it to him, as well.

"Thirty-five miles. Forty-six hours left," Declan replies. "I've already figured it. Three miles an hour, half an hour of rest every two hours. Sleep at the halfway point. That should put us at the border in less than twenty-four hours and gives us a little room for error." He glances over at Mia and me when he says this. She's looking down at her water as he sizes her up, but I see the way his eyebrows pull together. I know he thinks she'll hold us back.

I narrow my eyes at him. "You owe me," I mouth. For the elevator incident. For lying to me—repeatedly.

Declan tilts his head to one side. Lifting his bottle of water in a dramatic toast, he says, "I know."

Wesley grins and stares back and forth between us. "How've you two survived a few weeks together?" He twirls his CDS packet between his fingers. It's distracting and draws my attention to his dirty fingernails. I think of blood. Flesh-eater dens. His hands around my neck right before he—

I pinch myself.

"I lock him in my basement," I say, and Wesley laughs. It's deep and infectious—beautiful laughter that makes me smile, even though there's not much to smile about. Wesley's laughter doesn't belong to a flesh-eater or a violent boy. It doesn't belong in this game.

I'm going to have to get over myself and remember he's not the one who hurt me, because I don't want to miss out on learning to like him.

"Got any plans once you get out?" he says.

I feel three sets of eyes settle on me. My cheeks grow hot. A few weeks ago, before I met Declan and realized how much was possible, I would have said to get as far away from the border as I can. Now I'm not so sure. Declan has the equipment that can help me save the people I left several miles south of here. And once I'm out, if I can gather every ounce of courage I have…

"I'm getting the hell away from The Aftermath," I lie, meeting Declan's eyes. He looks away.

"What about you?" This time, Wesley speaks to Mia. She concentrates on crumbling a handful of leaves. "Where are you headed?"

She clears her throat. We're all quiet, leaning in to her, when she finally says, "Back to my brother. He's ten and I take care of him. He's still alive. I know he is. He has to be."

I shouldn't be stunned. I know she's not the girl I thought she was. But knowing the truth doesn't make it any less difficult to process. I hope and pray she finds her little brother when we get out of here. I really do. Still, I can't stop the heat that builds up behind my eyelids when I squeeze them shut. Mia has her brother, and Declan and Wesley have one another. And I've got nothing but a few scattered memories. I feel wretched for being jealous.

Yet I still feel cheated.

They're barely finished eating, and we have another five minutes of rest left, but I no longer want to sit. I'm ready to move. I take off walking just as they start packing up.

"Virtue, wait up." I roll my eyes at the sound of Declan's voice. I move my legs a little faster. They're sore from so much traveling. He catches up relatively quickly, pulling on one of my straps. "Hey, why did—are you crying?"

"No."

"Look, I'm sorry about lying about who I was. I just—"

I interrupt him. "Don't assume everything is about you." I stare down at the ground, at his shoes. Faint strains of sunlight make the bloodstains on them visible. I square my shoulders and sigh. I can hear Wesley and Mia coming closer, and I promise myself I'll keep my emotions in check, for her. "Can we just finish this?"

His lips pull into a tight line. He draws me slightly closer, so that our faces nearly touch, opens his mouth to say something. Or do something. I can't decide which it is, or which I want. Then Wesley claps him on the shoulder. "Ready to go?"

"Let's finish this," he repeats, to Wesley. His gray eyes never leave mine.

CHAPTER TWENTY-ONE

For our next break a few hours later, we stop inside a warehouse Mia spots off the main highway. She's skittish, but she has the sharpest eyes of us all. While they eat and share a couple of bottles of water—we're running low, since we only managed to snag a dozen or so from the flesh-eater den—I sneak away to the second floor. I hide in a corner between several stacks of crates and the wall as I check in on Olivia.

She's no longer with Dr. Coleman but is instead on a covered bridge. It's made of thick teal-colored glass squares with recessed lighting in the ceiling and connects two of the skyscrapers. A sea of faces surrounds us, coming and going. Advertisements play on every other block of glass. Injury and cosmetic regeneration in low monthly installments, LanCorp-prescribed games that are available for patients of every age and a vacation getaway in an underwater compound that offers everything from relaxation chambers to a genetics spa—whatever that is. But Olivia's eyes focus on just one thing—the thin boy walking right toward us with bouncy brownish hair. Landon. His striking blue eyes catch hers and as they brush shoulders, he slips something into her hand. Then he's gone. She doesn't glance behind us, but I can tell she wants to by the way she clenches her fists.

I hang on to her mind long enough for her to enter the building on the other end of the water. She goes into an enormous room and crouches between a gleaming white platform and table. So similar to the way I'm hiding it suffocates me. She opens her palm to reveal a flat rectangular chip. It's black and as small as the tip of my thumb. Olivia places the disk in the middle of her AcuTab, then lays it down flat on the platform. A hologram of Landon floats over us. He smiles at her. There's a little gap between his top teeth that I didn't notice when he sat next to us on the bench on the rooftop garden. She reaches out to touch him. Her hand drifts right through the projection.

"Archaic, I know, but I had to get this across to you. It's so hard being in the same province as you and not being able to see you or touch you or talk to you in person," he says, and she slumps over, her dark hair falling over her eyes.

"I can't wait until we're together again next week in our place. Somehow, someway, someday...it will be in person again. I love you, Liv."

"Wait, Landon, there's—" But the projection fades away, and Olivia supports her weight against the white table. "Ugh...what's wrong with me?" Breathing heavily, she rakes her hands down her face. When she pulls them away, I'm shocked to see that her palms are damp.

"I'm losing control," she whispers, her voice furious. "I'm going to lose everything."

She's crying.

My harsh, terrifying gamer is crying.

If Landon and Olivia's place wasn't The Aftermath and seeing each other wasn't a pretend romance between Ethan and me, I would hurt for her. As she smashes the chip into pieces with her foot, her tears blur what I'm able to see. Witnessing her in pain like this embarrasses me—I feel as though I'm an intruder. I release my grip on her brain.

And I come face-to-face with Wesley.

I scream and then clamp my hands over my mouth. "What are you doing up here?" I snap.

He holds out his hand, and I wince reflexively, but he pulls me to a standing position and stares down at me. I was wrong before—his eyes aren't quite like Declan's. They're pale gray. Like an overcast sky.

"Dec wanted me to check on you. He's running a simulation on his AcuTab right now to see if there's a quicker way to get out." He pauses for a second. "Claudia, are you okay?"

"I'm fine."

"You called out a name. Landon. You said 'Wait, Landon.' And why are you crying?"

I open my mouth to argue with him, tell him I'm fine again, but then I press the back of my hand to my cheek. Feel the dampness. For a long time, I look at him, mouth open with my hands on my face. Then I clear my throat, dry away the tears and wipe my fingertips on the hem of my shirt.

Why am I crying?

"It was a dream," I say lamely.

He shakes his head. "Are you sure? I mean, your eyes were wide-awake and your face looked like—" His hands ball up by his sides. It's as if he's fighting to get his words out. I touch his forearm, and we both take in a shaky breath.

"Like what?"

"Like a character. Not a person, but a character."

I imagine my face, void of any emotion, with tears streaming down it. I squeeze his arm and force out a laugh. "I'm fine. I swear." I don't bother looking him in the eye to see if he's convinced—I can't even convince myself—but as we head downstairs, I hope he won't mention this to Declan.

Wesley's not like Ethan. I can't simply boss him around—tell him to keep quiet—and expect him to listen.

We go to a room in the back of the warehouse. At some point before this state was evacuated, it must have been an office—there's a desk covered in stacks of paperwork that are yellow and crisp with age and a computer coated in a thick layer of dust. I sit between Wesley and Mia. Declan's across from me, eating. He cocks an eyebrow.

"You okay, Virtue?"

I draw a burning breath in through my nose. "Yes," I snap. I don't want to be asked if I'm okay anymore. I'm fine.

For the rest of our time in the warehouse, I make myself laugh when they laugh. Make myself eat another bite as they eat. Try my hardest to come up with something intelligent to say when Mia tells us stories about her brother, Daniel.

"And the day my foster mom turned us over to LanCorp because we couldn't afford the treatment, I saw their van before it even pulled into the driveway. I told him to run. He was—is—the fastest kid I know. He'll have made it somewhere safe." Her brown eyes are shiny, but this is the strongest I've heard her voice since Declan disconnected her link from her commissioned player.

We're all quiet for a few minutes. I imagine the thoughts running through my head are the same as theirs. Ominous vans coming after us in the night. Sick children and homeless people selling themselves to a company because they were born with an alleged gene that makes them dangerous. And I think of Daniel—picture him, a faceless boy with brown eyes.

Mia still believes he's ten and that she's only been in The Aftermath for a few short weeks instead of years. I don't have the heart to tell her I lied. Her brother is at least thirteen, and that's if he's still alive. If he's not in the game, too.

I'll tell her, but after she makes it out. And somehow I'll make sure she finds him if there's anything left to find. I owe her that much for me being a coward and keeping the truth from her.

She and Wesley take a head start once they're finished. I've a feeling Declan put them up to it, but I don't call him on it as we make sure we're not leaving anything important behind. "She's nice," he says.

My lips quiver, and I bend down to zip a compartment in my bag. "You're horrible at small talk, Declan. Just say whatever it is you want to say."

"I'm worried about you."

"Don't be."

"You haven't been the same since we broke out Wes and Mia. I realize I lied, but I need you all here."

Lifting my bag by the straps, I turn to him and smile. I start to speak, but he's in front of me before I manage two words. He covers my mouth with his fingertips. My lips part just a bit, and I involuntarily lean in close to him. "And stop doing that—smiling when you're angry. It makes you look like you've contracted dysentery."

I grab his wrist, pulling his hand from my mouth. He spins us around and pins me to the wall. "Well, I'm not angry," I whisper. "Now let me go."

He shakes his head. "You know, being so close to you...it makes me realize that—" He lets out a frustrated noise.

What?

"I realize that I'm more afraid to leave this game than I've ever been of anything else," he says.

He presses his lips to mine. Static tingles spread across my face—sweet and delicious. My body goes limp as he releases my wrists, skims his fingertips down my arms and to the small of my back. He pulls me even closer to him. So close I can hear and feel our hearts beating. So close every part of me is on fire and I'm not sure if that's a bad thing. All I know is that I don't want this to end. I curl my fingers into his hair. Memorize every angle of his face as his mouth moves against mine.

Gasping, he drags himself away from me. "I know you're tired and I know you're angry, but hold it together, Virtue." He touches my face, rubs the tip of his thumb over my lips once more.

I want to ask him how I'm supposed to do that. I want to know how he could do this to me now, just when we most need to focus. But I say nothing and leave with him, a foot of space between us and a million and one words left unsaid.

We come to a brick house with a pond behind it a few hours later and decide to make it our halfway point. It's quiet and off the beaten path. Nobody will find us here. While Wesley, Mia and Declan rest on the pond bank, I sneak off to see what Olivia's doing.

There's a pile of bricks at the front of the house, and I place my bag against it and sit down. Closing my eyes, I concentrate on getting into my gamer's brain. A moment later, I'm surrounded by utter blackness.

Maybe she's asleep.

Maybe…

Then I hear her murmur something and the world in front of me transforms. Instead of darkness, there's sunlight. Overgrown grass. She's leaning against a pile of bricks, and when she stands up, there's a ramshackle brick home behind her. Three people lounging a few feet away from a murky pond—two boys and one girl.

This is The Aftermath.

This is not Olivia's gaming room—there are no screens or projections or any of that—but she is definitely inside the game. And it's as real as if I were in my own head.

She's playing the game right now—in what must be some type of new gaming platform that makes it seem as if she's physically inside The Aftermath. And I'm not where she left me. Olivia pauses, probably trying to come to grips with what she's seeing. I hear someone ask her something in a frantic voice, but the words are too muffled for me to decipher.

"I've got it under control," Olivia snarls, and I can hear the sound of my own voice speaking in unison. "I can handle this myself, so don't do *anything*."

What is she going to do?

And then, to my horror, she makes me reach for the Glock. I fling myself back into my own mind just as she forces me to charge the gun.

I lock my fingers, dropping my weapon to the ground. My hand twitches. It stretches downward, toward the gun, and I feel as if my arm is being yanked from the rest of my body. I grit my teeth. Clench my fingers into a fist. Try to keep myself upright and my hand away from the—

Olivia forces me to grab the Glock. Compels me to walk several steps toward the pond. She plans to kill Declan and Mia and Wesley, and I can't let that happen.

I drag myself to my knees and dig my fingernails into the dirt and grass. I can feel her trying to maneuver my body and it burns. Like buckets of scalding water being poured over my skin. I have to bite my tongue not to scream.

I see Declan glance up at me and frown. I try to shake my head, but all I manage to do is twist my neck into an unnatural position. He rises from his spot beside the pond. "Don't," I make myself say as loudly as I can. But he doesn't listen. He's by my side before I can mutter another word, kneeling over me. Before I can stop myself—stop Olivia—my elbow jabs into his forehead.

He doesn't even falter. Grabbing my wrists, he stares down into my eyes and says, "Virtue?"

My foot draws up and kicks him in the knee. We both tumble to the ground. When his arms tighten around mine, pinning them to my sides, I'm not sure if it's for my own protection or to prevent me from hurting him.

"Leave me… *How could you be so stup*— Get out of… *You've ruined everything and now there's nothing*— Olivia, stop it!"

I scramble back into her head. I imagine all the horrible things she's made me do and say. All the characters she's forced me to murder. I imagine how I want to choke her right now. Her hands move up unwillingly and wrap around her own neck. The Aftermath dissipates, and now she's staring up at a sleek metallic white wall and a blue light flashing right above her eyes, gagging.

Declan was right. I can control her.

I concentrate on blocking her out of my mind, and I fall back into The Aftermath, landing in my own head. The hold over my body is gone, and I'm on my side, wheezing. Tears trickle down my face. "I wasn't paying attention— I should have known," I say to Declan. "I should have questioned what she was doing. Should have known to check in on her more."

When his eyes turn hard and he steps away from me, I know he's finally aware of everything I can do.

CHAPTER TWENTY-TWO

"You can see what she's seeing." Declan's voice is a low growl. I hear his footsteps come closer, feel the fury breathing down my neck. "Claudia...say something!" The pile of bricks to my right tumbles over. He curses sharply. My body tenses up as I carve half-moon indentations into my palms with my fingernails.

Then he touches my bare shoulder blades. I shiver because his touch contradicts his anger. It's soft as weightless cotton, and warm, too. Dangerous. I start to inch away as he trails his fingertips across my shoulders, but then he tugs me gently around so that I'm facing him. His face is red and pinched.

When he speaks again, his words hiss out between clenched teeth, like air seeping from a broken valve. "You know everything she does."

I tilt my head to one side and locate Wesley and Mia edging far away from us. They go around to the back of the house, toward the pond, pretending like they're looking for something. Wesley's gray eyes meet mine for a split second and he mouths something that looks like, "I'm so sorry." I can't be sure. Still, I want to mouth back, "Coward."

Mia never lifts her dark eyes from the ground.

"Not everything," I whisper at last. I want to break away from

Declan. Run into the woods and forget all this. Except then I'll be alone again.

"But you can get inside of her head? You can see what it is she's seeing?"

"Yes."

"Don't you think you could've told me?" he demands. "Do you know how useful what you do is? How could you be so ridiculously selfish?"

I feel as though everything in the game is crumbling around me. The old brick house Mia and Wesley dart in and out of as they try to avoid and listen in on our argument. The blades of scorched grass, sharp as they slice into my sunburned skin. The sun itself.

And suddenly I realize I'm shaking. I tremble as if it's thirty degrees out here instead of more than triple that. My ears ring.

I want to hit Declan.

A tingling sensation races through my head, from the center to my forehead. It's been so long since Olivia's actually managed to power me down that I've forgotten what it feels like. It's not at all pleasant. My head jars forward, then back, like a rag doll. One moment I see Declan's face and the next I see other faces—Dr. Coleman, the man with the moon-shaped scar, the group of men and women in suits from one of my first memories, the faces of people my hands are responsible for killing in the game. I press my fingertips to my temples, but it does nothing to stop the pain. "We should keep moving," I pant.

If I don't walk away, I will hit Declan. And Olivia has nothing to do with my urge to do it.

A strange sound hitches in his throat. He shakes his head. "Definitely not. Not until we—"

I shove my sweaty palms into his chest. He staggers back. Stares at me with wide incredulous eyes as I scoop my bag off the ground and stalk past him toward the house. Every step makes me feel as if my brain is on the verge of blowing up. I have to pause several times to gather my bearings.

"Wesley, Mia, we're going!" I shout, glaring at them through squinted eyes.

They're sitting on a brown floral-patterned couch in the den. Both are holding CDS packages but neither has opened theirs. "Didn't you hear me?" I ask. "We're leaving."

Mia wrinkles her nose at me and stands up. She puts her food into the pocket of her shorts before walking silently past me and out the front door.

Wesley gets up, too, and gestures toward the doorway with his chin. Declan is leaning against it, his face contorted and fists clenched. "Wouldn't you rather resolve your issues with him first?" Wesley asks, concerned.

I take a deep breath, and then I turn with my arms outstretched. Like I'm inviting Declan to take a shot at me. "Sure, why not." I hand my gun to Wesley, glaring at Declan all the while. "But just so you know, there's a psychotic gamer trying to get into my head at this very moment, and she's really, really pissed off." My words are slurred because the static current is creeping down my face. Declan takes a step closer when I drag my hands through my hair, screaming, but I back away from him.

"Don't touch me," I growl.

A muscle twitches in Declan's jaw. He comes over anyway. He waves his fingers toward the door and Wesley leaves, glancing at me over his shoulder as he steps into the sunlight.

This time, I call him the word that's on my mind. *"Coward."*

Flesh-eating, overly friendly coward.

"We're alone now. So come on, moderator—I want to hear what you have to say."

"You didn't have to lie to me," Declan says.

I shake my head, trying to let his words settle. They don't. "You're such a hypocrite. You knew who I was the moment you saw me. You evade the truth for weeks to get my help—you use me—and now you're angry with me for keeping this from you."

He swallows hard. "What do you mean I knew who you were?"

"I remember what happened back in the courthouse. I know you're the one who hit me, who made it possible for me to be like this."

His expression hardens. "I was trying to hit the boy. Ethan. I was looking for my brother, and I thought you were flesh-eaters." There's something different about his voice when he says this—something that I can't quite pinpoint—and I hug myself tightly.

"Then why didn't you just tell me?"

"Look, I—" But then he stops and shakes his head. "Claudia, there's a lot that I haven't been able to tell you… I hope you can understand."

He's looking at me so intently, and I know he's about to say something important. But the buzzing is back, starting in my skull and seeping down my spine. My hearing goes hazy, and my vision, too. I try to move my body, but I only manage to take two steps. I can't walk or flick my hand or turn my head. I can't do anything but stand perfectly still, with my fingers reaching out for something in front of me, and my lips parted. It's as though someone has shoved a needle into my veins, injecting ice into my bloodstream, freezing me.

Declan is by my side. He cups my face between his hands, says something. But I can't hear him. All I hear is a loud hum, like flies inside my head. I stare helplessly at him. Before I go under, my hands reach for his throat and Olivia makes me say, "I'll make you wish you were dead for betraying me."

I hover somewhere between delusion and reality for a few endless moments before I'm sucked completely into the dream—one where

I'm standing in the middle of a playground, the one from The Aftermath that Declan had taken me to. There's nobody else around, and the only noise comes from the swings as the wind rattles the chains, making a sound that reminds me of chimes.

It makes me feel cold.

Tentatively, I sit down on one of the swings and grasp the chain with both hands. "Wake up, Virtue," I whisper in a furious voice. "Wake up now."

A firm but gentle hand clamps over my shoulder. My heart feels as if it's jumped into my throat, and I jolt up off the swing. Stumbling around, I look at the girl standing behind me.

I'm staring at myself. The person I would be if I never entered The Aftermath. My face is filled out—there's color in my cheeks and the dark circles that have become a permanent fixture beneath my eyes are gone. My ear is whole, too, and my hair is long and brown, just like it was when the last memory hit me while I was here. Mesmerized, I take a step forward toward myself, expecting the hallucination to disappear.

It doesn't.

"Wake up now," she orders. "You have got to wake up."

"I'm trying to."

She shakes her head in frustration. "You're not trying anything. Get up. Break free. You've got to help yourself or they'll kill you first and ask questions later."

"Then help me," I plead. "You're me— You get me out of this."

"This is something you have to do yourself." There's a strange smile on her face as she says this. "Use that anger, that violence that got you here in the first place."

Even though I know this is nothing but a dream, I lunge forward. "I am not violent," I growl. I punch her as hard as I can, but my fist goes right through her body, banging into a metal post instead. Pain shoots through my arm, and I hug it to my chest.

The corners of the other Claudia's mouth lift up as she turns to me. "Yes, you are. We all are. So focus that energy and wake up *right* now."

"Claudia." I hear Declan's voice. It sounds far away and fuzzy, like a bad cell phone connection.

The hallucination grabs my chin, turning my face to hers. "Go back now!" she snaps. "If you stay here, you won't be able to leave and they will delete you. Is that what you want?"

"Claudia, come back." Declan's voice is a fraction closer this time. A hundred miles away instead of a thousand.

"You're taking too long," the other Claudia whispers. "And we're not getting killed. Not today. I'm so sorry about this—about everything."

"Sorry about—" But my words are cut off when her fist slams into my head.

Then my world goes dark.

I wake up on a couch with Declan hovering over me, shaking my shoulders. My breath comes rushing into me, and I gasp.

He presses an open water bottle to my lips. I drink it greedily, choking and coughing when I squeeze the plastic too hard. "Careful," he warns. He helps me sit up.

My brain is blurry, as though there's static humming through my head—in one ear and out the other.

"I thought you were—" he swallows hard, pinches the bridge of his nose and takes a tremulous breath "—dying. You stopped breathing a few times. And you kept swinging out at nothing. I didn't know wha—"

"A dream. A horrible dream of myself."

He sinks down onto his knees in front of me. Clasping my hands between his, he leans his forehead against mine. Out of the corner of my eye, I see strands of his dark hair intermingling with mine. "And what did she—or you—say to yourself?"

"I tried to punch her." I don't tell him that I actually wanted to hit him for all the lies, that I was taking all that aggression out where it was safe to let my anger loose. Because I'm *still* angry.

He gives my hands a tiny reassuring squeeze, and then he laughs. This is a good sound because it's the first genuine one I've heard from him in a while. I feel it vibrating through my entire body. "You can't hit what's not there, Virtue."

I clench my right hand, but the pain that raced through it on the playground is gone. "Look, before we leave I want to say I'm sorry," I say. "About before."

"Don't apologize for Olivia."

I don't have the energy to tell him I'm not apologizing for what Olivia said or did—I'm saying sorry for my own words and actions. So I give him a tiny ghost of a smile. He leans away from me, so that we are still eye to eye, and brushes damp strands of hair from my face.

"We had better go," I say.

"Claudia."

"It doesn't matter if Olivia knows. Or if she tries to get into my head every twenty minutes. I'm stronger than it—than her—I think. We can get out." Part of me still believes this. Another part knows I'm better off staying put, saving every ounce of my strength for the fight that's bound to happen.

"Claudia," he says.

"Where are Wesley and Mia? Where's my backpack? Where—"

He presses his mouth to mine, drowning my words. Drowning my thoughts. Consuming me. His lips are soft, warm, but I shiver none- theless. He moves his body close again, running his fingers up my neck and entwining them into my hair. And I decide something. I will stay in this smoldering room in this strange, uncomfortable position all day if it means he won't let me go.

But then there are several raps on the window, and I open my eyes. Wesley presses his face to the glass. He's grinning, saying something, but I'm too dazed to understand. I pull away and press my back into the corner of the couch. Shift my eyes to a large rip in the fabric.

Declan puts something heavy on my lap. My bag. "Claudia, I have to tell you something else. Something that—"

"No," I say. Because that *something* is probably just more lies. And right now I can't take not knowing if he's telling me the truth. I avoid his eyes. "Forget it, Declan. Let's just do this, get out, okay?"

"But—"

"Just leave it alone," I snap, and our intimate moment is gone. I stalk out of the brick house, into the open air. Declan follows, reluctantly, yelling for Wesley and Mia to join us.

And as we walk together, away toward the hazy horizon, my anger melts away. Declan looks at me and smiles questioningly, and before I know what I'm doing, I'm smiling back. His fingertips find mine. Gentle and hesitant. And I know this is as safe as I'll ever feel within The Aftermath—hunted by my gamer and probably by mods very soon.

CHAPTER TWENTY-THREE

I don't trust myself with Declan—hell, I still don't trust him after all the lies he's told me—so I break apart from him after a few minutes and walk next to Mia. Every couple hundred yards, she catches my eye and grins.

"I'm guessing you two will continue that once we're out?" she says, jumping up and tapping a low-hanging tree branch with the palm of her hand. "And don't make that face. Wesley told me what he saw."

When I turn my head to glare at him, Wesley waves cheerfully. We're in more danger than ever before, and they're all grins and laughter. But I suppose it makes dealing with the threat of capture a little less crushing. I shake my head. "I doubt Declan and I will see much of one another after this."

He can tell me a million times that he has no plan to disappear on me within the next twenty-four hours, but I've prepared for the worst. Once The Aftermath is behind us, there are no promises binding him to me. And as much as I want to kiss him again, I'm not sure that's a bad thing. I'm starting to think that I need to start over, away from his lies. Alone.

"Don't be ridiculous," she says. "Everybody needs someone. I have my brother."

I pick up a rock and skip it along the forest floor. My stomach churns. Sooner or later I'll have to tell her the truth and prepare her for the worst. I feel guilty. I've been so angry at Declan for lying to me for so long, and I'm doing the same thing right now, to Mia.

"Look, there's something I have to—"

"What the hell is that?" Wesley runs past us, maneuvering through the trees until he disappears. The rest of us race after him. I'm terrified, and my heart lodges in my throat. Twigs snag my hair and clothing and rake across bare areas of skin. At last I break through the canopy of trees with Mia close behind.

Towering piles of rocks and stones, every texture and color, lie in front of us. "You scared me like that because you saw a rock yard?" I hiss at Wesley.

He shrugs. Bouncing on his toes, he points behind the labyrinth of stones. "There's a building, too. If we're going to make it to the border before the mods start showing up, we'd better get rid of anything we don't need." He has a good point, but I scowl at him anyway. Declan slams his bag into his brother's chest.

"Don't run off like that again."

"Here, take mine, too," I say, hanging my strap on Wesley's wrist. He frowns at us, then trudges off toward the building. Mia catches up to him and takes my backpack, slinging it onto her back. I glance over at Declan. My lips tingle when our eyes connect. "I need to… check on Olivia."

"I'll wait with you… Besides, I need to talk to you."

But I shake my head. "Not now, Declan. This is something I have to do alone," I say. So far I've done a good job keeping her out of my brain, but I don't want to risk her taking control of me again with anybody nearby. I won't let them jeopardize their lives for me.

"You don't have to face this by yourself, you know. There are people who care about you. More people than you think."

Hearing him say that only puts more pressure on me. It leaves me feeling weighed down, as though there are ten tons sitting atop my shoulders right now. I feel as if I'm going to be sick. "I know," I say. "That's why I'm asking you to leave."

He touches his lips to my forehead. "If you need me—"

"I will," I whisper.

"Okay. But we're going to have to talk sooner or later, Claudia."

I wait until he disappears inside the building to lean back against a pile of rocks and try to access Olivia's brain. My head still hurts from the hallucination, but I manage to slip in just a bit. Even though I can't get a clear image of what she sees, I hear snippets of conversations.

"I can find her myself," Olivia growls. "I don't need your help."

"We're dispatching guards to—"

"She's *my* character! I'm responsible for her!"

I float halfway between my brain and hers, so when I hear the shuffle of footsteps, I'm not sure where it's coming from. But then I recognize the noise—Declan's boots. I release my grip on her mind and turn to him. "I told you—"

But this isn't Declan. It's a dark-haired man who's dressed like him. A real moderator.

The punch to my face literally sweeps me off my feet. I fall hard, my entire backside a dartboard for the jagged gravel. Getting hit doesn't daunt me. I'm so used to being knocked around, I don't feel the pain. He rushes me again, but I roll over and scramble to my feet. I swoop up one of the larger rocks—it's as big as my shoe—and hurl it at him. It hits him square in the forehead. Sends him collapsing into a bed of stone.

I don't have time to savor this small victory. Another mod with floppy blond hair comes at me, this time with a fist to my stomach. The air whooshes from my lungs. My body convulses. Dust flies into my face, sticking to my eyelashes and clogging my nostrils, and I realize I'm on the ground. Again.

The blond man digs rough fingers into my shoulders and yanks me up into a sitting position. He shakes me back and forth until my teeth clack together violently. Maybe he'll shake the block in my head loose. Or maybe he'll simply kill me now. "You'll be deleted for this," he growls. "Probably a public deletion. And I hope I'm there when they fry your brain to ashes."

I bring my knee to my chest to kick him, but he slams me back, pinning my wrists to the ground. Grinning, he sits on top of my stomach. I dry heave. When I catch my breath, I rasp, "Why wait? Why not kill me now?"

Olivia has corrupted me, made me into a stupid, reckless girl.

He chuckles and shakes his head. "After the stunt your boyfriend pulled last year when he escaped, you really think you deserve anything but a broadcasted deletion?" He leans in close to me and adds, "Besides, there's a bonus for whoever bags you and brings you in alive."

"What do you mean there's a bonus?" My words come out choppy and hoarse.

"Don't play stupid. You're a big deal to Lancaster and you know it," he says. When I draw in a sharp breath, he presses his face so close to mine our foreheads nearly touch. "You're sending me on vacation early this year."

This is not the first time that I've heard that I was a big deal. Hadn't Jeremy said those exact words to April when they were talking about Olivia and me weeks ago? I swallow hard. "Why?" I demand. "I'm just a character. I'm nobody."

The man snorts. "Maybe you really are stupid."

I writhe and struggle against the blond man. He squeezes my wrists harder, digging his nails into my skin until I shriek.

"Do you really think you can hurt me? Do you really think th—"

I swing my head up with all my might and bash my forehead into his nose. Blood spurts in my face, and he grabs his, howling. Survival instincts from three years of getting chased and beaten kick in. Bucking my hips wildly, I pull down on one of his shoulders and push up on the other, thrashing my forehead at his face all the while.

He falls off me, bloody and shouting obscenities. I clamber to my feet. He tries to do the same, but I knee him in the nose, knocking him unconscious. I grab my knife from the ground and a handful of zip ties from the dead mod's pocket. I quickly restrain the man's wrists and ankles. I'm tightening the last plastic tie just as he comes to.

"We'll just keep tracking you down!" he slurs as I stand up and back away from him. Narrowing my eyes, I shove the remaining zip ties in my back pocket and take off in the direction of Mia's screams. "We'll just keep tracking your chip, Virtue!"

He continues to yell at me, but I don't look back. I don't need to because I already have a sinking feeling I'll see his face again at my execution. My face has started to swell. It feels as if I'm traveling through a dark tunnel as I race toward the others, bumping into stacks of stones every few steps. Finally I emerge from the maze and see the rusted metal building.

Mia is pinned to the side of it by a female moderator who dwarfs her tiny body. Two large men are cuffing Declan and Wesley. Declan's dark gray eyes settle on me and his shoulders sag a little, like he's relieved. He casts a quick glance a few feet away from me, where his bag lies on the ground, the contents spilling out on the asphalt. I rush to it and pick up the electroshock gun. I've yet to use it, but I remember his instructions.

Release safety.

Wait for the light.

Pull the trigger.

And never touch the amp setting.

I crank the amps to as high as it will go, point it at the girl who's choking Mia and wait for the target light to blink. Then I pull the trigger. She lands facedown in a pile of gravel. I hold my breath as the breeze knocks the odor of burned skin into my face.

Mia staggers toward me, sobbing, but I whirl around and aim the gun at the other two moderators. "Step back with your hands up," I growl. "Or I'll send enough electricity through you to kill five people."

My heart is the only sound I hear as I wait for someone—anyone—to speak. The moderator holding Wesley down glances at me and says something. Then he reaches into his pocket. I pull the trigger once, twice, before he has a chance to remove his hand. He falls. The other man backs away from Declan, his hands stretched high above his head in surrender.

"Shoot him." Declan's voice thunders over the sound of my heartbeat. Slowly, other noises come back to me—my own breathing, Mia's quiet sobs, the blond mod shouting horrible threats from where I left him tied up in the stone labyrinth.

I stare between Declan and the moderator. They're both bloodied and ragged, breathing heavily.

"Claudia…"

I shake my head. "No. We're leaving. Right now." Keeping the electroshock gun focused on the moderator, I pull the rest of the zip ties from my pocket and drop them into Mia's hand. I jerk my head at Wesley. "Hurry up and cuff him." I want to get out of this place before LanCorp sends another group after us. I'm not sure how many others are here, or how they arrived in the first place, but I don't want to stick around to find out.

Declan gathers his belongings, then comes to examine my face. When he reaches out to touch my forehead, I flinch. I leave him to make sure the cuffs are secure. As I tighten the moderator's restraints, I catch Declan's eyes. He looks confused. Hurt.

I can't let him touch me, because I know now that no matter what I want, it might be impossible for me to stay with him.

We travel through the woods, putting a mile of distance between the moderators and ourselves before we stop to rest. Wesley says it will take LanCorp longer to find us this way because they won't expect us to stop so soon. I don't have the heart to tell him that, if the blond mod is to be believed, there's a chance LanCorp already knows exactly where we are because of *my* chip. So I stay silent, and I hope that the moderator was lying. As my group huddles beneath a towering pine to talk about our next move, I find myself moving away to protect them. From the mods. From Olivia.

And most of all from myself.

There's a vicious rattling deep within my head. I imagine it's like someone shaking a single screw around in a thin glass bottle. Still, I grit my teeth and carry on until I no longer hear Declan and Wesley yelling at each other and I can see a creek bed in the distance. I struggle to ignore the pain and the fuzzy thoughts that race through my brain, but finally I can't help but give in.

And the clarity of this particular thought—the images and voices—is strong enough to bring me to my knees.

"I hate this, Livvie. When's it my turn to play?" I ask. My voice is a whispery lisp. Sweet and childlike because that's what I am. A child. Hopeful.

Olivia's turned away from me, with her head bent. Bright red ribbons pull half her dark hair from her face. She drags a small digital tablet from her blue dress and places it beside her. "Beat me at chess first."

"You'll win. You always do."

"Then you'll never play the game, will you?"

Leaning against a tree, I vomit. Is this a memory? Or are the moderators simply screwing with my head—forcing thoughts into my brain just to slow me down? I wipe my mouth with the back of my hand and stand upright. As I wobble down to the creek, I pray it won't happen again.

Then someone touches my shoulder and I spin around, lifting my fists.

Declan stares down at me. "You saved our asses back there, Virtue."

But it was instinct. An ironic gift from my gamer. Even though Olivia has been controlling my movements, my brain retained every survival technique, every strategy.

"It was nothing." I try to relax, but it only makes the muscles in my shoulders tighten even more. Declan shouldn't be around me. Nobody should. He raises his eyebrow when I take a step backward, drawing my attention to an open cut that runs across his eyelid. "God, you're hurt," I whisper.

"It's nothing." But he winces. And I know that if we remain together, the next time he won't be so lucky. "We'll have to start moving again if—"

"The moderators found us because of me, didn't they?"

Silence. And that tells me everything I want to know. His nostrils flare as he drops his gray eyes to the forest floor to stare at a pile of broken leaves. I stand perfectly still, wringing my hands together.

It takes a lot of effort not to use them to attack him.

"How long were you going to wait before telling me that LanCorp was going to use my chip to track us down?" I ask. "Were you going to wait until Wesley or Mia got hurt or even killed? Or were you going to tell me as the mods dragged me away?"

"It doesn't matter what they can do because I plan to take down anyone who tries to hurt you."

A heavy weight settles on my chest. All hope that the blond man was lying about the mods using me to track us down disappears along with the little I have left of making it out of this game without being captured.

"You lied about not lying," I say. "But then, what's new?"

"Guess that makes two of us with trust issues."

I draw in a breath so deep it burns my nose. Digging my fingernails into my palms, I walk closer to him until he has no other choice but to face me, eye to eye. "Declan, I need to know if all that talk about being unable to disconnect my link to Olivia was a bunch of bullshit, too." I never thought I'd pray for something to be a lie, but I want to hear that I'm fixable. I want to be able to stay with these people.

"What do you—"

Before I can stop myself, I shove my hands against his chest, sending him stumbling backward a few steps. "Answer me! No more lies. No deflecting the question. Just give it to me straight, Declan. You owe me that," I shout.

Grabbing his chest, he lets out a hoarse noise that almost sounds like a laugh. Almost. "The entitlement. I swear you're just like—" But then he stops himself. Squeezes his eyes shut as he pulls in a harsh breath. "No, it wasn't bullshit. I've known from the day I met you that your link wasn't the same. That the connection between you and your gamer is something different."

I think of the way he rubbed the blue scanner across the crown of my head. The way he kept drawing his eyebrows together. My chest aches. "Then you must know why it's different."

"I didn't come up with the games, Claudia," he growls. "So, no, I have no explanation for why you're special, Virtue."

Something special that will get me captured—that will get everyone else killed. The moderators can easily track me because I'm still linked to Olivia. The longer I stay with Declan and Wesley and Mia, the more moderators and guards will come after us. My head will be the death of us all if I don't go.

"I'm going off on my own, Declan. And you're not going to follow me."

He cups my face in his hands, his gray eyes burning into mine. "Don't be stupid, Virtue. You need me with you if only to find your—"

But the longer we stay here arguing, the more likely it is that we'll be found. And I won't risk letting him or the others get captured. "I don't think you understand, Declan. I *don't* need you. I never have." Lowering my gaze so I no longer have to look him in the eyes, I clear my throat and then whisper, "In fact, I want nothing more to do with you now that I know the way out of here."

CHAPTER TWENTY-FOUR

Declan doesn't try to talk me out of leaving. It wouldn't work even if he tried, but it physically hurts when he turns his back on me and stalks away, leaving me with nothing. No goodbye. No more words of anger. Absolutely nothing.

It's better this way, I tell myself.

But if I'm so much better off, why does the knife in my chest twist deeper?

I say goodbye to Mia first. She cries. I pinch my fingers into the flesh on my thighs so I won't do the same. "I don't want you to go," she says.

"I don't want you to die."

She lunges at me, throwing her arms around my upper body and squeezing. God, I don't want to let her go. She smells dusty, like gravel, but it's the best scent I've ever inhaled. I want more time with her.

I draw back from her and take her face between my hands. "Listen to me, I wasn't honest with you. You've been in this game at least three years, and I'm so very sorry I kept that from you." She tries to speak, but I shake my head. "If I can get out, I'll find you. We'll find Daniel together." *If there's anything left to find,* I add silently, and I know she's thinking the same thing. The expression on her face leaves no doubt. She nods, and I hug her again.

Wesley walks with me for a quarter mile in the opposite direction, trying his best to get me to reconsider. "What the hell do you plan on doing?" he demands. "If they find you…"

"There's no if. The question is when they'll pick me up."

"I don't want you to go."

I don't want to go, either. But I smile up at him. His light gray eyes are narrowed. "Don't look at me like that," I say. "I'll just bring you guys down. You have a better chance of reaching the border while the mods are playing hide-and-seek with me."

"Claudia…"

"Which means you should go. Now. Before they show up. Why risk yourself?"

Tentatively, Wesley touches my ear and frowns. "Because I feel like I owe it to you."

He doesn't. His player owes me, but not him. I launch myself at him and squeeze my arms around him. "Go. Please?"

He hugs me back, pressing his cheek hard against the top of my head. Right on top of my Cerebrum Chip. I open my mouth to give him a message for Declan, but then I bite my lip and shake my head. "You never told me what you plan on doing when you get out."

His eyes are suddenly hard. "I'm going after Thomas Lancaster."

I leave Wesley, the boy who attacked me three years ago and now is my friend, standing in the middle of the road, dragging his hands through his short hair. I don't look back until I've walked a good ten minutes and the only thing behind me is a blurry empty road. Only then do I stop. I drink a bottle of water and shift through the contents of my bag. Three more bottles. Two CDS packets. And Declan's Triple C.

If I am going off on my own, I'm going to do things my way. I'm going to go back to that bar and save the people who I thought I cared about—since everyone else I care for is gone.

I am so thirsty I can no longer swallow.

Five hours ago, I stopped keeping track of how many miles I've walked. All I know is there's a lump in my throat, my muscles ache and every noise makes me twitch and look over my shoulder. I walk a little longer, humming a song that's both familiar and strange. I'm going crazy. By the time I'm deleted, I won't even feel a thing because I'll be so out of it.

The warehouse we stopped in right after deactivating Mia and Wesley comes into view. I hobble to it, hoping nobody has taken up shelter here since then.

It's empty.

I return to the little room we holed up in for half an hour. I huddle in the corner and rest my head against the wall. Crumbled CDS wrappers litter the cracked concrete floor, and I close my eyes tightly so I don't have to think of my friends. It doesn't help. I remember how the four of us sat around eating, talking. Sharp pangs grip my chest. The first normal conversation I can remember, and most of it was probably a lie. Still, I miss Wesley and Mia.

I take tiny sips of water through a split lip, struggling to stay awake, and hate myself for missing Declan, too. I leave the warehouse after fifteen minutes. I can't afford to stay any longer than that. Olivia hasn't tried to get into my head for hours. Another person might consider themselves lucky, but not me. I'm waiting for everything to come falling down around me. And I'm too afraid to risk going into her head to try to find out when that will happen. LanCorp might be trying to put me in Rehabilitation again. If I open myself up to Olivia and they succeed, Declan's not nearby to shake me out of my gamer's tight grip.

"This will all be over soon," I whisper as I break through the forest. I stare out at the asphalt in front of me, stretching miles to the west.

I walk. Farther away from the border. Away from Wesley and Mia. Away from Declan. Back into the poisonous cage.

The lights are on inside the bar. I didn't even realize the place had working electricity; it makes me pause. I crouch down in the alley across the street. There's a pile of clothes to my left that smells like urine, and I pull the neck of my shirt over the lower portion of my face.

What if my clan is no longer here? Olivia and The Aftermath's staff has known about my ability for a couple of days now, so that means my old friends—the characters—might know, too. Maybe they moved to avoid a confrontation. But then I shake that thought from my head. Olivia is proud. She'd never tell anyone that I escaped, especially her gamer friends. She cares too much about her reputation.

I sit unmoving, like a character whose gamer has signed off, as the sun sets. Then I see something move on the second floor. My heart catapults into my throat as Jeremy peeks out a section of unpainted window. They are still here.

I wait, counting the seconds to make sure nobody is around.

I'll go into the bar and deactivate their chips one by one. If I'm lucky, the majority of the other gamers will log off and I won't have to put up with a struggle.

And while I'm waiting for the characters to wake up, for their minds to leave Rehabilitation behind, I'll get into Olivia's head. Bait her. Maybe I'll take control of her again. That'll give my clan a fighting chance of escape while she sends the moderators or whoever after me. She may plan to delete me, but I already know it won't be right away. If that was the case, my life would have ended more than a day ago, when the moderators came after us at the rock yard—they were told to capture, not kill. She must want something else from me first.

I take out my gun and cock it. This has to be the dumbest plan I've ever come up with, more irresponsible than any raid I've ever been on. But I know that if I die after all this, I won't feel as guilty. Freeing the others won't make up for the people I killed while under Olivia's control, but it's better than escaping the game and leaving them behind to rot.

I dash across the street and into the alley. One of the windows is unlocked. I shimmy through it, groaning when I drop to the floor and pain shoots through my legs and hips.

It's dark inside, and I creep across the hardwood floor, feeling around with my free hand for anything I might bump into. I reach the stairs. I climb them slowly. When I reach the top, I turn in the direction of The Save. My body is shaking as I pull the door open and step inside.

I slip on something wet and sticky. The air whooshes out of me as I hit the floor, and it takes me a minute to gather my bearings enough to climb up on my hands and knees to see what I stepped on.

Blood.

My heart jumps into my throat—falls out of my chest—and I strangle a scream. It's still warm. When I cover my mouth quickly to hold back vomit, I can smell it and something else.

Charred flesh.

I scramble backward—away from the puddle. Away from death. My back bangs into the bed. A soft arm dangles into my face, smacking me in the forehead. A dead body.

No. No. *No.*

I stumble to my feet and look down at the person lying on the bed.

246

Short dark hair, a singed forehead and terrified brown eyes. Jeremy. I squeeze my eyes shut for a moment to stop the tears burning the corners. Then I open them, scanning the room to see if April and Ethan are here—if their bodies are here.

"We thought we'd find you here, Virtue," a voice says behind me. I turn around slowly to face a man. He's dressed differently from the other moderators—in a light-colored uniform with the LanCorp insignia on the front. And he's smiling. "If you'll kindly come with us so that nobody gets hurt, we have a few—"

I lift the Glock and pull the trigger, cutting him off midsentence. There's a look of surprise on his face as he falls next to the blood on the floor.

I don't really care that three other people come barging in and send electricity thrumming through my veins.

This time when I pass out, there's no other Claudia. No memories. No voices or out-of-body experiences, either. There's just me, suspended in blackness and silence and pain. Like a puppet dangling in a dark room with a million needles poking into her flesh. I don't have time to ask myself if I'm alive. Something shocks the back of my neck, and I convulse. I open my eyes, shrieking and choking on my own vomit, unable to move because I'm cuffed to a chair.

"Welcome back," a man says, placing one hand on either side of my seat. He leans down so that his face hovers right over mine. He glances at his watch. "You've been out for nearly half an hour, Virtue." My vision is hazy, and I have to squint so I can get a clear view of him. Short and stocky, with close-cropped auburn hair and a smooth face. He's wearing the same outfit as the man I killed upstairs.

As he smiles down at me with straight teeth, I picture him with longer hair that brushes his collar, gapped teeth and a pockmarked face. Before he's able to speak again, I hear myself murmur, "Bennett."

"Glad to see you remember me, Claudia. I'll be escorting you out of the game, to meet with Mr. Lancaster," he says.

I remember him almost too vividly. He escorted me just over three years ago, too. To a blue-lighted laboratory where I was surrounded by machines—some transparent, some stainless steel and others the same metallic white of the Regenerator. I'd turned to him, with tears streaming down my face. "What he's doing to me is wrong."

"You're a character now in LanCorp's newest game." He'd avoided my eyes, but when I tried to jerk away from him, he'd pressed an electroshock gun to my rib cage. "And if you try something reckless, I will electrocute you, Virtue. I don't care who you are."

As the memory dissolves, I look up into his eyes. "You killed Jeremy," I whisper accusingly. I won't say anything about the memory. Why bring up something that doesn't fully make sense to me?

He leans back. "Well, you killed Anthony, did you not?"

I don't even flinch when he tells me the name of the person I shot. Nor do I point out that Jeremy was dead before I made the move to do it. I swallow hard and choke out, "Where's April and Ethan?"

"Where's Hastings?"

I stare at him, unblinking. Unsure of what he's talking about. After a moment of silence, he grits his teeth and shakes me. The cuffs around my wrists bite into my flesh. "Where's Hastings?" he repeats.

"I've no idea who the hell you're talking about," I say.

He hits me. So hard I taste blood and spit. "Don't be an idiot, girl. Declan Hastings, the boy you've been traveling with. Dark hair, gray eyes—a sarcastic little prick?"

Declan. Of course that's who he's talking about. I feel stupid for not catching on to Bennett immediately and even more ignorant for never asking Declan what his last name was. Funny to halfway fall for a boy when I don't even know his full name.

But even if I'd asked, what's to say he would've told me the truth? Just about everything that came out of Declan's mouth was a lie.

"I don't know where he is."

Seething, Bennett draws back to hit me again, but then he catches himself. Balls up his fist. He looks over his shoulder to where the two other men stand at attention with their hands behind their backs and feet spread apart.

"Get me the other two characters," he orders.

My heart jumps as the men go into the basement. They wouldn't bring back dead bodies. Ethan and April must be alive. A few minutes later, my thoughts are confirmed when the rest of my former clan is led into the bar. The men force them down on their knees and position electroshock guns on the backs of their heads, execution-style.

I try to keep all emotion off my face. If I pretend as though these people mean nothing to me, they won't be hurt. I narrow my eyes. "What are they here for?"

Bennett gestures to the man behind April, and he nods. He tangles his hand into her red hair, then jerks her head up. Her face is bloody, bruised. And when our eyes meet, there's fear in hers.

She's sentient.

I draw a painful breath into my lungs. Shift my eyes away from her quickly. "You get off on torturing someone who's helpless?" I ask, my voice cracking midsentence.

"Where's Hastings?"

"I. Don't. Know."

April lets out a scream that echoes throughout the room, and she sags forward, her face down toward the floor. I can see her tears dripping onto the hardwood.

"You would go off with a stranger with no clue where he's going?" Bennett demands.

"Of course I knew where he was going. The border. Out of the game."

"And after that?"

I shrug. "Why would he tell me that? I told you—I don't know."

Bennett flicks his hand, and there's a loud thud, followed by Ethan coughing. Out of the corner of my eye, I see him curled into a ball, holding his stomach. He's spitting up blood.

I cringe and squeeze my eyes shut. "Stop it."

"I don't know how," Bennett says, mocking me.

The two men begin beating April and Ethan. Kicking and punching until their fragile bones give, the crunching sound even more deafening than the cries for help. I don't know if either of them realizes that the men have drawn their electroshock guns, but I do. And a moment later, the scent of burned flesh mixes in with the odor of blood and vomit.

I can't watch this. Can't stomach it. But Bennett knew that all along.

"He's going to kill Lancaster," I gasp. "Declan's going to go kill Thomas Lancaster. Are you happy?"

Bennett holds up his hand, and the men stop. "Now was that so hard?" He grins down at me, winking. "We've already caught them, by the way. Your boyfriend and the other two are in custody. In a holding facility."

Suddenly, my chest is on fire and I can't catch my breath. These men just beat my friends—and for absolutely no reason. And LanCorp has Declan. I force myself to breathe in, breathe out. I look up from my lap just as Ethan glances up. Our eyes lock. There's so much fury in his, anger directed toward me, it almost knocks me breathless again.

Then Bennett says to the two guards, "Take these two back to the cellar. Ms. Virtue and I have to catch our ride."

CHAPTER TWENTY-FIVE

In the past several weeks, I've had hundreds of fantasies about the day I would leave The Aftermath. In each and every one of my fantasies, I exit the game happy—utterly unsure of my future but so ecstatic that I made it to Olivia and Declan's world, to the Provinces, away from the horrors of The Aftermath, that nothing else matters.

I am leaving the game now in a car, one of those self-driving vehicles I witnessed once before through my gamer's eyes. I'm so close to the border that if my wrists weren't shackled, I could reach out the car window and skim my hand along the metal. But I'm not happy. I'm not free. Instead, I'm preparing myself.

For whatever will happen to me at The Aftermath's holding facility.

For meeting with Lancaster himself.

For more torture and pain.

For death.

The gates rattle open, and the car speeds through it. For some reason, I expect to feel something—a tingle in my head or a temporary loss of consciousness—but nothing happens. I rest my head against the window. Stare out the tinted glass into the night. There's nothing but forest on either side of the highway. It looks just like the game, and my chest goes numb. Was I fooling myself, thinking that the outside world was something worth fighting for?

Was everything in Olivia's head my imagination—some other sick effect of the injury that started all this?

I feel heat behind my eyes. I drag my gaze down to my fingers. The inside of the car is dark, but I can see the bruises on the backs of them, running up my wrists and forearms. Knocks from the moderators I fought off with Declan and Wesley and Mia. Blows from the guards who killed Jeremy—who may have killed...

Just thinking about my friends sends me reeling forward. I cast a glance at Bennett sitting on my left side. Does he know if the rest of my friends are still alive? Or would he tell me they're gone already.

Deleted.

Dead.

Casualties of The Aftermath.

A few minutes later, the car rolls to a stop in front of a building— the only one around as far as my eyes can see—that must be at least 150 floors high. The wide tinted-glass doors at the lower level slide apart, and the car moves forward, parking on a lift. Is this the holding facility that Bennett had mentioned?

I bounce in my seat to try and peek out the car window as the lift rises up, but Bennett sinks his fingers into my shoulders, slamming me back. Out of instinct, I clasp my hands together and fling them up at his face in an attempt to shake him off me.

He grabs his forehead, and I clamber to the far side of the bench seat. I see a bright green light reflecting off the glass—the lift is on floor number seventy-nine and steadily climbing. Is the creator of The Aftermath waiting for me on one of these floors?

Something slams into the left side of my face—it feels like a brick—

and I sag down with my head spinning. Bennett's face hovers over mine, contorted with rage. There's a gash in the middle of his forehead where the sharp part of my shackles hit him. Blood trickles from it, making a thin line down his nose.

"I will use force against you if necessary," he says. There's a dangerous edge to his voice, and I notice his fingers are wrapped around the hilt of a knife. My knife. I hold back a whimper. "Stay put until we get clearance to go inside."

Waiting for this to happen seems to take an agonizingly long time, and by the time two guards come to the car for me, I'm shaking. They escort Bennett and me into an elevator and take me down more than one hundred stories to the ground floor of the building.

And into a large white cell.

Before Bennett slams the cell door in my face, he says, "Get dressed for your meeting with Mr. Lancaster."

Then I'm left alone. Cold and shivering, with my head spinning from everything that's happened and my stomach in tangles from the quick ride here. I'm so alone it hurts my chest. I sit down on the corner of the small bed in the far corner of the cell. I drag the neatly tucked white quilt over my shoulders. Drape it around my body.

My cell is an extravagance compared to the shelters I lived in while I was in The Aftermath. It's large—the size of four of the prison cells. There's a large square piece of glass on the wall to the left of me and beneath it is a desk complete with a cushiony chair. In the opposite corner of the room is a standing shower with frosted glass. And hanging on the door handle is a towel and a mesh bag with some sort of digital tag attached to it. I'm so dazed that I'm not even aware I've gotten up until I stare directly down at the text scrolling across the thin screen.

Name: Claudia Virtue
ID #: 001-002
Location: THE AFTERMATH
Procedure: Inpatient/Chip Configuration

I know I should be freaking out right now, wondering what the procedure means. But all I can think about is the day I met Declan and how I made up an ID number when he questioned me. Maybe I'm an idiot for thinking about him at a time like this, but there's nothing I want more than to have the chance to tell him he was wrong. There are identification numbers!

I don't think I'll ever get the chance to rub it in. Angry and hopeless, I let the tag drop to the floor and step on it. It crunches under my worn sneakers, a tiny pile of broken machinery on the polished floor.

Someone clears his throat. I spin around, dropping the bag, but there's nobody behind me. Not physically anyway. The glass above the desk shines. A hologram of a man comes out of it and walks across the room toward me. He's staring at me intently. "Good evening, Claudia." Surprisingly, his voice isn't cruel. It's hesitant, questioning.

I take a step in his direction. When I hesitate, stopping halfway between the shower and him, he motions me forward. "Please, come closer. I promise I won't bite."

I comply. Even though he's a hologram and I know he can't possibly hurt me, I keep some distance between us. Hell, even if he could hurt me, there's not a thing I can do to stop him. I'm caged in. It's impossible for me to run. "Who are you?"

"You don't recognize me?"

I do. He's the same man I saw in my gamer's mind the day she complained about the newest version of the game being inadequate. He sat next to Dr. Coleman and he was just as angry as Olivia. But he's not referring to that day. He expects me to have memories of him from the past, before The Aftermath. I don't.

I barely remember myself back then. The few memories that have flitted through my head the past several days are so foggy, I'm unable to separate reality from illusion.

Maybe it's all a fantasy.

When I don't answer him, he says, "I'm Thomas Lancaster. Do you...remember me, Claudia?" I shake my head, and his lips curl down in disappointment. "Are you afraid of me?"

"Are you afraid of me?" I counter.

He chuckles—a sound so creepy, it sends a harsh shudder through me. "Of course not. You're a child, my dear." His expression turns serious and he rubs his chin. "But I'm happy to have a conference with you as soon as I come to the premises. Your...glitch caught me off guard."

A conference. He makes it sound as if we're business partners instead of a diabolical game creator and one of his characters. The corner of my mouth quirks up. "Sorry, maybe next time I glitch I'll try and accommodate your schedule."

"Oh, no, Ms. Virtue. You'll never glitch like this again."

My breath whooshes out of my nostrils as though I've been punched in the stomach. I wrap my arms across my chest. It helps control my trembling. "You're going to delete me?"

"Don't be ridiculous, Claudia. We've had this conversation before, remember? Now, be a good girl and get dressed. The guards will bring your dinner along in an hour or so and I'll be there to speak with you very, very soon."

I've got so many questions. When did we have this talk before? And if he's not going to delete me, what will happen to me? Before I can murmur even a syllable, he holds his hand up and shushes me.

"Do as I've told you," he says. Someone must be speaking to him, because he turns his eyes to the right and shifts his head down slightly, as if he's listening to something. He frowns and growls a command before he addresses me again. "And, Claudia? No fighting the guards. Let's do this without anyone getting hurt. We've already wasted a large sum of money tonight."

Then the image disappears, and the screen looks like thin glass again. "I'm dead," I say over and over again as I stand beneath a heavy stream of hot water in the shower, letting motorized arms that extend from the tile walls wash my body with soft sponges and soaps and perfumes.

I dress in the clothes I find in the bag—baggy underclothes and oversize starched pants and a shirt. There are white sandals, too, that hurt my blistered feet when I slide them on. I wait huddled on my bed until there's a high-pitched sound at the desk and a tray of food comes up on a stand. When I pull the tray off the platform, it disappears, and the wood closes back together. As I turn to go back to my bed, I catch a glimpse of Bennett outside my cell door. I rush forward.

"Is Lancaster here yet?" I ask, but he shakes his head. He's covered the gash on his forehead with a large white bandage. Probably just a placeholder until he can get to a Regenerator.

"Eat," he orders. Then he disappears.

I don't want to eat the food. Thomas Lancaster puts kids and anyone else he can find into role-playing games to be controlled by other people. There's a good chance he's lying about not deleting me, and I don't want to take anything from him. I return to the bed, where I curl into the fetal position.

But when the screen lights up again and a woman starts talking, I'm lured to the desk. And I can't resist popping food into my mouth as I sink down into the chair.

"A leader in defense and medical technology, LanCorp introduced cerebrum links to the public over five years ago with War, the first reality role-play game in history," a woman says. Her voice is soothing, melodic. It almost makes up for the footage on the screen. Blood and death and violence. The same images from the memory I had the day Declan told me about deletion in the playground by the bar.

"Today, LanCorp continues to provide quality characters and a variety of games tailored to treat those diagnosed with the various violence disorders, including The Aftermath, the number one reality RPG for three years running, designed for patients with VG-B."

Clips from The Aftermath alternate with promotional images. I see a boy and a girl sneaking stealthily into a parking garage—there are visible shadows in the windows and I gasp. They're the Survivors we saved, just before I almost prevented Olivia from killing Reese.

Next comes an image of some gamer girl smiling in her white screened room with her thumbs up. She wears a shirt that says, "Honor, VIRTUE, Loyalty: The Aftermath."

The video flips to a cut scene of a girl with short blond hair, green eyes and a deformed ear turning a Glock on two flesh-eaters. My mouth freezes midbite. I feel as if my stomach is balling up on itself as I rub my fingertips across my ripped ear.

The last image is the side of a building that's been transformed into an enormous promotional glass poster for the game. The same thing that was on the girl's shirt is written on it, except at the very bottom of the poster, it says, "Choose Your Clan with Care."

And in the middle of it all is a picture of me, holding a knife in one hand and a gun in the other. Eyes narrowed into slits. Hair flying around my face as though I'm in the middle of a fight.

Now, the blond moderator's words and Declan's initial surprise when we met and some of the other characters' reactions to me all

CHAPTER TWENTY-SIX

They take me to the room that reminds me of a black diamond. The one with the windowed walls that show game footage. I've seen this room before in Olivia's mind. "Don't try anything stupid," Bennett warns, shoving me into one of the thin metal chairs.

There's not much damage I can do in here. Aside from the table and the chairs, the room is bare. "I'll try my best," I say. I consider making a joke about jumping out the window, but he starts to leave, and I decide I'd rather not have him stick around. Besides, the windows are outrageously thick. I can see that even from where I'm sitting.

The door locks behind Bennett. I wait about a minute to make sure he won't return; then I pace the room, from column to column, up one set of stairs and down the other, like erratic connect-the-dots. Every few moments, my feet snag the hem of my starched white pants and I have to roll the waistband again.

"You're looking well, Claudia."

I twist around, pressing myself to the side of a column. Lancaster stands above me at the top of one of the stairways, a serene smile on his face. He glides down the steps toward me. My eyes flick to the open door, but he wags his finger to one side. "You know you'll make it no further than the elevator. Why try it again?"

An image of Thomas Lancaster, surrounded by a group of men and women in business attire, slithers through my mind. His hand was cupped over the left side of his face and he was cursing. "I'll kill you," I had said as guards pinned me to the glass wall. My voice was scraped raw from screaming. "Can't you see what you're doing?"

Blood oozed through his fingers as he bellowed, "Sedate her."

I shake the memory from my head. I want desperately to hold on to it—to try and remember more—but there's too much at stake right now, I have to keep focused on the present. "I've no plan to try to escape," I say. He's so close I can see the scar I put on his face. And every curve of the electroshock gun in his hand. It looks much more lethal than Declan's. I've no doubt he'd be willing to use it on me. "I'm not going to attack you, either."

"Compliant, are we?"

"No. Just tired."

He chuckles, motioning me to approach him. I dig my nails into my palms, raking them back and forth, and fight back the bile in my throat before I obey. He smiles down at me. Placing a hand on my shoulder, he says, "Would you like to see the newest testing programs?"

"In here?"

His eyebrow lifts in surprise. "No, dear. Out there." He points to the open door.

There must be some type of catch. Why else would he take me around the facility? "Why are you doing this?"

"Because I promised you last time you were here that I would and I didn't follow through. We had certain...distractions. And, after all, you deserve to see this," he says. He holds out his arm and jerks his head toward the door. "Your friends are excited to see you, my dear."

I go completely still. My heart pounds violently in my ears.

Boom.

Boom, boom.

BOOM.

"What?" I demand.

He casts a satisfied smirk at me and nods. "Yes, they're here. Wesley, Mia."

Wesley and Mia are alive. I let out a sigh of relief, and then I whisper, "Anyone else?"

"Are you referring to Declan Hastings?" I look up at him helplessly, and he continues, "Because he's facing imprisonment and likely death."

"Declan's here," I croak.

Mia and Wesley—Declan—are all still alive.

Thomas points to the door again. "Shall we go?"

I keep my face down, but I watch him carefully as we walk into the hallways. He wears a tranquil smile, one that makes me cold and nauseous. It makes me want to knock him down, but then I catch a glimpse of beige out of the corner of my eye. My guards are right behind us.

We stop at the elevator. He presses his fingertips down on the reader and then types in a numeric code: 951208. The steel doors fly open. Thomas places his hand on my elbow, squeezing it, and guides me inside. I yank away from him and slink to the corner of the box.

Bennett nudges my shoulder with the tip of his electroshock gun. My eyes jolt up to his face. He nods to the back wall of the elevator. "Turn around, Virtue." His hand is on the opening to the door, so that it won't shut. I don't think he'll let go until I turn to face the wall.

Like a prisoner.

I follow Bennett's directions because I just want to get whatever horrible thing that's going to happen over with as soon as possible.

The elevator comes to a stop on the fifth floor. I hear Thomas punching in his code and the doors reopen. This hallway reminds me of Olivia's original gaming room. It's warm and empty and pristine white. And it makes me feel dead inside. "What's with all this white?" I ask.

"It promotes peace and pure thoughts," Thomas replies.

Maybe that's why he seems so passive when it comes to his line of work. He surrounds himself with a sterile white space so he doesn't feel guilty about creating The Aftermath, selling humans to other humans for the sole purpose of entertainment. No, that's not what he calls it. Rehabilitation and therapy.

"You're a monster, Lancaster."

"You've told me that before, right before you tried to kill me." Shrugging, he stops in front of another door and opens it. He looks at me out of the corner of his eye. "If I hadn't made the games, someone else would have. Now, no more questions. Welcome to The Aftermath facility's deletion chamber."

I feel as if someone spit in my face. This is the last place I want to be. "Why are we here?"

"So you can see a deletion," he says. He smiles over his shoulder at the female guard. "Initially, I planned to show you on a screen upstairs, but I want you to see what you've done. You'll watch from the other room."

No.

Please, no.

Bennett presses me forward into the windowed room on the other side of the deletion chamber. It's freezing, and I rub my hands up and down my arms to warm up. I'm surprised I don't exhale condensation. "Enjoy, Claudia."

I squeeze my eyes shut. "I don't need to see it— Take me back upstairs. Take me anywhere else." Just please don't make me watch this. Please. But Bennett closes the door behind them, leaving me.

A moment later, the door opens again and the sound of footsteps thud across the hard floor. "Claudia?"

My eyes fly open as Declan stumbles toward me. He's wrecked and battered, with bruises and cuts covering his face, but he's alive. I race toward him. "You're all right. Thank—" he starts.

I throw myself into his arms, knocking the air out of his lungs. "I thought you were dead. I thought—" But then I remember Thomas's words about all my friends being excited to see me, and fear claws through me. "What about Wes and Mia?"

"They're fine. We're all fine for now." He covers my lips with the tips of his fingers. "But, Virtue, you've got to get out of here. You've got to go now."

"What?" Then something hits me. "Declan, are you being deleted?"

A strangled noise comes from the back of his throat, and I feel my chest freeze up. Before I can say a word, something flat and rectangular presses against my stomach, and when I glance down between us, I see that it's Declan's tablet. "I stole it from the guard," he whispers. "As soon as you get out of here, you need to enter the code 734598. Find the file with your name—it will tell you everything."

I shake my head. "But what about you. What about—"

"I'm sorry, Claudia. For lying to you. For getting you into this mess." I gasp when he spins me around and his forearm locks around my neck. "I'm sorry for this."

"What are you—"

"Shut up. Just be quiet—and when we reach the lower levels, run." He drags me over to the observation window. "Hey!" He bangs on the glass with his free hand. As all the faces in the other room turn toward the sound of his voice, I feel cold metal press against the crown of my head.

"Declan," I plead.

"Struggle," he orders in a soft voice. So I do. I scream and flail, kick against him until finally the doors on both sides of the room open.

Thomas Lancaster races into the room, his face a mask of fury. "Put the gun down, son." He puts his hands up defensively and takes a few steps toward us, two guards following right behind him. "Put it down."

Declan moves us closer to them. "Not on your life, Lancaster. What you've done to her—to all of us—is sick. She's better off dead than having you sticking her back in that game just so you can make even more money."

"Put the gun—" Lancaster's words are cut off the moment the current hits him in the chest, and he crumbles to the floor. Declan releases his hold on my neck as one of the guards fires his own electroshock gun at us. The jolt hits me in the knee, and I stumble away as Declan takes down both guards.

"Get their weapons, Virtue. Hurry. They'll get back up at any moment and we've got to get you out of here."

Grinding my teeth, I limp toward the bodies on the floor and grab the guards' guns—and one of their knives. I hand one of the guns and the knife to Declan as he joins me at the door. Grabbing my arm, he jerks me into the hallway, firing at a guard who rounds the corner. "The entrance to the building is on the first floor. As soon as we reach that staircase, you keep going until you're out of this building."

"What about you?" I rub my hand across my neck where he had gripped me. "What about—"

"I'm going back for Wesley and Mia. But I need you on the outside."

We race down the hall, firing at anyone we come in contact with until we reach the staircase. The loud pounding of boots follows us as we race down the steps, but we keep running. It's ironic when I think about it—that the same people who put us in a game where we were molded into mindless, deadly creatures are feeling the effects of that now.

"Almost there," I choke out, struggling to breathe, dragging in so much air that my lungs burn.

When I drop my gun as soon as my foot hits the final step and turn to pick it up, Declan pulls me in the opposite direction. "No time to stop," he wheezes as we burst through the parking garage door.

Declan kicks out one of the back windows of the third car we find—a sleek black sporty thing that looks as if it could fly. He opens the door and unlocks the rest, resting his electroshock guns on the floorboard. As he dusts glass onto the concrete, I say, "What am I supposed to do?"

He wipes his eyes with the back of his hand, shaking his head. Something loud crashes behind the parking garage door. "Nothing if we don't hurry up," he says.

"Get out of the vehicle!" a voice says.

I turn to see a guard standing several feet away from us. His gun is positioned right at my chest. "Surrender, Virtue. Then nobody gets hurt," the guard says. He takes a hesitant step in the direction of the car. "No sudden movements, either."

I have no way to fight. The electroshock guns are in the car. I'd have to bend over to reach them and by then the guard will have fired at Declan or me or both of us.

Declan catches my eye and he shakes his head slightly. He lowers his eyes, and I see his knife where it has fallen on the ground… right next to my feet.

"Virtue, step away from the car, or I'll be forced to shock you."

I slip my toe under the knife and kick it up. I catch it, wrapping my fingers around the hilt, keeping my eyes focused on the guard.

"Where are the rest of you?" I demand.

He sneers. "Oh, they're coming."

I blink away tears, and, just as I open my eyes, I see his trigger finger move. I act without thinking. I act like Olivia. The knife sinks into the hand holding the electroshock gun and he drops it, screaming.

The car engine comes to life and Declan jumps out. "Go, Claudia," he orders, shoving me into the driver's seat. "I'll be...I'll be fine."

"What do I do?" I shriek as he closes the door, leaving me alone in the car. He's condemning himself, and there's nothing I can do about it.

"The code is 789312," he says quickly. It's not the same code he gave me in the building, but I say nothing as Declan continues, "Type it in and hit the *Chauffer* button. It'll take you where you need to go." He looks down at me, his gray eyes full of emotion, and I lose my breath. "And, Virtue? I'm so sorry." The sound of more guards rushing into the parking garage pulls him away from me. "Go!" Declan yells.

Trembling, I touch the flat screen, swiftly entering the six-digit code. "Welcome, Phoebe Coleman," the AcuSystem's robotic voice says as a menu appears on the screen. I jab the flashing *Chauffer* button, and the engine revs. The words *Park* and then *Drive* flash across the screen, and a second later, I feel the car lurch forward.

As the car speeds off, I see Declan crumble to the ground in the rearview mirror.

CHAPTER TWENTY-SEVEN

It takes several minutes for my sobs to subside long enough for me to remember the tablet that Declan gave me while we were in the holding facility. As the car speeds down the road, passing gleaming skyscrapers and turning on its own down wide, winding streets, I shakily type in his code.

I scan through the files, dragging my fingers across the screen slowly until I find the file he told me to look for. It's labeled "Virtue."

As soon as I place my finger on the icon, text flashes across the screen telling me to set the tablet down. The moment the tablet makes contact with the seat beside me, a life-size hologram pops up.

"Declan?" I whisper, and he turns his face toward mine.

It's prerecorded, and judging from the concrete walls behind him, it was made while he was staying in the basement at the bar shelter. "If you're listening to this, Virtue, I've either been captured or killed or both." He smirks. "But for your sake, let's hope I'm not dead."

"You're not funny," I snap, bringing my knees up to my chest. I wrap my arms tightly around them.

Rubbing his hand over his face, Declan sighs. "I haven't been entirely honest with you. I'm not a moderator. I'm a former character."

I listen closely as he recounts to me everything that I already know.

How he escaped LanCorp just before being deleted a year ago, how he broke into the game and how he tricked me into helping him save his brother, Wesley. But then the hologram of Declan tells me something that turns my blood to ice:

"The truth is, Virtue…I was sent into the game to find you."

"What?" I whisper, even though I know he can't hear me.

"I was hired to break into The Aftermath to recover you. I…was supposed to grab you from a mission and take you right to the border. You should have been alone—you were supposed to be alone—but you weren't that day. I panicked, tried to knock out the kid you were with, but things didn't go so well."

I sink my teeth into my bottom lip until I taste blood. So that day in the courthouse was no coincidence. He was coming after me with a purpose, and Ethan stood in the way. But why?

Who hired Declan to come into the game to get me?

As this thought tumbles through my head, the car turns down a narrow alley and comes to a stop in front of a small building at the end. Shakily, I gather all my belongings and stumble out of the car. I walk to the front door of the building, hobbling because my leg is still burning from the shock I received back at the holding facility. The moment I reach for the doorknob, I hear the screech of tires behind me, and I whip around to see the self-driving car speeding off in reverse down the alley.

No. Please…no. Despite the pain racing through my body, I chase after the car. With each millisecond that the car gets farther away from me, my heart pounds harder, faster. And then the car is gone, and I'm left alone, watching as it speeds down the street. Holding my breath so I won't release the sob threatening to come out, I return to the building in the alley.

If this isn't where I'm supposed to be—if Declan has held anything else back from me—I'm screwed.

But the doorknob turns easily for me and the heavy metal door swings open. Hesitantly, I step inside, into the darkness. I keep walking until I reach the center of the room, and then all the lights come on.

"Hello?" I call.

"Back here! Just have to put in the code and then we can go." I spin around to see a girl standing by the front door. Her back is turned to me as she types in a code on the security panel, but once she's done, she turns to me.

My heart drops to the floor.

Once again, I'm staring at myself. That dark-haired, undamaged version of me. The me from my dreams.

"You look like you've seen a ghost." She walks toward me, the heels of her boots clicking on the hard floor. She tucks a long brown lock of her hair behind her ear. "Actually, you look like you're going to throw up."

I know that voice. Why do I know that voice? "I'm dreaming again." I take a step backward. "I was killed back at that holding facility, or drugged, and I'm dreaming, and—"

She leans forward, placing her face—my face—close to mine. She squeezes either side of my shoulders and gives me a rough shake. "Oh, trust me—you're alive, and this is anything but a dream."

"Who are you?"

She draws back, her green eyes narrowing into a thin line of disappointment. "You don't remember?" When I shake my head, she continues, "Declan didn't tell you?"

I drop my gaze down to the floor. "Declan didn't tell me much of anything," I mumble.

Releasing my shoulders, she begins to walk away, so I follow her toward the back of the building and out another exit to where another car—this one silver—is waiting. "I'm your sister, Claudia. Your twin sister, if that's not obvious enough to you." She jerks up a dark eyebrow. "Get in the car."

But I shake my head. Pressing my back up against the closed door behind me, I jab my finger at her. "I'm not going anywhere until you tell me what's going on here."

She opens the car door and begins to get in, but then she groans. "We don't have time for this crap. Just trust me when I tell you that there are people after us. People who want to use us. You can save your questions for later." Slamming her small body down in the driver's seat, she tilts her head to the side and glares up at me. "Where did Declan take the car you broke out in?"

The mere mention of Declan and breaking free of the facility makes my chest hurt, and I swallow hard. "He didn't make it out."

My sister drags her hands through her dark hair and snorts. "I told him to stick to the task. I told him not to let his emotions get in the way of—" The sound of a siren stops her words, and she casts a warning look at me. "Get in the car, Claudia."

I comply because, once again, I have no other choice. As I buckle my safety belt, I turn to her. "Can we help him? Can we save him—and Wesley and Mia?"

Releasing a harsh sound, she starts the car. "I need Declan Hastings, so yeah, we've got to get him out. And I have a feeling he won't be doing anything without his brother—he's made that much clear with all the crap he's pulled. Though maybe he'll be deleted before we rescue Declan, and then—"

My gasp cuts her off. "And then *what?*" My sister wants Wesley to be deleted? Just so dealing with Declan will be easier?

She gives me a look that makes me feel as if I'm an idiot, but then her features immediately smooth into a sympathetic smile. "I wasn't being serious, Claudie."

Claudie. The nickname—which is so obviously something from our childhood—should bring about some kind of memory, but it doesn't. And I hate that. I hate it almost as much as feeling like my sister just lied to me.

She meant what she said about Wesley, but why?

I dig my fingernails into my palms. Now isn't the time to grill her about Declan or Wesley—not when LanCorp is after me and there's the chance that Olivia might try to get into my head, even from out here. "What about our parents? Can they help? Isn't there anyone—"

The corners of her mouth tighten. "Our parents might as well be dead."

As she starts to move her fingers along the flat screen on the center console, I let those words settle into my head. I have a sister. I have parents...even if it sounds as if they won't be much help. I have...

But the sight of her entering her six-digit code freezes all my thoughts: 117908. I've seen that code once before, and I turn toward my sister slowly. "You...you went as far as to steal my gamer's information?" I demand.

As the car takes off, she stares down at her lap for several seconds. Finally, she lifts her green eyes to me and gives me a sad smile. "You don't remember anything?"

"No, nothing."

She drops her head back against the headrest. "Well, that's disappointing. After everything I've done for you? After I lied and dated that crybaby for years, just because his parents had information?" She takes a deep breath and turns her head until her green eyes lock on to mine. "After I *killed* for you, Claudia?"

I grip the armrests. Shake my head from side to side. I welcome the denial even before my sister leans in close to me and opens her mouth to finish speaking.

"Claudia...I was your gamer. I'm Olivia Lancaster."

* * * * *

ACKNOWLEDGMENTS

Writing *The Aftermath* was such an amazing experience for me, and I'm so grateful to all the wonderful people who helped me along the way.

Thank you from the bottom of my heart to my wonder-agent, Mollie Glick. You are brilliant, and your enthusiasm and hard work are fantastic. Thank you so much for believing in *The Aftermath*. Thank you to the Foundry Literary + Media team, especially Katie Hamblin, Emily Brown and Emily Morton. I'm so appreciative to you three for always being so quick to answer my emails and questions (and sometimes there were many!).

Many thanks go out to the incredible team at Harlequin Teen. I've been in love with Harlequin novels for many, many years, and to be a part of this family still amazes me. To Natashya Wilson, thank you for taking a chance on my book—you made my dreams come true! And to Annie Stone, my patient, butt-kicking editor, your editorial insight is wonderful. *The Aftermath* has grown so much because of you.

One of the first people to read my book (back when it was called *The Way the World Ends*) was my critique partner Michelle. Thank you, lady, for always being so honest with your critiques and taking me seriously when I said, "Rip it to shreds!" I appreciate all of our long chats and the jokes—you're awesome, friend.

Another huge thanks goes to Taryn Albright, owner of The Girl with the Green Pen. You read *The Aftermath* so fast, and so many times, and gave me such detailed feedback. You are insanely talented!

Last, I have to thank my family. I once read that a writer's most important tool is a strong support system, and I'm so proud of mine. To my parents, who call or email to check on my word count every other day; my younger sister, who reads everything I write; my grandparents, who are always willing to volunteer to babysit; and finally, to my wonderful children and husband. I'm so blessed to have you all. I appreciate your love and support more than you'll ever know.

AUTHOR'S NOTE

The concept for *The Aftermath* came to me after staying up late to play a video game and the horrible dream that followed. After sharing the nightmare with my husband, who very sleepily told me to write it down, I began to put Claudia's story on paper. Although the book has changed quite a bit over the past two years, one thing remained the same: the role video games played in my creative process. As a big fan of video games, I'd like to share with you some of my favorites. I promise no characters were harmed in the process.

10. "Lightning Returns: Final Fantasy XIII"

I'll admit it—I wasn't the biggest fan of the previous "Final Fantasy XIII" installments, but the conclusion of the trilogy is spectacular. It doesn't hurt that Lightning is a butt-kicking heroine. The ending has been a bit controversial, but I may have said aloud, "Best. Ending. Ever."

9. "Lost Odyssey"

I preordered this game the day I saw the trailer, that's how excited I was. Not only did it not disappoint, I still have my fingers crossed for a sequel. Immortals, great world building and a solid plot—what's not to love?

8. "Resident Evil 2"

When this baby came out, I was still living in the Stone Age of video game consoles. I played this at a friend's house, and I was hooked. I needed a PlayStation. I had to have one. It took a little convincing, but eventually my mother caved. Thanks, Mom.

7. "God of War: Ascension"

You think Claudia has issues with her dad? Meet Kratos, son of Zeus. He's easily the best antihero I've ever seen, and the "God of War" games are some of my favorites.

6. "Assassin's Creed II"

I have a bad habit of starting video game series out of order, and that was the case with the "Assassin's Creed" games. I've since played the other games in the series, but Ezio's story will always be #1 in my heart.

5. "Final Fantasy VII" and "Final Fantasy VIII"

Remember that PlayStation I had to have? Well, it played a huge part in some of my most memorable gaming moments as a kid. "Final Fantasy VII" and "Final Fantasy VIII" were two of those games I discovered for PlayStation, and they feature some of the best characters in the entire series!

4. "Contra"

This was the first first-person shooter game that I ever played, and I can still vividly recall the code for thirty lives. The characters looked like Arnold Schwarzenegger and Sylvester Stallone, and it was such a cool game. Come to think of it, maybe it's time to find that old Nintendo and pull this game out….

3. "Final Fantasy X"

I didn't think I liked this game at first, but then I played a few minutes longer. And then a few hours more. Before long, I couldn't tear myself away from what was happening on screen. "Final Fantasy X" was visually stunning, with a solid plot and lots of romance. Needless to say that when I discovered this video game was being remastered in HD for PS3, I immediately preordered it!

2. "BioShock"

I've played quite a few first-person shooter games, but this one definitely tops my list. The story line was amazing, and it's one of those games that I've played multiple times.

1. "God of War III"

Kratos is back, and he tops my list of favorite games! I'm not going to tell you how fast I played this game (I'm embarrassed to admit it), but I will tell you that it was addictive. Kratos is definitely one of my all-time favorite video game characters, and I'm hopeful that another installment will follow!

QUESTIONS FOR DISCUSSION

1. In this novel, live-action games like The Aftermath serve as treatment for young people who are prone to violence. Putting aside the moral implications of using human beings as playing pieces, do you feel that this kind of treatment would be effective? Can games be used as more than just entertainment? If so, how?

2. At the end of the book the reader discovers that Olivia's motivations are quite different from what Claudia had thought. Does the fact that Olivia is acting to help her sister change how you view her? To what extent do her motivations justify her actions? What would you have done in Olivia's place?

3. Another character with noble intentions but imperfect actions is Declan Hastings. How would you compare and contrast the characters of Declan and Olivia? Does one character seem to be more morally upright than the other, and if so, why?

4. The Aftermath is a futuristic game created to eradicate violence within the American population. If we were to develop the technology to screen children for a "violence" gene, do you think people should be genetically sorted and subjected to treatments in order to prevent violence? Why or why not?

5. What obligation, if any, do Claudia and Olivia have to the victims of LanCorp's games, given their family's involvement with the creation and implementation of this "treatment"?

6. Declan explains to Claudia that games like The Aftermath are partially a result of several civil wars that had a devastating impact on America as we know it currently. Do you think it's realistic that the American government would resort to extreme techniques such as these live-action games to keep its citizens from rebelling a third time? Are there periods in history you can point to where extreme policies have been implemented after a period of violence?

7. Put yourself in Claudia's shoes at the very end of the novel. What would you do next?